SAVING SCHRÖDINGER'S CAT

Mark Jenkins

*This novel is dedicated to my mother Thelma,
who taught me empathy, compassion, and resilience.*

*Brush off your boo-boo, stand up, and get back out there.
Learn, grow, and always respect others.*

Acknowledgments

I wish to acknowledge all of the wonderful teachers I have learned from, especially during my formative years of high school and university.
I've been influenced by superb instruction in math, science, literature, music, and swimming.
I was challenged: I grew.
I wanted to learn more, and they gave of themselves to challenge me further.
For this I am eternally thankful.

*

I am grateful for the shared life experiences with other kind souls I've met on my journey. Whether brief or long — family, friend, patient, or stranger — all of these experiences have strengthened me as a human being.

*

Connect with Mark:

markjenkinsbooks.com

Books by Mark Jenkins:

Klickitat - and other stories

Saving Schrödinger's Cat

Help fuel further adventures by visiting my website and signing up for my periodic newsletter, where I'll share updates, backstory, tidbits, and more.

*

The delicious cover art was brilliantly crafted by ©Mars Dorian www.marsdorian.com

ACT 1

1

"Few are those who see with their own eyes and feel with their own hearts."
~ Albert Einstein

I was five years old when I learned I was sick, but I never thought my hallucinations — the dreams of trees, the sky, oceans, and animals — would lead here.

Proteus's hands began trembling and soon were shaking too much to continue packing. He stopped, stepped back from the table to look around the sterile white preparation chamber, and tried to center his thoughts.

Alone, and promised privacy in this moment before his journey, he nevertheless knew the sensors projecting from the smooth surface of the symmetrical room were recording everything. He couldn't blame them. His last moments in the twenty-fifth century were a time of anticipation for the Colony. No one sent had been successful — or lived — but there was hope that it would be different this time.

Proteus was an aberration, a genetic misfit. Institutionalized in childhood — and then removed two years later, after a serendipitous accident involving another had shown that a human with his mutation could survive time travel — he'd spent the past two decades training for this moment.

He looked down at the spectrum/data unit held white-knuckled and began a breathing exercise to calm his nerves.

3

Swallowing saliva, he looked at the largest knobby black sensor on the ceiling. He wanted people to know he was confident but couldn't think of a gesture or a word. *Soon I will be on the surface and I will see the sky for the first time.*

Proteus returned to his preparation. He placed the SDU in a brown suitcase, then checked the other pockets within to verify that everything was in order: five gold bars, clothes, a knife and tools, med-kit, and the retrieve-unit.

A chime sounded, signaling it would soon be time to depart. Proteus closed the suitcase and hefted it to feel the mass. *Soon I will see nature for the first time.*

Deep beneath the surface of the Earth, the Colony held the last remnants of humanity, and the weight of who he was and what he must do pressed down on him like the mountains he'd dreamt of but never seen.

Bile rose in Proteus's throat as he thought about the early lies he'd been fed about his hallucinations. His dream was genetic — an ancestral memory of nature — but the mutation that allowed his genes to tap into these rudimentary echoes of the past also marked him for an early death. None touched in this way lived a full life.

Institutionalization of those who would eventually die raving about nature was a safeguard for the rest of the Colony. Everyone must be made to forget that nature ever existed. The lessons had been bitter. The dwindling Colony was devoid of any reminders of Earth's past. Proteus now knew that this was to protect the population from the truth: humanity had once lived on the Earth's surface.

There were once forests, lakes, mountains, oceans, and animals beneath a sky that could be blue or stormy. He'd never seen any of this but had learned from the simulations. The simulations — which were forbidden to ordinary citizens — had also uncovered the meaning behind his dreams.

Proteus looked up at the clean white ceiling. The fiery Cataclysm that ravaged the Earth over a hundred years ago was still churning above, beyond the hundreds of meters of rock overhead. No one could survive up there. This room — part of the wormhole complex — was the closest he'd ever been to the surface. Perspiration trickled down the side of his face as he thought of the magma flowing above.

He would soon be on the surface — not the one above his head at present, but one in the past — to prevent the events that led to the Cataclysm.

4

The sliding door behind him hissed open, and he turned to see a handler in a protective bio-suit and helmet step silently into the preparation chamber. The silver faceplate hid the person's face, and Proteus wondered what the individual was thinking, what they were feeling. Hope? Fear?

The door hissed shut, and the handler stood motionless, hands pressed to the sides of their thighs, spine erect, like a soldier. Proteus smiled at the handler, who displayed no sign of acknowledgment. He looked at his own reflection, distorted in the silver face-shield, and fidgeted in his anachronistic clothing: a shirt with buttons, a necktie, a grey suit with buttons, and matching trousers (also with buttons). The clothing pulled at his skin and bunched in odd places when he moved. It was strange to actually wear the clothes he had seen during his historical studies.

He wanted to ask the handler what he or she was thinking, but the protocol was clear: once scrubbed, sterilized, and prepped, these last moments in the year 2420 would be without meaningful human interaction. There could be no physical or social contact; a virus might be passed to Proteus, or a conversation might distract him from the task at hand. Too much was at stake.

"I am ready," said Proteus and slipped on a long black overcoat.

The handler turned and passed a gloved hand over a security panel, which blinked twice. The door slid open. Proteus followed his escort into the hallway and saw another handler waiting there. One end of the hallway hummed.

The two handlers pointed Proteus in the direction of the deep, bassy sound, and as he approached it, flanked by the handlers, a reverberation grew in his bones. The clunky, hard-soled shoes on his feet slapped the floor, sending sharp echoes off the walls and almost drowning out the swishes of the soft booties and bio-suits of the people following him.

Proteus's left shoe flopped, and he stumbled. He stopped, looked down to find a loose lace, and bent to tie it. *Did I not do it right to begin with?* Embarrassed, he stood and looked over his shoulder; he was startled to see his escort had grown to seven, all standing in the exact same posture, mirrored face-shields directed towards him. Waiting.

He adjusted his clothes and then continued along the corridor. The humming grew louder. The wall signs indicated he was approaching the nexus of the power conduit, which would anchor one end of the wormhole.

The humming noise intensified the closer he came to the nexus. Each step he took in the corridor was heavier and harder than the last. Tingling played along the hairs of his arms and head as small pops and cracks of static electricity built and discharged. *Twenty years of preparations leading to this moment and to what will follow. But where and when exactly will I land?*

The boomerang path of the wormhole would put him in direct physical contact with the surface of the Earth, but there were unknowns. The Heisenberg time-shift corollary meant that the time and the place of his arrival in the past could not both be precisely calculated. Winnowing down one variable to an extremely specific value came at the expense of growing uncertainty in the other. The power required to open a wormhole was staggering, and precise manipulations of the waveform that would guide his journey were constrained by the immutable physics of space-time.

Picking the exact day but dumping him in the middle of an ocean would end the mission quickly, as would a number of other combinations. The planners and scientists had narrowed the place to London, which gave him close access to his objectives, and centered the time-window around 1918, plus or minus five years.

The humming changed pitch and then began pulsing. The tempo was slower than his footsteps at first but became faster as he drew closer to the source. It throbbed into the base of his skull and the roots of his teeth. Faster, until it outpaced his racing heart.

A handler stood at the end of the corridor, before a door, beckoning Proteus.

It was time.

2

"In an honest search for knowledge, you quite often have to abide by ignorance for an indefinite period."
~ Erwin Schrödinger

He stood in darkness in the middle of a boggy field, heavy suitcase in hand, trying to remember who he was and what he was doing here. He shivered and inhaled the smells of wet grass, soil, and soot. Blobs of murky yellow light dotted the periphery of the darkness, and a cold mist drifted into his face.

His thoughts came slowly and had to be picked over carefully to extract concepts that made sense. A wave of vertigo assaulted him, and he dropped to his knees in the fog. The spinning in his head made it harder to grasp the snatches of coherency trying to form there.

I'm ...

... Proteus.

The thought made sense. *Yes. I am Proteus.*

Wetness penetrated the knees of his trousers, as he tried to recall more. He frowned and then looked down at the earth, at the grass sticking up.

He marveled at each blade.

The journey ... I came from someplace else.

He recalled the sensation of being repeatedly stretched and squashed, as if the dimensions of his body had flipped between infinitesimally small and impossibly large. One moment, he was a subatomic speck, watching sparkling particles collide; the next, he was elongated to thousands of light years, seeing galaxies stretched out before him. Zero to infinity and back, he cycled.

Proteus leaned over, braced his hands on the ground, and retched.

After the nausea had passed, he sat back and looked up.

He raised his hands overhead and spread his fingers wide at the predawn clouds swirling above. *The sky!*

As his brain fog and vertigo ebbed, a memory of an instruction solidified: *Your first sight of the surface and nature will overwhelm you.*

Proteus forced out the breath he'd been holding and reflexively began a mind-centering technique, linking the timing of his inhalations and exhalations to his heartbeat. Slow breath in. Slow breath out.

Adaptive discipline.

And then more memories of instructions came to him. *Cycle through each sensory organ slowly, and breathe. List the sensations and understand the significance from your memory. Proceed methodically.*

Proteus looked away from the sky and towards the sounds that spilled in from the edge of the dark field: rumbles of mechanical engines, voices, and the honk of a horn. He began to shiver again. Bells sounded in the distance, ringing a four-note melody that he knew. And then four deep chimes.

Big Ben? London!

He squinted into the darkness, looking toward the murky yellow lights in the fog, and saw dim shapes moving. *People.*

In the background, high above the ground, were rows of arched windows glowing amber in the charcoal silhouette of a spiky, towered building.

The simulations in the Colony had prepared him for the sight — but not the experience of being on the Earth's surface. It was beyond anything imaginable.

It's real. I'm in the past.

Proteus resumed his slow breaths, and his shaking began to subside. *I can't believe this!*

He breathed in — and shuddered again.

Come on, get up. Follow your training. Survive.

He pushed himself up from the turf to stand, uncertain of how long he'd been kneeling.

Proteus grasped his heavy suitcase and grunted as he lifted it. He walked over the squishing grass toward a street. His balance shifted slightly with each step as his boots sank into the turf. As he passed under the boughs of a tree, he stopped suddenly and turned to face the trunk. He set his suitcase down and stepped closer, extending his right arm toward the trunk to touch it with his fingertips — then stopped, pulling away before contact.

He recalled more instructions, emerging like phantoms from the fog. *Discover your exact location and date and find a goldsmith.*

As he walked toward the blobs of light at the side of the field, they resolved themselves into lamps on tall poles. Soon the surface underfoot changed to crushed gravel as he found a path. Following this, he found a street. When his shivering began again, he retreated into the darkness of an alley.

He hugged his arms around his body and leaned against the brick wall of the alley. He was as alone as when he was institutionalized as a child, plucked from his parents, whose faces he could barely recall. Out of habit his right hand touched the numb area on his left elbow. The washcloth-sized patch extended along his forearm, and he had a similar one on his right knee. Both had developed a year ago and were a symptom of his disease and a harsh reminder of his mortality.

What if I'm trapped? What if no one understands me?

The cascading *what-ifs* threatened to overwhelm him, and he retreated into the safety of his training to keep a grip on this new reality. He spoke the mantra he'd been taught: "Remember discipline. Observe. Think. Learn. Adapt." He repeated it — again and again — until the pounding in his chest subsided.

Proteus stayed in the alley for over an hour, studying people, buildings, and traffic while his mind continued to clear. The cobbled streets glistened in the reflected glow of bright electric lamps, dim gaslights, and the slowly sweeping headlights of motorcars. He was curious about everything, but especially the people: what they wore, how they moved, and what their function appeared to be.

Ψ

Overhead, the darkness began to yield to the coming dawn, and when Big Ben chimed six o'clock, Proteus began to move again. He recalled the term *pea-soup fog* and wondered if the populace understood that this was the result of carbon particles belched out from millions of coal fires, serving as seeds for the condensation of water vapor.

He tasted the soot as he breathed in.

Walking along the pavement, studying signs and trying to further orient himself, he came across a boy hawking newspapers. He had no coin to buy one, but he stopped and glimpsed the date: May 1, 1921.

He paced and considered the implications of this date for his mission. The scientists of this era had, at this point in time, already identified the electron, and Ernest Rutherford had just discovered the proton. The identity of the neutron would remain hidden for another decade or so, but the physicists experimenting with radioactivity would keep chipping away until they found it — unless Proteus was successful in his work.

Taking a step back from the larger mission objectives, his thoughts turned to his most immediate next steps: find a goldsmith to exchange his gold for pounds sterling; buy clothes; and then secure lodging at a hotel. Once he was safely alone, he could access the SDU. Amongst the wealth of other historical data it contained were stock tables from the London *Times*. He also needed to drill through the specific mission details for 1921. Although he'd memorized the overall plan to disrupt Ernest Rutherford's research into the structure of the atom, there were specific details to guide him now that he knew it was May 1, 1921.

Proteus was pulled from his thoughts as the sidewalks and streets filled with people, buses, motor taxis, horse-drawn carriages, and vendors' carts as the morning blossomed into a crush of commuters and commerce. The bustle, cacophony, and odors hit him in waves as he walked. The sky lightened more and he saw the River Thames carving a big bend through the city. He soon saw a sign for the Royal Bank of England and knew he could find a goldsmith in this area.

He approached a small sign reading *King's Honest Gold, Ltd.* He opened the door of the premises, and something rang above his head. He ducked, then looked up to see that it was a small bell.

A pot-bellied man with ruddy cheeks, glasses, and bushy eyebrows eyed Proteus from behind a counter as he approached and set his suitcase down on the floor.

Proteus unlocked the case and extracted the gold bars. "I'd like to exchange these, please," he said as he placed the bars on the counter, one by one.

The man frowned as he inspected the bars. "I'll need to test these," he said. "Where'd you come across them? There's no mint stamp."

"My grandfather bequeathed them to me. He was a reclusive Greek."

The goldsmith looked at him as if expecting more information. A clock on the wall ticked. Proteus kept his face an impassive mask and said, "Yes by all means, please test them. You will find they exceed 99.99% gold."

He broke eye contact and looked around the store: a large sign stated the monetary rate for gold, silver, and platinum; glass cases behind the counter displayed coins; the wall-clock read 9:15; and a large man standing near the front door was watching him.

He turned back.

The goldsmith smiled through thin lips. His eyebrows crawled up onto his bald forehead like red caterpillars as he said, "The assay and weighing will take a few moments, Mr. ... um ... ah..."

"Proteus."

"Hmmm ... Greek, you say?"

"Yes."

"If I may say, you don't look Greek," said the goldsmith, tilting his head to peer over his glasses. Pale brown irises stared at Proteus. "And your accent is hard to place."

"Family name," said Proteus. "And I'm American."

"Ah, I see." The goldsmith watched him for a moment before shrugging and shuffling off to the back room with the gold bars.

Proteus had been taught that saying he was American could help head off, or untangle miscommunications and social blunders in the UK. By explaining that he was from across the Atlantic, he might recover from linguistic or cultural faux pas. Not that Londoners cared much about Americans, the historians had explained — rather, they found them strange.

A time of change, thought Proteus. *Recovery from the war was interrupted by economic depression.* He delved deeper into his memory of the early 1920s. The Great War had left countries in ruins. Large swathes of the population had been slaughtered or maimed. The butchery of trench warfare was orders of magnitude worse than any prior war: massive artillery barrages; waves of soldiers running across minefields into barbed wire and overlapping machine gun fields; bombs dropped from airplanes; and new gas weapons. Farmland, livestock, villages, and cities were decimated. The warring sides scorched the earth to drive their opponent into submission, resulting in starvation, death, and disease. Even when the hostilities stopped, the death toll rolled along as an influenza pandemic raged. Governments had invested heavily in science and technology to yield greater destructive power to crush the opposition and win the war, and it'd paid off — but not in the ways they'd thought.

And from those ashes had risen discovery, hope, and darkness.

The goldsmith returned. He coughed. "Well then, Mr. Proteus, with the current exchange rate, minus the one percent commission, the total sterling value of your gold is two hundred and thirty-two pounds and fifty-one pence." When he smiled, his lips seemed to disappear. "In what notes would you like the currency?"

Proteus did the math in his head and realized it was off — he was on the short side by a full percentage point beyond the commission — but decided to let it pass. "Tens, please."

The corners of the goldsmith's lips twitched up, and he turned to the till upon the counter. He sighed as he counted out the money.

He probably expected me to object and then barter, thought Proteus. *Now, I imagine, he feels profound disappointment at not trying to rip me off for more. Well, I was warned that the twentieth century revolved around cash and power.*

"Two hundred and thirty-two pounds and fifty-one pence," concluded the goldsmith as he finished counting out the notes. "Would there be any further exchanges I can help you with?"

"Not at present."

"Well, I hope you keep me in your mind in the future, Mr. Proteus."

"I certainly will."

The tiny bell above the door jingled again as Proteus left the premises.

Back on the street, the sky was dark and weeping a fine grey drizzle. The tainted droplets settling from the murk above beaded on his long, black overcoat and formed small rivulets that ran through the folds.

A man in a stained and worn suit, standing on the sidewalk, turned toward him and held out a large wooden tray displaying bootlaces, cufflinks, and other gentlemanly necessities. Defeated, dirt-rimmed eyes looked up at him.

Proteus gave the man a pound note and then waved him off. He had no need for anything the man was selling, but the sadness in his face spoke of his plight. These men were seemingly everywhere, scratching out whatever cash they could. The money Proteus had given him was probably equivalent to half a month's income. The man stared at the note in his hand uncertainly, then bobbed his head and said, "Thank you."

Proteus moved on, resuming his study of the people on the street. A boy swept a gutter with a broom, occasionally bending over to pick up some tidbit. Two men leaned against the wall of a stained building, sharing a cigarette; one was missing an arm. An artist sat on a wooden box in front of a small easel, painting a picture of a tower with a clock face. A musician played a tune on a flute. Farther along, a man turned a crank on a music box, which trilled off-key piping noises, while a small monkey in a buttoned red jacket and matching hat held out a tin cup to passersby. Proteus stopped and clanked a few coins into the cup, and the monkey tipped his cap.

It's marvelous and strange, thought Proteus, but then frowned. Depression, dirt, and despair seemed to permeate everything. It was different from the holo simulations.

Beyond the scavenging he could see, he knew that others were driven to crime. Although trained in combat, he reminded himself that the best defense was to spot trouble in advance and avoid it.

He thought about *Homo sapiens'* incessant, dark yearning for ever more powerful weapons, which had not been slaked by the Great War. In fact, despite four years of ceaseless horror, the seeds of the next war had already been planted — and the call for even greater means of destruction could not be long ignored.

Big Ben chimed its song, followed by ten deep peals.

Proteus watched two men in American uniforms enter a coffee shop and recalled that postwar London had a surge of American jazz, GIs, and gonorrhea. It was a time of excitement as new technologies such as intercontinental flight and radio took off, but it was also a time of depression. The dichotomy between the poor on the streets and the wealthy young adults attending lavish parties typified the roaring twenties.

Proteus looked at his own clothes in the reflection of a store window. They were an adequate simulation of period clothing but out of necessity were generic. In 1921, they wouldn't necessarily denote the style of the wealthy young gentleman he needed to portray in order to open doors and gain influence.

I should find a clothier, go shopping, and then check into a hotel.

He turned westward, taking in everything he could. Adrenalin amped up his senses and chills coursed through his body at the realization that he was exploring a city coming to life in its past. London had survived famine, pestilence, bombs, and blitzes. It had always endured.

Until the Cataclysm buried it in ash.

13

Ψ

Proteus reminded himself to hold his chin up and shoulders back as he left the clothier and strode along the sidewalk in his new attire. The wool suit, bowler hat, and cane made him appear more like a gentleman of the period. He'd watched several of them in the store and had memorized how they moved and spoke. And as he continued westward along the north edge of the Thames, he emulated their walk and their talk.

He'd taken more hours exploring than he'd intended and was now looking for the Strand, on which the Savoy Hotel was located. The tailor told him it was a posh place to stay, befitting a gentleman who enjoyed the nightlife. Everything of interest could be found there, and it all sounded fine to Proteus.

He stopped in a few more shops and then found the Savoy just beyond a bridge called Waterloo. Big Ben chimed seven as he walked up to the entrance; two blue-suited bellhops with pill-box caps held open the double doors. *They're dressed like that organ-grinder's little monkey,* he thought, but as he walked inside, it occurred to him that it was probably the other way around.

The lobby was spacious, with dark wood-paneled walls, grey marble floors, and a carmine carpet. A large glass chandelier was suspended above the center, and light from bright, mustard-yellow electric lamps sparkled off mirrors and polished wood furniture. It was as opulent as the backstreets were scruffy.

Music, laughter, and voices flowed in from a large ballroom off to one side. A woman wearing a floppy hat, a string of pearls, and a knee-length dress walked past Proteus and giggled as she hooked arms with a man in a wide-striped blazer, who was waiting for her. She looked over her shoulder and smiled as they went into the ballroom.

Proteus turned away and saw his reflection looking back at him from a plate-glass window. His throat went dry as he imagined himself naked, exposed, allowing all to see him for who he was. He looked down and repeated the mantra he'd been taught: *Observe, think, learn, adap*t.

When he looked up again at his reflection, he saw a confident gentleman, someone who appeared to belong. He returned his attention to the social interactions and setting — and what he had to do next.

I fit in. And I'm learning.

After several more minutes of observation, Proteus followed the carpet to the front desk, approaching it with a bounce in his step. Each personal encounter and each transaction became easier with time, and the new clothes looked good on him. *Soon I'll blend in and be one of them.*

Proteus went to the check-in counter and was greeted by a pleasant young man in a three-piece suit who gave him a form to fill out. On the line above *Surname* he wrote Proteus but then was brought up short by the lines for *First* and *Middle* names.

"Initials are fine, sir," said the young man.

Uncertain, Proteus thought of everything he'd just been through. *A journey backward in time and I'm tripped up by something simple. A journey backwards ...*

He wrote *A.J.B.*, signed the bottom of the form, and passed it back. The man offered him one of their *better* suites on the top floor, and Proteus paid in advance for four weeks. The man called over one of the ubiquitous bellhops in blue, who helped him with his suitcase and shopping boxes.

They walked together a short distance and then stopped in front of a brushed-metal door. The bellhop pressed a brass button on the wall, and machinery whirred and hummed.

"I thought my room was on the seventh floor," said Proteus.

"It is, sir," said the bellhop. "This is the lift."

"Oh," said Proteus and waited as an embarrassing silence stretched on. He was about to ask a question when he was interrupted by a squeak and a loud thud.

The metal door in front of him ratcheted open to reveal a small space with a mirror on the back wall and a small boy wearing a blue suit with a double row of brass buttons and a cap. Proteus hesitated at the threshold as the bellhop carried his things inside the tiny confines of the lift.

"It's all right, sir," said the bellhop, displaying the fearless grin of youth. "This is one of the newest lifts in London. Hardly ever malfunctions."

Proteus wiped sweaty palms on his trousers and concentrated on the mirror as he entered the lift. He heard the steel door close behind him and locked his eyes on his reflection. The words *hardly ever malfunctions* echoed in his mind as the lift shuddered, groaned, and

15

creaked upwards.

He recalled the smooth simulations of the twenty-fifth century and clenched his jaw. This ride up was nothing like that. It was claustrophobic terror. *Hardly ever malfunctions* was twentieth-century speak for the careless application of technology. Nothing he'd seen so far inspired any confidence, despite his teachings, and the thought of being trapped…

They arrived at the seventh floor, and Proteus was first out as the door opened. He straightened his clothing, then followed the bellhop along the hallway to room number 707. The bellhop unlocked the door, carried the packages in, and gave him a brief tour of the suite.

"Would you be needing anything else, sir?"

"No," said Proteus.

Finally alone, he locked the door and sat down heavily on the bed. He removed his uncomfortable new shoes, within which painful blisters had already formed. Then he placed the suitcase on the bed and unlocked it, eager to tap into the information in the SDU.

He extracted the unit, pressed his thumb onto the black obsidian-alloy surface, and said, "On." The faintest of vibrations passed through his fingertips as he set it on the bedside table.

"Holo."

A translucent green cube, a meter along each side, appeared, hovering at eye level.

"London Stock Exchange. Daily summary, 1921 to 1928."

The green holo-cube filled with ninety-six neatly sliced white planes as it accessed information pre-loaded into buffer storage. By touching a corner of a plane, Proteus could extract any month he wanted and then expand it into individual stocks and price data, each presented in its own separate holo-cube.

The data component of the SDU used synthetic DNA for memory. Although it held over four exabytes of information, the biological transcription of data into a useful binary format was slow — it could take hours, or even days. Unzipping and compiling a data request was too slow to be useful in real time, so a storage buffer was used to keep a searchable index and recent data requests available. The buffer was large enough that as long as Proteus anticipated his needs and planned ahead, the glacial pace of the DNA memory access would not be an obstacle.

The first thing he did was scan for large inflection points — indicating extreme price fluctuations. Up or down didn't matter.

"Quantitative analysis. Identify sigma-two plus."

Red blips and swatches appeared in the white planes.

"Optimal strategy. Time start: May 1, 1921."

The cube fuzzed and then showed three planes of data, which Proteus cycled through: a buy/sell/short list of individual stocks by date; a graph of profits; and a probability graph of the trades being identified as suspicious. The thought of accusation, and subsequent incarceration, chilled him. *I'm here out of need, not greed.*

"Plot."

The cube fuzzed, rotated, and then displayed a two-dimensional plot marking weekly timepoints along the x-axis and pounds sterling on the y-axis. Each data point consisted of a buy/sell/short icon, company name, stock ticker, and the number of shares. Proteus followed the irregular saw-tooth line running from the bottom left to upper right, showing the growth of his hypothetical investments.

"Tabular."

The plot disappeared and a table appeared. He took out a pencil and a sheet of paper to write down his investment plan for the next three months.

After he'd finished, he said, "Switch to mission goals. May 1921."

He watched as a series of interconnected dots beginning in 1921 branched forward through time as they populated the 3D display. Red trefoil symbols marked important scientific advancements.

Proteus's target was Ernest Rutherford. Regardless of the exact date in the early 1900s into which he'd arrived, he had to find him and disrupt his work. Whether that was at Manchester or Cambridge didn't matter; Proteus had been trained for either place.

He studied more details relating to May 1921. Rutherford was at Cambridge and had just discovered the proton. In addition to refining his gas experiments, he was revisiting his gold foil scattering investigations from over a decade earlier. With advances in the sensitivity of his equipment (lower-pressure vacuum tubes, higher-resolution microscopes, and phosphorescent screens) — as well as higher-purity radiation sources and high-voltage equipment — Rutherford hoped to dig deeper into the structure of the atom.

"Off," said Proteus, and the cube winked out. He unpacked his shopping bags and smelled the leather of the satchel and the latched, leather-bound book he'd purchased. The aroma sickened him. The chemical smell combined with the thought of animals being stripped of their skins to be fashioned into bags, clothing, and accessories illustrated the barbarism of the period.

Proteus went to the sink to pour a glass of water. He turned on a tap — and flinched at the brown-tinged water that flowed out. He let the tap run for a few moments to clear the rust before filling his glass, which he inspected in the light.

He could still see a trace of brown but raised the glass to his lips and drank.

He frowned at the faint metallic taste. He knew he would get used to it, but it was the worst water he'd ever tasted.

He drank the rest and then went back to the main room and picked up the leather-bound book he'd purchased. A wide strap and buckle secured it closed, and the words *Holy Bible ~ King James Version* were embossed in large gold lettering on the brown cover. He unbuckled it and then removed the Bible. The dimensions were snug, but the SDU fit inside the cover. Pleased, he put the Bible on a table and the now leather-bound SDU into the satchel. He had no intention of letting anyone see it, and the cover would withstand casual scrutiny should some accident occur.

Exhaustion began to set in, and Proteus got ready to turn in for the night. It was warm, so he opened one of the windows — then held his breath in awe at the sight of dusk falling over the city. Noises of street traffic and parties floated up from below.

The shifting sky flowed from copper to rust to umber, mesmerizing him. Proteus remembered his childhood hallucinations and gripped the sill to stabilize himself.

But this is real.

He turned, shuffled back to the bed, and sat down — then collapsed backwards to stare at the ceiling.

Proteus soon descended into the depths of dreams.

He walked in a tunnel connecting nodes in his Colony beneath the Earth's surface. Symbols and high-energy warnings marked the smooth, cylindrical passage deep within the Engineering section, near the fusion reactors.

Sensors blinked

He went deeper.

Ahead was an Atmospheric Integrity Node where scrubber units scavenged carbon dioxide for reuse and electrolysis units split water into its constituent elements. Oxygen was cycled into the Colony's air circulation, and the hydrogen was destined for fusion generators or chem-synthesis. Underground natural water and energy were effectively limitless.

He walked. Closer, now, to the AIN.

Klaxons blared and strobes flashed: *Fire!*

The door before him slammed shut. He ran forward, but in slow motion, gripped by the dream.

Warmth bathed his face as he neared the door. The tunnel heated.

He neared the door. A faint pounding came from the other side. Muffled shouting.

He pawed at the surface, trying to find something to free the people trapped inside. The door became too hot to touch. He clawed at it.

The noises on the other side stopped. Tears blinded him. A scream welled from deep in his soul; Proteus staggered away with blistered palms.

3

"How wonderful that we have met with a paradox. Now we have some hope of making progress."
~ Niels Bohr

Before dawn, Proteus was awakened by tremors in his arms and legs, just as had happened every morning for the past several years. Another symptom of his nature-dream disease, they rarely lasted more than half an hour, but until they went away he would be unable to put on clothes or even hold a glass of water.

Over the rustling of the bed sheets as he twitched, he picked out the faint noises of traffic on the street below. This was his second day in the past, and he was eager to begin.

After what seemed like an eternity, the tremors faded, and he got up from bed. Proteus knew that his disease would slowly worsen over time. The tremors would last longer, more numb patches would develop, and his vivid nocturnal dreams would eventually progress to daytime hallucinations. He had perhaps twenty years left until the disease robbed him of a functional existence. He hoped to finish his work here in the past long before that and — if he was lucky — return to his time to discover they had a cure. But now was not the time to dwell on such things, and he busied himself preparing for the day.

When he was dressed and ready, Proteus put the SDU and stock-list into the new leather satchel. Then he retrieved his black overcoat, bowler hat, and cane, and studied himself in the room's mirror — and adjusted his necktie. He imagined himself a proper English gentleman.

Satisfied, he grabbed the satchel, flicked off the light switch, and left his suite. He locked the door, pocketed the key, and strode down the empty corridor to the lift, where he pressed the brass button. An electric bell rang, and machinery began groaning.

He monitored the lift's progress on the analog half-circle dial mounted above the door and estimated its velocity at seven seconds per floor.

Half a minute later, it arrived. The grinding noise stopped as it clunked into place, and the door slid open. Reluctantly, Proteus entered the claustrophobic space, hoping it wouldn't malfunction and plummet, taking him and the monkey-costumed elevator boy to their deaths.

He announced his destination. "Lobby, please."

The lift moaned all the way down to the lobby, then lurched to a halt. The lift boy slid open the door. Proteus tipped him as he exited into the lobby, which was subdued compared to the previous night. He walked past the shoeshine and toward the front entrance.

The Royal Bank of England was less than thirty minutes' walk away; he was soon up the steps and through the glass and polished-brass doors. Two men flanking the doors eyed him as he entered. Proteus's boot heels clicked, and his cane tapped on the polished marble floor as he walked toward the counter, where two cashiers watched him through the bars.

Proteus stopped, looked around, and swallowed dry saliva, suddenly feeling out of place. He fidgeted with his new trousers.

Project arrogant confidence, he reminded himself. *That's what gets attention in these times.*

He strode toward the nearest cashier and stopped at the caged window; he rapped the end of his cane on the floor and said, "Bully! Good day to you, young sir. I wish to open an account."

The cashier tilted his head slightly and put on a half-smile. Dressed in a pressed white shirt, suspenders, and a thin black tie, he peered over a pair of *pince-nez* spectacles and said, "How will you secure the account, sir?"

"What?"

The cashier sighed and fixed his grey eyes on Proteus. He enunciated each word slowly as he said, "You will need to deposit *something* to open an account, *sir*." His gaze flicked over Proteus's shoulder toward the front door.

"Oh … yes, of course." Proteus reached into his coat pocket to retrieve his money clip. He counted out bills, laying each one on the counter with an exaggerated thump of his index finger. "Two hundred pounds."

The cashier's eyes widened, and he said, "Yes, sir!" He reached for the bills. "I can help open an account for you." He picked up a fountain pen from its resting place and dipped it in an ink well. "What is your address?" He poised the tip above a lined piece of paper and looked expectantly at Proteus.

"I'm renting a suite at the Savoy, 707."

"Very good, sir. Would you like printed checks with your account, sir?"

"Yes," said Proteus and began tapping his foot on the polished stone floor. "Be quick about it, young man. Do I look like I have all day?"

"Yes, sir," said the clerk, and Proteus caught the young man rolling his eyes as he turned to walk into a back room. Proteus busied himself by looking around the bank. The security guard by the door eyed him up and down; Proteus turned to look elsewhere.

After a few moments, the clerk returned and approached the counter.

"Here you are, sir, ten checks and your account information." The clerk handed Proteus a small leather binder. "Also, we have safety deposit boxes available for a fee if you have the need."

"Not at present, young man," said Proteus. "But I am interested in buying shares in the London Stock Exchange. Can you give me directions?"

"I'm the bank manager," said a voice behind him. Proteus turned to face a man in a charcoal-grey pinstripe suit with slicked hair. "I can help you with that inquiry, sir. We have a strong brokerage presence in the *exchange*."

"Yes, that'd be great," he said, and smiled at the manager.

"Excellent. Shall we discuss in my office?"

Proteus nodded and followed the manager. There was a twinge of guilt at knowing the outcome of the stocks in the market, but his instructions about ethics had been clear: *It's all relative, because humanity and the planet are doomed if you fail.*

Ψ

An hour later, Proteus left the bank and returned to the Savoy. He picked up a copy of the train schedule for Liverpool Street station and studied it in the tea room as he snacked on small, triangular sandwiches and drank Darjeeling tea. *Elevenses*, they called it.

He held up the *Times* and flipped through several pages.

He rehearsed the logistics for his trip to Cambridge as he scanned the paper for relevant news. A tingle went down his spine. He'd planned and practiced for this first foray into the laboratories for years and could recite almost every detail about his objectives. But now, on the cusp of action, it was different.

As he read the paper, he found himself less certain about his chances of altering the past, despite the reassurances he'd received in the twenty-fifth century. Soon his eyes were simply skimming the print and he was no longer reading.

The scientists' information about time travel had been hedged with hesitations and caveats. They were certain about one thing, though: despite the dozen or so time travelers sent back, nothing about their current understanding had changed. Sensor readings showed the same volcanic infernos and ash heaps that had characterized the Earth's surface for almost two centuries.

Most scientists believed in a closed time-loop reality. And the principle of self-consistency meant it was impossible to create a paradox: you couldn't go back and kill your father when he was a child. The probability of success dropped to zero; time itself would push back to make this violation physically impossible. But pick a flower destined for someone else — then what?

Others said space-time could have many threads or parallel instances. Within this reality, Proteus could only affect the time-world he was presently in. The people dying in his time-world of origin would still move to extinction regardless of his efforts in any other time-world.

Now that he was here in twentieth-century London, the uncertainty seemed moot. *They wouldn't have sent me unless they thought I could change the past and affect the future.* This line of thinking led him to consider the known deaths of some of the initial time travelers — a fate that his genetic mutation should prevent him from sharing — and he shuddered.

Pushing this morbid thought aside, he returned to the problem of the paradox. Given that a large-scale change in the past, such as an assassination of a key historical figure, was thought to be physically impossible, he'd been instructed to make minute incremental changes over time and then observe the effect on research into the atom. The scientists called it the *butterfly effect*. A series of seemingly random, alternative outcomes in small events might generate enough of a realistic probability-wave that desired larger outcomes might occur naturally. This was their best hope.

But Proteus had to be careful. In a closed system, time would resist being altered — and that might manifest in multiple ways, from subtle to severe. Too much success, and too quickly, could result in him being winked out of existence or killed in an *accident*. He had been advised to proceed slowly and be on the watch for subtle anomalies. Even minor feelings of *déjà vu*, or its opposite, *jamais vu*, might herald incipient Time-resistance.

His trainers had also taught him that modern ethics, morals, and laws held no covenant over him — nor did those of the twentieth century — and that he was authorized to use any means necessary to delay the discovery of nuclear fission. The survival of humanity and the planet were paramount.

He ground his teeth at the irony. Physical laws prevented him from assassinating Rutherford and other scientists — and finishing his mission in a fortnight — in a barbaric twentieth century where violence and murder were the rule.

Ψ

After Proteus had finished his tea, he went up to his room, gathered his gear for his evening venture, and headed back down to the lobby. He exited the hotel and stood under the shelter of a wide awning as a concierge popped out from a booth to the side. Beyond the shelter of the awning a fine, grey mist drifted down, leaving a sheen on the street and sidewalk.

"What can I help you with today, sir?" asked the concierge.

"A motor taxi, please," said Proteus. "Oh ... and a paper."

"Right away, sir," said the concierge; he reached into the booth and then handed Proteus a copy of the *Times*. He raised his hand, looked up the street, and then turned back to face Proteus and said, "The Savoy is hosting a big shindig tonight. You wouldn't want to miss it."

Proteus thanked him and walked to the motor taxi that had just pulled up. The driver was already out and running around the front of the vehicle in the slick, sooty drizzle to open the passenger door. Proteus thanked him, climbed into the vehicle, and studied the controls as the driver closed the door and then scurried back around the vehicle. As he plopped into the driver's seat, Proteus felt the suspension springs shift.

"Where to today, sir?" asked the driver, a young man with dark, curly hair spilling out from under a black eight-panel hat. He smiled, and his blue eyes studied Proteus.

"Liverpool Street Station."

The driver grabbed the large stick protruding from the floor of the vehicle and then manipulated the pedals; the taxi coughed forward.

"Here on holiday, sir?"

"Business."

"Oh. What kind of business is the gentleman in? If you don't mind me asking?"

"Academics," said Proteus.

"Oh, so headed on the train to Cambridge?"

Proteus opened his mouth to reply —

— and was pitched forward; he braced himself against the dashboard as the driver stomped on the brake pedal. The vehicle slid to a stop as the driver mashed the button for the high-pitched, warbling horn.

"Bloody sheep!" said the driver. "You all right, sir?"

"Fine."

"Sorry 'bout the language."

"It's of … no concern," said Proteus. He looked through the windscreen at the policemen and the shepherds trying to clear the intersection of the herd of sheep. There seemed far from universal agreement about how this should be accomplished.

As they idled, waiting, the driver said, "You know what I think? The sheep can't read the bobby's hand signals — and the shepherds ain't much brighter than the bobby and the sheep combined." A smirk twitched his lips.

Proteus parsed out the language, then smiled in response. He wondered: *Is this humor? Am I supposed to laugh?*

The driver chuckled. Proteus followed a second later.

"A laugh is good," said the driver. "My name's Conrad." He shifted into gear, and the taxi lurched forward.

"Nice to meet you, Conrad," said Proteus. The taxi thrummed over cobblestones, jarring his words.

"So, what're you investigating, sir?"

"I beg your pardon?" said Proteus. His grip tightened on the satchel.

"I mean, what kind of academics?"

"Oh. Physics."

"Ah. Like Sir Isaac Newton," said Conrad. He slowed and turned at an intersection. The taxi picked up speed. Conrad grinned. "You know, I read a lot, and I think there's something special about Cambridge. They've got it figured out up there." He pointed to his head.

The taxi slowed and pulled off to the side of the road.

"Well, here you are, sir. Cambridge-bound trains are usually on the number four and five platforms, but check the boards."

"Thank you," said Proteus. He paid the fare, plus a tip, opened the door and stepped out of the motor taxi.

"Thank you, sir," said Conrad. "Best of luck with your investigations, and unless I've pegged your accent wrong, I'll quote your Mark Twain to you: *The two most important days in your life are the day you are born and the day you find out why.*"

Proteus had one foot on the curb, but now he stopped. He replayed the quote in his mind and turned to look back at Conrad.

"It's quite good, I think. Spot-on, sir," said Conrad. "I'm a dependable driver. Would you be needing a taxi when you come back from Cambridge?"

"No," said Proteus and closed the door.

Under a weeping graphite sky, Proteus joined grey people on a grey sidewalk, walking toward Liverpool Street Station.

Ψ

A stationmaster's whistle blew. A sequence of bangs reverberated through the carriages as the train bucked and then began to roll forward. Proteus surveyed the people in the sparsely populated carriage. Workers, farmers, and students he guessed by their attire. He looked out through the rain-streaked window as the train left the station.

As they rolled past warehouses and factories, heading northeast, the side-to-side sway began to make him feel nauseated. He closed his eyes and tried to ignore it, but this made it worse. Proteus opened them and stared at the ceiling of the railcar.

His thoughts drifted to the sickness that had killed every previous time-traveller who'd been successfully retrieved. Most of those who journeyed back in time never triggered a retrieve and were presumed missing-in-time, fates unknown. A successful retrieve heralded a wave of hope in the Colony — but then immediately afterward, despair. All that was ever retrieved was a dead or dying body.

The necropsies had the same finding: each cell's nucleus had withered from within. Time travel had triggered the death-program in the DNA: apoptosis. Programmed cellular suicide. The theory was that a time journey disrupted a cell's recognition of itself as healthy and viable, triggering the program.

It hadn't seemed possible for a human to travel back in time and survive, but then someone with the nature-dream genetic aberration had escaped confinement and run screaming into the wormhole just as they were fully energizing it. He disappeared, and they'd scrambled to reverse the wormhole to bring him back.

The retrieve was successful. He came back alive, brambles stuck in his hair, thorn scratches covering his body, a full beard, and eating a fistful of blackberries with a wild look in his eyes.

Because of the asynchronous flow of time, the scientists had no idea how long he'd actually been in the past. They searched for the Time-sickness that would kill his cells and drown him in organ-system failure, but they found none. He was physically healthy, and his mind, long gone to the dream-mutation, was unchanged.

More puzzling was the change in his genome. Cellular scans and biopsies demonstrated high metabolic energy in segments of dark DNA, noncoding genes that made up most of the human genome yet had no known function. Supposedly dead, some of these sequences had come alive in him. Were the dark genes the remnants from past evolutionary cycles or placeholders for future ones? They didn't know. But they knew he'd survived.

All further attempts at sending people back in time were halted, and the doctors looked for others with the rare nature-dream disease. They needed someone young and malleable — long before the eventual neurological decline and madness overtook them. Someone who could be trained.

The train slowed and braked to halt, the fifth stop on this trip. Proteus shivered and looked out the window: the sky was brighter, and the rain had stopped. People scurried off the train. The station placard read *Cambridge*.

Proteus jumped up from his seat, bumping his head.

"This is my stop!" he announced, heart pounding, hoping it would prevent the train from leaving the station. He grabbed his satchel and scurried down the aisle to the exit. The train lurched, nearly pitching him into an empty seat. Recovering his balance, Proteus made it to the end of the carriage, opened the door-latch, and hopped down onto the station platform.

As the train continued to chug away and pick up speed, he scowled. *That train ride wasn't anything like my holo-training.*

After taking a moment to orient himself, he located the signs pointing to the university, just over a mile away. Proteus swallowed and began walking. The contrast with London was immediate: the air didn't taste of soot; the narrow streets felt spacious; and there weren't crushing crowds filling every available square meter of space.

The afternoon sun warmed his face as he passed one- and two-story buildings along St. Andrews Street. The shops, pubs, tobacconists, and bakeries appeared to be doing a good business, and the people he encountered on the sidewalk seemed less rushed, less pinched in the face. And they smiled. Time felt slower and more pleasant.

The shift in architecture ahead announced the university well in advance of the banner in the breeze bearing the Cambridge coat of arms: four gold lions on a red background, split by a white cross. Weathered stone ramparts, archways, and walls flanked the street as two- and three-story structures loomed in the background. Some looked like Gothic cathedrals, whilst others seemed more like squat blocks.

Proteus passed though a wrought-iron gate, and from here he could walk to his destination with his eyes closed, so many times had it been rehearsed in simulations. Since his exact arrival date in the twentieth century wasn't known, he'd had to fully plan for Rutherford's prior two institutions as well: McGill in Canada and Victoria University of Manchester. Rutherford was an intellectual giant and a powerful catalyst for others researching the atom, and Proteus had been meticulously prepared for any of the three laboratories where he might encounter him in the early 1900s.

Ahead was Free School Lane, which led to the Cavendish Laboratory. Before long he arrived, stopped, and stared at the peaked stone archway at the front of Cavendish.

Proteus trembled in confused wonderment. He'd had this building's image in front of him for so many years, he wasn't sure what to think.

Two decades of training and four centuries of time-shift led him here. He closed his eyes for a count of twenty as he slowed his breathing cycle and heart rate and then opened them again.

It was still there. Despite the momentary flashback to his training, he knew this was no hologram. Cavendish was solid and real.

The intricate stone scrollwork surrounding the entrance to the three-story building must have meaning, but he couldn't fathom it. His intense training had focused on the technical and practical aspects of the mission: science, transportation, language, finances, and martial arts. Some of his knowledge of twentieth-century culture — especially religion — contained gaps.

Proteus paused to call-up the photographs, floor plans, and holo-sims of Cavendish that he'd committed to memory. In the mission details, the basement was the most likely location for all of Ernest Rutherford's various radiation-scattering experiments, but the exact location was unknown. He recalled the mess: wooden benches were jammed together and overflowing with glass vacuum tubes, electrodes, clamps, and large flasks; and in between the benches were narrow passages, which were themselves hazarded by metal pipes, hoses, and wires, high-voltage gear, and electric pumps.

Proteus considered that the photos were likely taken on clean-up-for-the-press day, and he expected the dangerous clutter to be much worse than had been recorded. And — in addition to the jumbled mess of scientific gear — there would be considerable radioactive contamination.

Proteus stood to the side of the archway and watched the sparse foot traffic flow into and out of the building. Across campus, chimes sounded the Big Ben song, followed by three bells. Only a few more hours to wait.

His mouth was dry with the anticipation of his first mission, and thick saliva clung in his throat.

Deciding that further time spent gawking at the academic building he was going to break into after sunset might appear suspicious, he shouldered his satchel and moved on. He paced around it once, evaluating the entry points he'd been taught, before moving on to explore other aspects of the university. And to find something to quench his thirst and settle the hunger pangs in his stomach.

There was much work ahead before catching the train back to London in the morning.

4

"That which is not measurable is not science. That which is not PHYSICS is stamp collecting."
~ Ernest Rutherford

"Yes. Yes!" said Ernest Rutherford in response to a soft knock on his office door. He disliked being interrupted when deep in thought. "Come in."

"Sorry to disturb you, Professor, but—"

"It's quite all right," said Rutherford. He capped his fountain pen, setting it on a pile of papers that was threatening to overwhelm his desk. Outside, rivulets of water ran down the leaded windowpanes, creating ripples in the grey morning light entering the room. A brass pendulum clock on the wall tapped its rhythm. He stood and smiled at his graduate student. "It's a lovely morning, Marco!"

Marco flinched visibly at the volume of Rutherford's voice, and several loose window panes rattled.

"Yes?" said Marco.

"Yes, indeed," said Rutherford and wondered if this man would be one of the washouts. "The Royal Society have accepted my paper, and I've been formally granted the distinct honor of naming the particle I've discovered as the proton."

"Y–yes?"

"After Prout's Hypothesis. Blast it, man. Do try to keep up. You're new here, but you won't last long unless you snap to it." Rutherford spun to face the chalkboard. "You're certainly familiar at this point, after three months, with this!"

As Rutherford gestured with his hand at the equation on the board, he toppled an Erlenmeyer flask, which fell and shattered. He ignored it and stabbed a thick index finger at the equation: $\alpha + {}^{14}N \rightarrow {}^{17}O + p$

"The alpha particle has collided with a nitrogen and been absorbed, turning it into oxygen. But in the process, it's chipped a little piece off the atom, and that little p is exactly the same mass and charge as a hydrogen atom without its electron."

"So nitrogen has been transmuted into oxygen," said Marco.

"Don't use that word!" said Rutherford, and Marco shrank back. "They'll call us alchemists and heretics. Call it *transformation*."

"Transformation," said Marco, and his Adam's apple bobbed as he swallowed and nodded.

"You came in my office for a reason. And I hope that reason was to show me the results of your experiments. Where are they? We can't keep students on board who don't produce results. And I can't wait around while you stand there with your mouth open, gaping like a fish. I have experiments to do before my conclusions are fully accepted."

Rutherford went back to his desk and sat down, rifling through the mounds of papers in search of his pen. "Blast it, the pen keeps disappearing," he said. He looked at Marco, then remembered something. "Ah, I have a project for you. It will give some direction to your early wanderings and build upon the work of Geiger and Marsden."

"Yes?"

"The refinements in our equipment permit greater accuracy, and the more enriched radiation sources from Curie will yield deeper insight, I believe. There's more in there! The atom hasn't fully revealed its secrets to us," said Rutherford. "Probe deeper into the metal-foil experiments and tell me what it shows! That is your task. Now, let's get some results."

Rutherford rose and walked toward the door. He left his office singing "Onward Christian Soldiers" as he paraded past a large sign reading *Quiet please — Experiments in progress.*

The people he met in the hallway smiled at the Prof's good mood, even as they shrank back a bit in response to the decibel level of his voice. He didn't care. He knew there were secrets to uncover, and his purpose was to find them.

At the end of the hallway, as he descended the stairs to his laboratories, he was already well into the second verse.

5

"Life is not easy for any of us. But what of that? We must have perseverance and above all confidence in ourselves. We must believe that we are gifted for something and that this thing, at whatever cost, must be attained."
~ Marie Curie

For an hour, Proteus walked around the campus, letting his curiosity lead him. He explored buildings, looked at statues, and read bronze plaques describing the histories of pivotal luminaries. He then sought out the Trinity College Chapel, which was easy to identify by its Gothic pinnacles and crenelated roof, and went inside to find the memorial to Sir Isaac Newton. The life-sized marble statue stood in the antechapel; Newton looked thoughtful as he gazed upward in his flowing robes. At the base were the words *Qui genus humanum ingenio superavit*: "who surpassed the race of men in understanding."

Proteus stood motionless for several minutes. From Newton's three laws of motion, Rutherford had pulled together knowledge of electromagnetism and radiation to deduce and tease out structures comprising the atom. Rutherford was leaping forward at breakneck speed. Newton had once said, "If I have seen further, it is by standing on the shoulders of giants." The statement certainly applied to Rutherford as well.

Then Proteus chuckled as he recalled Newton's pursuit of alchemy and the philosopher's stone, which could transform base metals into

35

precious ones. Ironically, Rutherford's 1908 Nobel Prize was awarded for demonstrating that radioactive decay was a process that fundamentally transformed one element into another. *The man is a genius, but he needs to be stopped. Nuclear fission must be delayed.*

After several more minutes, Proteus turned and left to continue his self-guided tour of Cambridge. The campus featured a fascinating collection of architectural styles from over half a millennium. Still wandering, he passed through a gate into a busy street, and his eyes were drawn to a wooden sign hanging from two chains. On it were three icons: a man in robes with a long stick ending in a curved hook, a sheep, and the mathematical symbol, Π. At the bottom of the sign were the words *Public House.*

Intrigued, he walked up the steps to inspect it more closely, but then jumped back as the wooden door swung toward him. A man in a wool cap and sweater exited, and from inside the building wafted savory and sour odors, and Proteus heard burbles of conversation spiked with laughter. The door closed slowly, sealing off the noise and the smell. Proteus stood still, uncertain if he should go inside. Above the door were written the words *Welcome to the Shepherd and Pi.*

It seems inviting, he thought, and his stomach growled again.

"Going in, mate?" said a voice from behind him.

"Oh ... yes," said Proteus, and he pulled on the metal handle. The door was heavy but moved easily. He stopped and absorbed the smells, warmth, and buzz of the voices as his eyes adjusted to the light. The man behind him squeezed past, brushing against the coats and jackets hanging along a wall, and Proteus looked around the room full of people. Some were sitting on tall stools along a polished wooden bar; others were seated around shorter tables; some smoked pipes. Everyone was either engaged in serious conversation or smiling and laughing.

Glasses full of amber liquid clinked, and darts thudded into a board. Two men sitting in the corner were huddled over a chessboard. Even above all the other noise in the pub, he could hear the thwack of the wooden pieces and the players' taps on top of the dual-faced wooden clock as their hands flew back and forth. Proteus stepped closer to watch them. He'd played against the computers in his century and didn't care much for the game or count himself skilled, but this was a joy to watch: a blitz of strategy and tactics.

Suddenly, one player resigned, and then they both looked up. One gestured with an open palm, inviting Proteus to play, but Proteus shook his head, and politely backed away. A waft of smoke stung his eyes, and he turned away, squeezing them shut. When he looked up, he saw that he was standing under a glass frame mounted high on the wall. It encased a protractor, a compass, and a sheet of yellowed parchment with mathematical equations calligraphed in black ink. The sight was the closest Proteus had come to a religious experience. *An original Newton document on calculus!*

His reverie was interrupted by a man behind the bar. "What can I get for you?"

Proteus turned toward him, and said, "Something to eat and drink, please."

The barman pointed to a chalkboard on the wall, and said, "That's our food menu, and on tap we've got stout, lager, India pale ale, and bitter."

Proteus studied the menu, and then said, "Two scotch eggs and a lager, please."

"Yes, sir," said the barman. He filled a pint glass and placed it on the bar as Proteus sat down on a stool. "Be right back with the eggs."

The beer was crisp and cool, and the carbonation tingled his tongue. The barman returned with the food and set a plate in front of Proteus.

Proteus studied the food a moment before slicing into one of the scotch eggs. It consisted of a sausage meat-casing around a boiled egg, and the layers made him think of an atom, with the yolk being the nucleus. He was still getting used to the taste of animal flesh, but these were quite delicious, and he soon finished off the meal.

He checked his watch: 7:10 p.m. It was time to get on with the evening's work. Rutherford was a stickler for getting his assistant professors, postdoctorates, and graduate students out of the laboratory by six, to be home for supper. But Proteus was certain that some of them disregarded that order, especially if they were in the middle of a critical experiment. This meant that he needed to be on high alert for people — in addition to the radioactivity and the clutter of dangerous equipment.

He was in for an intense evening.

$$\Psi$$

In his century, Proteus had been inoculated against infectious, toxic, and radioactive agents, which would provide a relative degree of protection — but he knew that the best mitigation strategy against radiation was time-based.

In the 1920s, they knew next to nothing about the deleterious effects of radiation exposure on the human body. Even at this moment, women were licking the tips of paintbrushes dipped in radium to better paint the markers on glow-in-the-dark watches. Thorium was put into toothpaste.

The physicists had devices to measure the energy in their experiments but physically experienced nothing when handling radioactive sources. They only used shielding to isolate the radioactive stockpile from interfering with sensitive experiments — not to protect themselves.

You're being paranoid, aren't you? an internal voice chided him. *You won't live long enough with your mutation to worry about radiation sickness — and that's if time-travel sickness doesn't get you first. You don't really know that you're safe from it.*

Proteus clenched his fists, angry at the punch in the face his higher reasoning center had just dealt him. It lent a sense of urgency and reminded him to focus on what he could change. The anger was self-pity, and he had no time for that. He knew his most immediate danger would be found in the high-voltage equipment in the labs.

It was not yet twilight, but a misting rain made it seem darker as Proteus made his way from the pub to Cavendish. His black overcoat repelled the moisture as much as it helped him blend into the shadows. There were few about as night settled upon Cambridge, and he circled the building, making certain he wasn't observed.

Moving into a dark alcove, he extracted the SDU and scanned with the infrared wavelength, looking for human heat signatures. Finding little beyond what he'd seen visually, he flipped to the gamma radiation sensor, calibrated it, and then scanned Cavendish — and almost dropped the SDU. One corner of the basement was ablaze.

Proteus's breath caught and his gaze flicked up from the screen, but from a hundred yards away, Cavendish sat quiet, dark, and serene. He rechecked the SDU, wondering if he'd set the gain incorrectly, but it registered accurately. He scaled back the sensitivity and looked at the building again. The hotspots confirmed the basement location of the experiments.

Proteus put the SDU back in his satchel. In addition to the Data-Cube, it had another important function: the ability to emit particles and photons of high energies across the electromagnetic spectrum.

Touching the obsidian flat top accessed both the Cube hologram and the EM-projector; he intended to use the latter to adulterate the radiation experiments of the period.

The microfusion power source could generate up to one million mega-electron-volts, well in excess of the eight MeV needed for fission and similar in output to the massive synchrotrons and particle accelerators that would only be created decades in the future. But at seven kilograms, it was considerably lighter than those field-sized behemoths that would weigh upwards of five thousand tons.

Proteus emerged from the alcove and approached Cavendish. He was delighted to find that the front entrance was unlocked. Inside, he soon found the stairs to the basement.

The lights were out, so halfway down Proteus paused to pull out the SDU and tuned it to sense infrared. He continued down the stone staircase, watching the screen.

Despite the lights being off, he was careful not to make any noise lest there be someone working on an experiment. Some of the work involved peering into a microscope to look for transient flashes of light on a fluorescent screen. The light emitted when a radioactive particle collided with the coated screen was so faint that the experiments were often conducted in total darkness.

He ducked around a large pipe on the landing and continued down. At the bottom he paused, peered into the darkness of the large room, and listened and scanned, counting to thirty.

There didn't appear to be anyone present, so Proteus continued into the room. He stepped over a set of pipes running across the floor and explored deeper into the maze, cautious of the electric wires and benches creating obstacles to his movement.

After several minutes, when he was satisfied that no one else was there, he switched the SDU to a low-lumen visible spectrum. He looked around the laboratory at the piles of equipment, jars, vacuum tubes, and wires. This wasn't yet the location he sought. He exited into a narrow corridor that led in the direction of the radiation source he'd glimpsed from outside.

He stepped inside the room and checked the SDU, which indicated widespread radiation. The device registered alpha, beta, gamma, and X-rays, of which the scientists of the time were aware, but also other electromagnetic spectrum bands of which they were not. None of the different forms of radiation were in quantities sufficient to present a short-term risk, but Proteus knew that working there over time was not safe.

He readjusted the device to alert him should it encounter more intense levels. *I wonder how many suffer from some form of radiation sickness or will develop cancer?* But even as the question formed in his mind, he already knew the answer. Henri Becquerel first measured radiation emissions from uranium salts in 1896, won the Nobel Prize for this discovery, and then died shortly after that from a mysterious illness at the age of fifty-five.

Ever since Becquerel let the cat out of the bag, humans had been playing with radiation, trying to figure out what it was and what it signified. They found more mineral sources and began purifying the radioactive elements within for their experiments. Soon, they began zapping almost everything with it.

They'd jumped too far, too fast. They were like toddlers playing with hand grenades, amazed at the energy but not comprehending the danger. But one would be the first to pull out a pin.

The jarring thought of the Cataclysm returned Proteus's focus to searching the laboratory.

Upon a table in the corner of the room was a low, semicircular wall of loosely stacked matte-grey bricks rising a few feet in height. Proteus went over to inspect the bricks and hefted one of them, which was much heavier than it looked. Lead. There was a gap at one end of the lead-brick wall; cautiously, he eased his device around the corner. The SDU flashed a warning, and he withdrew it. *Hot stuff here.*

Proteus marked the location in the SDU and continued his exploratory rounds. After confirming there was no one present, he began diving deeper, opening drawers and cabinets, and inspecting closets. He took inventory as he went, quietly dictating to the SDU.

He came across a metal box in one of the drawers, pulled it out, and placed it on a table. Inside were small sheets of gold foil, each roughly four square inches. There were about a dozen of these, and other types of metal foil as well — silver and lithium. He picked up one of the gold foil squares, analyzed it with the SDU, and found it to be four microns thick, approximately one hundred atoms.

The scatter-experiments conducted in Cavendish focused a beam of alpha radiation, He^{++} atoms, at thin metal foils, while an observer looked through a microscope and measured the tiny blips of light on a phosphorescent screen as a tiny percentage of the alpha particles, roughly one in 300,000, were deflected by the atomic nucleus. Since atoms were mostly space with a tiny nucleus, the scattering angles and frequencies helped Rutherford deduce the size and composition of the nucleus.

Proteus's plan was to alter the metal foils in such a fashion that the scatter observed would push Rutherford and his team off their previous observations and hypotheses — and introduce the seed of doubt.

By splitting some of the gold atoms in the foil into lighter atoms, he would create a stencil: whatever pattern he etched was what they would see, although quite fuzzy. He thought of the outlines to inscribe, rehearsed in his training, and then began populating the template in the SDU with a series of irregular circles and ovals. These geometric shapes should result in a scatter that appeared natural yet be too blurry to recognize in detail. When he finished the template, he began the micro-etching process.

After several hours, he was confident he'd attended to all the metal foil samples: lithium, silver, and gold. Proteus began to cover traces of his presence before deciding the whole place was so messy that no one would ever notice he'd been there. Even if he were wrong, no one would spend energy trying to piece together his intrusion.

There were a number of other experiments he needed to sabotage, but they would have to wait until future evenings. He was pleased at what he'd accomplished this evening, and it was approaching time to go. However, before he left, he at least wanted to locate the next apparatus he needed to sabotage.

After a while, he located an array of compressed gas cylinders standing like upright torpedoes and a large vacuum tube mounted on a bench. Rutherford had recently used this to discover the existence of protons. High-energy alpha radiation from thorium couldn't travel very far, but it blasted the protons off nitrogen. These protons travelled farther than alpha radiation could, and as they struck a zinc-sulfide-covered glass screen, tiny flashes of light betrayed their presence.

Proteus's sabotage here was to irradiate the zinc sulfide with high-energy neutrons, transforming stable zinc isotopes into unstable, radioactive ones. These unstable isotopes would no longer have phosphorescence when struck with radiation, rendering the experimenter effectively blind to any effect of the radiation source used. On a future trip, he would zap all of the glass screens, as well as the stockpile of zinc sulfide they used to make them.

It was 4:00 a.m.; time to go. He crept cautiously back through the laboratory. On his way out, he couldn't resist stopping to marvel at the simplicity of the device that would lead to so many discoveries and ultimately spin off into newer technologies: Rutherford's scatter experiment. At one end was a lead box with a thin slit that allowed a narrow slice of alpha radiation to emerge from the shielded thorium and into a vacuum tube. Air needed to be pumped out to as low a pressure as possible in order to eliminate any contaminants, and the glass walls needed to be thin enough to allow the radiation through. Although highly ionizing, the relatively large alpha particles didn't have the penetrating power of beta or gamma radiation. The desire for thinner tubes and lower vacuum pressures explained the piles of broken glass.

Suspended in the center of the vacuum tube was a piece of thin metal foil. Mounted on the other side of the foil was a piece of glass coated in zinc sulfide, which would briefly fluoresce, like a faint pixel on an LCD screen, when an alpha particle hit it.

Dawn struggled through thick clouds as Proteus arrived at the foyer and peered cautiously through a small glass panel in one of the doors. He stifled a yawn and shook off the sleepiness. This was no time to let his guard down.

He took a deep breath, pushed on the brass bar, and walked out into the feeble morning light. There were only a few pedestrian early birds walking under the slate sky that threatened rain, and they seemed intent on reaching their destinations before the skies opened up.

He glanced back over his shoulder and caught sight of a large man standing in the shadows of a building. From fifty yards away, Proteus couldn't make out any of his features, but he was certain the man was looking at him. Proteus turned away and increased his pace. *A janitor, perhaps, or a gardener.*

Proteus retraced his path from yesterday along Free School Lane, back towards the train station, occasionally turning to see if he was being followed. The town began to emerge from its slumber. He thought of all the recurring work he would need to do here over the next several weeks and months to disrupt the research. He looked around one last time before deciding he was in the clear.

$$\Psi$$

Proteus merged like a sheep into the herd as he left the morning commuter train at Liverpool Street Station and went down a steep double staircase into the Underground. It was half-past seven, and the claustrophobic tunnel was flooded with souls entering the depths beneath the city.

His necktie seemed to constrict as he descended, and he stopped to loosen it.

On the other side of the tunnel, people rode up an escalator. They were slumped and looked dejected.

Tobacco smoke burned his eyes and throat. His chest tightened. Perspiration dripped off his nose, and he used his handkerchief to wipe it away. Turning to look back up, he could no longer see any daylight. Below, there was no sight of the train platform. The walls of the tunnel seemed to move toward him, squeezing—

So many people. Too many. It's tight in here!

Proteus gripped the railing, closed his eyes, and slowed his breathing: *Find your center, there's nothing to fear.* People swarmed around him and clumped downward. The cacophony of shuffling feet and voices echoed in the deep passage.

After several minutes of calming breaths, the claws of claustrophobia receded. Proteus released his white-knuckled grip on the railing and slowly put one foot in front of other, stepping down toward the exit at the bottom, repeating to himself that he was safe.

Nearing the end, he heard the squeaking of wheels and felt the whoosh of an acrid ozone breeze as a train pulled away from a platform. He searched above the shuffling masses and found signs pointing out the platform he wanted.

When he arrived there, he found it was much more crowded than the line leading away from central London. He waited for the next train to the west, toward Piccadilly.

After several minutes, a dirty metallic serpent rattled along the rails into the station and stopped. The nearly full train disgorged people onto the platform. Proteus stood back, out of the way, then boarded.

As the train left the station, Proteus looked out of the dingy window. Bright sparks flashed off the tunnel walls, and the compartment rocked from side to side as the train picked up speed.

Just several stops to the Temple tube station, and then I can escape from this tomb.

6

From his workbench in the backroom of Father Time's Watches &
Clocks, the watchmaker heard the small bell ring out as the front door
of his store opened and closed. Footsteps sounded on the wooden
floor; he sighed and stood. His assistant was not yet at work, so he'd
have to attend to the customer himself. He removed the magnifying
loupes from his face and stretched his sore back.

After a glance at the chessboard that displayed his current
correspondence game in progress, he shuffled through the narrow,
curtained doorway and into the front of the shop.

"Morning," he said to a man in a black overcoat and black porkpie
hat, dripping with the morning rain. "How may I be of service, sir?"

"My pocket watch has stopped and won't wind," said the man.
"Can you repair it?"

The watchmaker stood under the sign advertising *New, Used, and
Repairs*, and said, "Yes, that is what I do. I craft, I build, and I repair.
May I see the timepiece, please?"

The man's hands shook as reached into his pocket and approached
the counter.

The watchmaker turned on a gooseneck lamp and gestured for the
man to put the watch on a board covered in taut black felt. He put on

pince-nez glasses as the man set the watch down.

"Let's have a look, shall we?" said the watchmaker. He picked up the gold lozenge and read the lettering on the white face of the dial. "Ah, an Omega, 1918 model. These are known for having weak springs. Did you drop it?"

"No. I don't think so."

As the watchmaker inspected the bezel and then turned the watch over, looking for signs of damage, he thought about all the other repairs he had lined up. His fingertips explored the surface, finding small scratches. He ran an index finger lightly over the edge of the backplate. In the tiny nicks in the gold surface, he recognized the pattern of long and short scratches. *Code. A message.*

The watchmaker looked closely at the taller man before him, taking in the details of the face: flat nose, handlebar moustache, and worried brown eyes. He was certain he'd never seen him before.

"W–when should I come back?" the man asked.

"These can be difficult to work on, but if it's just the spring, then it should be straightforward," replied the watchmaker. "I can have an estimate by close of business tomorrow."

The man stared at him, his face frozen. Clocks ticked in the background.

"Please fill out your name on the repair ticket. And come back *tomorrow* before six o'clock," said the watchmaker and handed over a slip of paper.

A shaking hand reached out, scrawled something, and handed it back.

The watchmaker knew the name was fake. He tore off the number at the bottom of the ticket and passed it over to the man. "You'll need this number to claim the watch," he said. "Don't lose it." *He must be new, but displaying such fear is a dangerous weakness.*

The man exhaled slowly and nodded. "Thank you."

"If it looks like it'll take more than two weeks, I can loan you a watch until yours is ready. Remember, I close at 6:00 p.m., sharp. Punctuality is purity, as my dear mother used to say."

The man nodded again, then turned and left the shop.

The watchmaker glanced as the shadow passed the frosted window. *Weakness will get you killed.*

He went into the back room, carefully set the watch down on a felt cloth at his workbench, and pushed aside the other work he'd been doing. *We shall see what this means.*

The doorbell rang again, and the watchmaker went to the doorway to see his assistant, Paul, enter, precisely fifteen minutes early for his scheduled shift. He smiled. *To be early is to be on time.* "Good morning," he said.

"Good morning, sir," said Paul. He began the task of checking, winding, and setting each timepiece displayed in the shop.

The watchmaker observed his young, smartly dressed assistant, pleased at the thoroughness with which the young man attended to his duties. *The customers must see that each and every timepiece is running and that all display the exact same time.* In the beginning, he'd said these words daily to his assistant, but the lad was a quick study, and it was no longer necessary. He watched a moment longer and then said, "I've some delicate repairs to do. See that I'm not disturbed."

He returned to the back room, pausing to pull a thick blackout curtain across the doorway. At the workbench, he noted the time frozen on the face of the Omega and wrote it down on a notepad. Next, he turned the pocket watch face down on the soft cloth and reexamined the pattern: four scratches, each a quarter of an inch in length, and three pinpoint dots. Easy to mistake for accidental, unless you knew it for what it was.

The watchmaker began unscrewing the back plate. After a moment he had the back plate free and adjusted his magnifying loupes to peer at the mechanism inside. A small white lip attracted his eyes, and he reached in with a pair of tweezers, gripping the edge of a tiny fold of paper jammed into a gear. He extracted the paper carefully and unfolded it in his palm, smoothing it gently.

The watchmaker placed his glasses on his nose and then adjusted the lamp. He scanned the small, neat letters, and copied each one onto a piece of paper, each a finger-width apart. After he was finished, he went to an array of three dozen clocks and watches hung on the back wall: each was silent, hands unmoving, and dangling a red-marked repair ticket. He looked for a timepiece displaying the time corresponding to the one on the stopped messenger watch.

When he found it, he wrote down the three letters on the repair tag: *FXH.* In the safe was a thick, sorted sheaf of invoices, one of which had these three letters at the top. The "invoice" was part of a matched pair known in cryptography as a *one-time cipher pad*, filled with the transpositions that would allow him to decrypt the message, and only this message. And because it had been coded by Red-Bear using the exact same one-use key, it couldn't be broken if intercepted by British

Intelligence.

The watchmaker was soon back at his bench, decrypting the message. He worked through the letters, meticulously determining each one and then repeating the process to be certain there were no errors. Anticipation gnawed at him like change in the pocket of a child in a sweet shop.

He finished the message — *R-B 3 d 445 meet* — and then opened the iron grate of the coal stove. He stuffed the papers into the fire and watched them burn as he thought through the message and its implications: *Red Bear, one of my operatives in Cambridge, is requesting to meet in three days, at a quarter to five.*

It was unusual, and the context and timing implied something important. Cambridge was important, too. It provided access to new research and technologies, as well as the opportunities for recruitment — both those who understood the call of a workers' revolution and those who could be unwittingly bent to the cause.

In the stove, the paper blackened and split into glowing yellow-edged fragments — which then crumbled, fell, and turned to ash.

The watchmaker went back to his bench, wound up the Omega, and verified that it worked before reattaching the back plate. He then wrote the cost of the repair and then the letter *Y* on the attached ticket. *Yes, we shall meet in three days.* Again, he wondered what information Red-Bear would have for him. He didn't know the name of the messenger who'd dropped off the Omega, or if someone different would pick it up, but he was certain the affirmative response would make it back to Red-Bear. *Our tradecraft has now grown beyond that of the English, and they don't know how deeply we've penetrated.*

He looked at the chessboard; he was black, playing the Slav defense in response to white's Queen's gambit. The game had branched into the Alapin variation, which was as familiar as his repair tools.

Time is on my side. He's boxed in and clueless to the real threat.

7

Proteus read the *Times* as he ate a breakfast of bangers and mash in the restaurant of the Savoy. He tried not to think about what was in the sausages, though he wanted to scan them with the SDU for radioisotopes, heavy metals, organic chemicals, and bacterial toxins. But of course, he couldn't do that in a public setting, so he slipped a sausage in his pocket to scan later and continued his meal.

Hopefully, the Savoy's kitchens were relatively hygienic and sourced their ingredients from reputable establishments — but if he was going to eat here on a regular basis, he needed to be sure. Relatively was the key word, and applicable to everything in this century. Any foodstuff made four centuries before he was born was apt to be suspect compared with the sterile food processing in his century. But provided it didn't sicken or kill him, he had to get used to the food of this period. He looked at his plate again. The taste of animal flesh was new and strange, but at least the potatoes were familiar. He scooped another forkful and held it in front of his face to inspect before putting it in his mouth.

The idea of harvesting animals for food, clothing, or tools was as barbaric as the chopping of trees. Something in the abject waste and thoughtlessness toward the future — and the precious things he'd dreamed of — made the meal taste bitter.

He pushed the plate away and returned to the paper, scanning a section on events:

> Crown Prince Hirohito of Japan concludes official UK visit
> First golf tournament between the States and the UK to play

May 22nd

> Royal Society announces lecture by famed German physicist
> Buildup to the Derby June 1st: Daily Updates

Proteus turned to the section on the Derby and read more about England's most prestigious horse race. It was a time of fairs, picnics, celebrations, and heavy betting. In his training, he'd been warned to avoid gambling, large crowds, and parties, since these introduced too many opportunities for potential conflict and might jeopardize his safety.

Perhaps another time, he thought and rose to leave.

Ψ

Back in his room, Proteus opened the SDU and recorded into his personal log:

"It's been two weeks, and I'm still alive. I've made a half-dozen trips to Cavendish and have disrupted a number of their critical radium and thorium scattering experiments. And although I don't yet know how effective, my hopes are high.

"My health remains good, with no signs of illness. My eyes and throat are raw from exposure to tobacco smoke, coal smog, and dust.

"I haven't yet seen any conclusive evidence of Time-resistance. I had the same motor taxi driver three days in a row, and the déjà-vu was troubling, but then I reasoned it was my regular schedule and large tips that propelled his behavior. Nevertheless, I remain on guard."

Proteus finished the recording and secured the SDU in its biblical binding. He stretched out on the bed, closed his eyes, and visualized the mission parameters and his experiences in this time period to date. Frustration built as he thought of the difficult uphill challenge he faced. Sneaking into labs to sabotage experiments and discredit researchers, while disruptive, could simply not overcome the momentum of scores of scientists across many nations — especially when funded by governments and scientific bodies obsessed with the pursuit of power.

He sat up and stared at the hotel wall, trying to fathom how he could apply more influence and guide the research onto a different set of rails. Everything in this time period revolved around money and control of others.

Money and control of others…

The money Proteus was accumulating through his stock portfolio was to fund his sabotage and living expenses, but what if he could leverage things from a different angle? He had been working on the pinnacle of the pyramid, the sharp point where the experimentalists did their work, but what if he eroded the base and undercut the foundation as well?

He looked at the paper again and read the article about the guest lecturer, the German physicist. The Royal Society was a magnet for the best and brightest scientific minds. It controlled both the purse strings of researchers in the UK and their publication prestige — while also serving as the pot for a primordial soup of new ideas and international research.

Rutherford was not only the director of the department in Cavendish but would also become president of the Royal Society. If Proteus could become a full-fledged member and raise enough capital, he could influence the direction of scientific research.

$$\Psi$$

The watchmaker told his assistant he'd be back by half past five. It was a short walk to Battersea Park, and the summer afternoon sun warmed his back. He strolled into the park and continued walking until he arrived at a pair of benches, backs nestled against one another, and sat down on the one facing the Thames.

He reached into his pocket and tossed a few seeds to the pigeons as he waited and checked his watch: a minute away from a quarter to five. Red-Bear, like all of the assets the watchmaker handled, was punctual; none of his charges lasted long if they weren't.

Soon he sensed the bulk of Red-Bear easing into the bench behind. The back-to-back arrangement meant they could talk freely while observing 360 degrees around their location.

"Red sky at night, shepherd's delight," said the watchmaker.

"Time waits for no man," said Red-Bear in his deep voice.

Proper code having been exchanged, they engaged in talk about the sunny weather, the FA Cup win by Tottenham over Wolverhampton, and the poor quality of English vodka. Throughout it all, the watchmaker listened for the code word that meant their spy network had been compromised, but it wasn't there. He smiled, tossed a few more seeds to the disgusting pigeons, and said, "Proceed."

Red-Bear dove into the information: someone had been sneaking into the Cavendish laboratories several nights a week; and he relayed what he knew of the man.

"Are you certain?" asked the watchmaker after Red-Bear had finished his report.

"Yes."

"How?"

"I followed him. After being in the laboratories all night, he took the morning train from Cambridge to London. It was crowded and difficult, but I followed him through the Underground to the Savoy."

"Who is he?"

"I don't know … but my contact at the restaurant says he speaks like an American."

"An American … hmm," said the watchmaker. "This is most irregular." *American dandies at posh hotels are only interested in women, booze, and jazz.* "You have done well. I want you to keep tailing him. Figure out what he's after and report back in two weeks."

"It will be done," said Red-Bear, and then stood and left.

The watchmaker threw a few more seeds in the direction of the pigeons, which were cooing and stalking around his bench looking for handouts. He hated the filthy flying rats, but the English seemed fond of them, and it would never do for him to be seen trying to stomp on one. So he smiled and tossed seeds and analyzed the information he'd just received.

An American sneaking into Cavendish. These are indeed strange times.

8

"You should never bet against anything in science at odds of more than about 10-12 to 1."
~ Ernest Rutherford

Proteus sat at the desk in his room and reflected on his rejection by the Royal Society. The chief steward had been polite at first but then had turned surly at Proteus's braggadocio. It was puzzling. Bluffing or money had worked in every other circumstance thus far — just as the historians had told him it would — but the Royal Society was flatly unimpressed. And insisting that he was a preeminent scientist, and even hints of "large donations," had only resulted in Proteus being shown the door. In the end, the chief steward had told him to come back when he had a Nobel Prize, wished to bequeath an estate, or became a lord — and then he had smirked.

I'm going to need more clout. A lot more clout.

Proteus picked up his copy of the *Times* and looked at the front-page article, which was all about tomorrow's Derby. He then checked the Data-Cube index of *Times* headlines and found the one for the second of June, where he found the picture of the winner, Humorist, splashed all over the front page.

It wasn't really gambling if you knew the outcome. All he had to do was decide how much money to bet, make the trip to Epsom, cash in — and then figure out what to do with the winnings. So, his next step was to look for a short-term, big move in a stock. Filtering through the Data-Cube's stock algorithm, he found his candidate: a coal-mining company was about to find diamonds in one of their mines — and in ten days' time, its share price was going to go through the roof.

He whistled as he got ready to go to the bank to make a withdrawal. To his ears, he still sounded off-key. Despite his practice, he hadn't yet figured out how people formed the correct shapes with their mouths to hit the proper notes. But it didn't really bother him; making music was still making music. And he was happy to have a plan to work around the roadblock at the Royal Society.

ψ

Proteus boarded the Epsom Express at Victoria Station and was almost overwhelmed by the crush of people in their suits, long dresses, and gaily decorated hats, all headed to Epsom Downs for the Derby. He reminded himself to pronounce it *Darby*. As the train chugged out of the station, the buzzing conversation, peals of laughter, and brightly colored clothing were a welcome tonic to the guilty thoughts he harbored.

Some of these people — most of them — were going to lose money betting. Some would shout and get angry. Some would get drunk. And some would fight.

But that would be later. Right now, they were on the cusp of the day's enjoyment, with the enthusiasm of expectation: the uncertainty of a great English horse race; the promise of a large fairground packed with food, drink, and entertainment. Proteus looked through the window as the train picked up steam, heading southwest into the English countryside.

The soot-covered buildings became smaller, fewer, and less carbonized as the train escaped London. And as the Express powered along, the built-up, dense environments yielded to villages, hamlets, and then farms.

The farther from London the train went, the more the green fields opened up to distant ochre hills, cloud-dotted in the morning light. The sight of the horizon and blue sky transfixed Proteus, and he cupped his hands to shield his eyes and pressed his forehead against the vibrating train window in wonderment.

The name of the horse that would soon win was Humorist.

Tomorrow, he could hold a copy of the London *Times* in his hands with that headline — just as he'd seen in the digital archive of the Data-Cube. The name tickled him. All these people laughing, and Humorist, a long shot, would win. It was also terrible, because he knew the horse would die of pulmonary hemorrhage shortly after the race.

And I'm betting the farm, thought Proteus. Or is that an American idiom?

The train had stopped accelerating, and he relaxed in the swaying carriage as steel wheels clacked over track sections. Inside the car, conversations rose to compete with the train noise. Outside, green hills rolled by. June was in full bloom and the rich smells of hay and flowers blew in through the open carriage windows. Proteus became lost in thought as the terrain flowed around the train.

The train rounded a bend, and sunlight suddenly blinded him. He shut his eyes in pain and turned away. A bright after-image hovered in his retina and triggered a memory — the Hiroshima fireball from his teachings — and he recoiled in horror as the video images played in his mind.

He snapped back into his surroundings and noticed the train was slowing and the burble of voices was growing. A small child seated between her parents, was studying him from across the aisle. The child's mother looked across at Proteus, and he waved and smiled. The child waved back and began giggling. The mother said something to her daughter, and the girl clapped her hands and bounced in her seat.

Proteus clenched his teeth and turned away to look out through his window again. He couldn't remember the face of his mother or father, so young had he been when he was separated from them.

Tents and crowds were stretched out as far he could see. Wood and coal smoke drifted into the carriage, carrying the odor of spices and cooking. The slowing train lurched to a halt, and suddenly everyone stood and began talking at once. Proteus decided not to wrestle with the crowd and waited until the throng had thinned before getting up from his seat and disembarking.

Outside, a drum and pipe band marched by, playing a rousing tune as children skipped alongside and clapped to the beat. All of the musicians wore tall black furry hats and tartan skirts (*kilts*, Proteus reminded himself), and they strode by in perfect step in the wake of one man with a big stick. A crowd followed along behind as the band marched toward the fairground, which was impossible to mistake for anything else. Colored pennants flapped and waved in the breeze above giant tents and steam-powered rides. Children towed parents toward the rides like motorboats pulling barges on the Thames. Even from half a mile away, Proteus could hear the cheers of the crowd.

The fairground, though, was not his destination. He scanned and quickly located the grandstand. He moved forward and then stopped to sneeze several times. Pulling out his handkerchief, he blew his nose; then a chill snuck along his spine as he wondered if he might be coming down with an illness.

Proteus resumed his approach, still watching the people in the crowd, and soon the grandstand towered over him. From his perspective at one side, it looked like an enormous cheese wedge terraced with rows upon rows of people. His eyes drifted to the large central, enclosed booth in the middle of the grandstand and then down to the track. He couldn't quite see the surface, but the hedges and fence clearly marked the boundary.

In front of the fence was a series of elevated wooden platforms. Upon each one was a booth, some with roofs, and all decorated with ribbons and half-circles of red, white, and blue cloth. As Proteus got closer, he could read some of the signs: *Bobby's Honest Bets*; *Whinny's Winners*; and *The Golden Pony*.

In front of each platform stood a cluster of men — some gentlemen and some commoners, judging by their attire. Proteus looked at the nearest platform. Before the booth was a red-faced man in shirtsleeves, gesticulating to the crowd.

The man on the platform shouted out something, and several hands in the audience raised in reply. Proteus was soon close enough to see that money and paper tickets were changing hands.

He got in line in front of The Golden Pony and studied the board hung behind the barking man. It listed all the horses and then a series of numbers. He scanned down the list until located the name Humorist, and beside it the numbers *10/1*. Proteus watched the proceedings and listened to the men placing their bets, trying to fathom out how to do it properly when his time came.

The line inched forward, and Proteus experienced a chill despite the bright noon sunshine. *Anxiety*, he thought and tried to project composure. When it was his turn, he said, "Two hundred pounds on Humorist to win."

The barker repeated the order, looked at Proteus, and said, "Big bet at ten to one. Let's see the sterling, mate."

Proteus handed him the cash. The barker counted it out, flashing a quick side glance at his helper. He scribbled on a paper ticket and then handed it to Proteus.

"Are you sure you don't want to pick Humorist to show?" asked a man from behind him. "He pulled out of the Royal Ascot because of a cough. Not a well horse, that one."

Proteus turned to face a short man in a tuxedo and tall silk top hat. "I'm fine with my bet on Humorist," he said, raising his voice so as to be heard above the din.

From behind the top hat, a man in an ill-fitting suit and a Panama hat stepped forward. "Humorist — that's a good one," he chuckled and nudged his mate in the ribs. "*Funny* to think that one'd win."

His companion chortled, spilling his beer, and joined in on the fun. "Oi. Here's a punny horse!"

Proteus looked at them, trying to decipher what was so humorous. His expression itself must have been funny, because they guffawed louder, and one began slapping the back of the other, spilling more beer.

"Never mind them," said Top-hat. "Ruffian rugby louts." He beckoned Proteus aside and leaned close. "If you really want to win at the horses, you need a good betting strategy. The odds must be calculated and downside risk mitigated."

"That makes sense," said Proteus. The back of his neck was sore, and he reached his hand to rub it. His heartbeat tapped in his temples.

"I have a foolproof system," said Top-hat. "You're clearly a gentleman of means. I would be happy to share my betting scheme with you—"

Proteus sneezed, started to speak, then sneezed again. He retrieved his handkerchief and blew out copious amounts of mucus.

Top-hat flinched away and asked, "Are you unwell?"

"I think not," said Proteus and wondered if he'd answered the enquiry properly. "Fine," he added. A pounding began in his temples.

"I lost a nephew to the Spanish flu," said Top-hat. "Can't be too careful, I say."

"Exactly," said Proteus and sniffled.

"Which is why my analytical system is so precise. It's based on statistical probabilities. And my methodology is one I would only share with a fellow gentleman," said Top-hat. "It's guaranteed!"

"Then why talk to me?"

"Because for a small fee you can participate in my system."

"Thank you, but no," said Proteus, and he sneezed again. The headache gripped his skull like a fist. "I think perhaps I am getting ill after all. Best keep your distance." Without waiting for a reply, he turned and walked away.

"Perhaps after you've lost some of your money, you'll come to your senses. I'll be right here should you change your mind," shouted Top-hat.

Proteus kept walking, looking for an unobstructed view of the track, away from the crowds. He eventually found a section of track on the final curve, looking along the straightaway to the finish. The view would provide neither the elevation nor the side perspective of the grandstand, but he no longer wished to be around people. *Have I picked up an infectious disease?*

A bugle sounded, and the loudspeakers around the track crackled to life. A man's voice, amplified and distorted, named and thanked a number of individuals, though Proteus couldn't quite make out the names. A high-pitched screeching and metallic echoes drowned out the next words. This was followed by several loud clicks and then silence.

After a moment, the loudspeakers came back on, and this time the man's voice was much clearer. He called out the horses, jockeys, and trainers one by one as the muscular, lean horses were led out to line up in front of the crowd. Proteus studied the horses and picked out Humorist, both by his number and the white blaze on the face, visible even from this distance. After all the horses were introduced, the crowd cheered.

"All stand," said the announcer, and a hush descended over the grandstand.

"It is my distinct pleasure to present to you His Majesty King George the Fifth."

Loud cheering and clapping erupted, and Proteus saw heads in the grandstand swiveling to look up at a booth draped with large flags.

A bugle sounded again, and the jockeys mounted. The noise of the crowd stopped, and a band began playing "God Save the King." As the final notes sounded, the masses erupted again. The jockeys rode their mounts to the starting line, and Proteus saw that Humorist was prancing about and wouldn't settle down. Eventually, two men ran out and helped the reluctant horse into his spot and stood next to him; the announcer made a quip, and the audience tittered.

Everything quieted, and then there was a loud bang, and the horses took off. As they were running away from him, Proteus couldn't see much. The enthusiastic announcer was shouting so fast that Proteus couldn't make out the words. A roaring built from the throngs in the grandstand. People within the inner ring of the track ran across to the other side to catch a second glimpse of the horses. It was the movement of these people that told Proteus how the race progressed around the track.

Soon he saw people running back, and he knew the horses would soon exit the back stretch, begin the final turn, and enter Proteus's field of vision. Moments later, he saw a cluster of horses galloping into the turn, hugging the inner rail. He couldn't see Humorist; his mouth went dry.

Where is he? He can't lose.

Then, with the thundering of hooves, and amid the sleek beasts that raced toward him, he saw the white blaze: Humorist was in fourth place and boxed in. Proteus's throat tightened as he yelled at Humorist to run faster. "Come on! Come on! Run!" *Humanity is counting on you.*

The horses flashed past, and then he saw Humorist jump to the inside as the race entered the home stretch. In the grandstand everyone was on their feet, yelling.

Proteus could see Humorist's hindquarters now. The horse held the inside position, but Proteus couldn't tell if he was ahead or behind the leader. The announcer was somehow managing to squeeze in ever more syllables per second, which Proteus still couldn't understand. The voice reached a crescendo, and then there was a jubilant cry over the loudspeakers: "Humorist has won! Humorist has won!"

Trainers and handlers ran onto the track as waves of burbling energy passed through the grandstand. A circle was roped off at the finish line, and three wooden blocks were brought out, the tallest of which was decorated in blue ribbons. Proteus turned away from the ceremony and sought out the betting platform. It was time to collect his two thousand pounds winnings and head back to London. The excitement hadn't washed away his headache, and his muscles and joints hurt.

The barker accepted the ticket and eyed Proteus as if reappraising his initial assessment. It took him half a minute to count out the money as onlookers ogled and murmured.

When he left with his prize money, Proteus was trailed by a small group of men and women. Their voices sounded close on his heels: "Buy a lady a drink"; "Oi, I've a mate who's got the inside scoop on the tables, if you'll follow me"; "Where's the party?"; "Can you help a fellow out?"

He ignored them and strode onward, past rows of cars, where

drivers honked horns that sounded like electric sheep; past tents big and small; past throngs of people clustered around brass bands playing marching tunes. Proteus shot a glance over his shoulder and saw that his entourage had dwindled to a pair. Once they realized that he wasn't going to stop, they too gave up.

The farther he got from the track, the louder everything seemed to become. He stopped to puzzle it out. In the midst of the swirling cacophony of shouting, laughter, music, and car horns, it occurred to him that the next phase of entertainment for the day was only just beginning. A longing tugged at him. To circulate and watch the people of this era celebrate at this enormous event was an enticing thought, and his headache was fading, but his mission depended upon the money he'd just won, and he knew something was not right with his body.

He resumed walking and soon reached the fairground, then slowed to a stop at the entrance. He checked his watch; the sun was still several hours from setting, and he'd have no trouble getting onto one of the many trains headed back to Victoria Station. Children's voices shrieking in delight attracted his attention to the steam-powered rides, and he walked over to have a look.

When he got closer to a small roller-coaster ride, a group of gleeful children burst from the exit and circled to surround him. They sang, joined hands, and began dancing. Their circle rotated clockwise and then counterclockwise as they chanted the words to their song:

Ring-a-ring-a-rosies
A pocket full of posies
Ashes! Ashes!
We all fall down

The king has sent his daughter
To fetch a pail of water
Ashes! Ashes!
We all fall down

The robin on the steeple
Is singing to the people
Ashes! Ashes!
We all fall down

The wedding bells are ringing

The boys and girls are singing
Ashes! Ashes!
We all fall down

Each time they sang the word *down,* the children tumbled backward on the grass, giggling, then got up, joined hands, and circled in the other direction for the next verse. Proteus was helpless to do anything but watch from the center of their circle for the duration of the performance, such was the joy on their faces. Despite his pain, he smiled and then laughed with them. *A childhood I was denied.*

When they'd finished, they came running to him, chattering and smiling, their little hands reached up, clapping, and patting his clothes. And then the tallest girl in the bunch shouted, "Over here," and the troupe went running off after her.

Proteus watched them run off and then turned to head to the train back to London.

On the horizon, dark clouds gathered

9

Proteus arose early, still excited about the Derby, and went down to the lobby. It wasn't raining, and he decided to stretch his legs and explore a bit of sleepy London before it woke up. He had plenty of time before he needed to catch a motor taxi to Liverpool Station for another trip to Cambridge.

He stepped out into the street and—

—pain exploded in his head as he was blindsided by a huge, hairy object. Proteus bounced and rolled on the cobblestones and lay still.

From his fuzzy perspective at street level he tried to understand what had happened.

Trotting away was the horse that had hit him and the carriage it was pulling.

Proteus sat up slowly and reached up with his right hand to explore the pain in his temple. Blood dripped and ran over his hand. He found the painful gash in his scalp and pressed his handkerchief to the wound.

"Crikey, wha' a dumb sheep!" said a boy's voice. A street-sweeper in a floppy cap was pointing at him and laughing. "Always look both ways, me mum says."

Proteus rose to his feet. Blood dripped onto his clothes.

How could I not have seen that carriage?

He held the handkerchief against his head and probed the wound.

He needed to stop the bleeding, and still make his train. Proteus fastened his cloak to hide the blood on his clothes and wedged his stiff bowler hat down against the handkerchief to staunch the bleeding, turned and limped back to the Savoy.

There was still a full night of sabotage ahead, and he needed to get the wound taken care of and change clothes. He retreated into the lobby and then up to his room, trying to ignore the stare of the lift boy.

Ψ

After irrigating the wound with water, Proteus dressed it with gauze bandages from his med-kit and then changed out of his rumpled and bloody attire and into clean clothes.

He checked his watch. There was ample time, but he was agitated by the accident. A random event like that could have killed him.

An uncomfortable sensation in his stomach supplanted the pain in his head. *What if it wasn't random?*

The thought stopped him in his tracks.

He replayed every second of the accident — sights, sounds, and smells. He'd sensed nothing and yet — on a clear street — an enormous draft-horse hauling a huge milk-wagon had *suddenly* run him over. It was improbable.

Resistance from Time?

Proteus's heart pounded.

It must be true. Am I now a target?

He fumbled through getting ready and then forced himself to slow down and breathe.

With shaking hands, he packed his gear. *Breathe.*

He checked to make sure everything he needed was in his satchel and then hurried out of his room.

Ψ

Exiting the lobby, Proteus spotted Conrad's motor taxi, waiting where it always did. The vehicle drove over to him.

"Blimey, what's happened to you, sir?" asked Conrad as Proteus climbed into the vehicle.

"Nothing of note," said Proteus. He sat down. "A horse hit me. I'm fine. Do you know if the trains are running on time?"

"As far as *anyone* can know, yes," said Conrad. He put the motor taxi in gear and glanced at Proteus. They pulled out into the light traffic. "You know, sir, a gentleman of your means, with all your travelling, shouldn't have to risk himself in the streets."

Proteus bounced in his seat as the vehicle hit a pothole.

"With your own car and me as your driver, you'd have freedom and security," said Conrad. "And I've been driving these streets for almost two years now. I know the good spots and the bad — and how to get you there safely."

"I see," said Proteus.

Conrad stopped the taxi at an intersection, and while waiting for the signal, he turned to Proteus and said, "Trust me, sir. I'll take care of you. In fact, I know an excellent dealership run by my cousin Mick. He'll get you a good price on a brand new motorcar."

Proteus thought about the gentlemen he'd seen being chauffeured around London. It would fit the persona he was cultivating and provide better mobility and less danger — at least from horses. He thought through the instructions he'd received: *Don't engage too deeply with the people of this time period; they're not to be trusted.*

His head throbbed, and the wound reminded him of risk.

Perhaps it was time to halt his direct sabotage for a period and work on raising his social status and capital. He had no certainty, but Time-resistance might lessen if he focused his attention on mundane tasks of wealth accumulation, showing it off, and climbing the status ladder. Other gentlemen seemed to be doing it with impunity.

They're barbarians, yet some seem honest.

Proteus decided on his gut instinct and said, "Conrad, I think you have an excellent idea. Let's go to the dealership. You're officially hired to be my driver and assistant."

"Are you pulling my leg?" said Conrad after Proteus had described the duties and pay. "That's three times what I make now."

"I'm telling the truth," replied Proteus. "I need a good driver and assistant."

"What's the catch? Are you doing something illegal?"

"No. I won't ask you to break any laws," said Proteus. "The work may be tricky at times, and we should be on guard against interference. But I'll never knowingly put you in danger."

"Who'd want to interfere? And why?"

"The information I possess is valuable, and there are some who wish to get it from me, but as long as we're attentive, we should be able to stay several steps ahead."

"Are you a spy?" asked Conrad.

"No," said Proteus. "But my knowledge might be used by America's and England's enemies. As long as we're smart about it, we should both be safe."

"Ah, so it concerns research technology," said Conrad. "At Cambridge."

A shiver went through Proteus. *I'm deep in it now.*

"Yes."

"Off to cousin Mick's then," said Conrad. "You're a bit vague on details — if you don't mind me saying — but there's a good nature about you. So, I'm your driver."

Proteus's stomach rose and floated as Conrad drove over a bump in the road.

"Tourists love that one," said Conrad and laughed.

"I'm sure."

Ψ

The next morning, after another evening spent in Cavendish, Proteus flipped through the *Times* in his hotel room as he considered his next steps. He'd had little sleep, and his head throbbed; but he needed to think this through carefully.

Although he'd been apprehensive about hiring Conrad, each passing minute gave him more confidence about the decision. The young man was sharp and seemed to know the streets. If Proteus kept him out of the fray then any resistance from Time should spare him. He should be safe.

The motorcar Proteus had purchased was called a Vauxhall. He hadn't seen it yet, but Conrad and Mick had been quite enthusiastic and promised he'd love it. The Vauxhall was due to be delivered and ready to go in seven days' time.

In the interim, he should lie low. Proteus's calculations also suggested that he should switch locations. Staying in the Savoy for too long — with all its fops, spies, crooks, and gamblers — might tempt fate. It was time to move on. He looked through the paper for a flat to rent — ideally, someplace secure and out of the way. After several minutes, he'd found and circled several options.

His thoughts returned to the Royal Society. He needed an estate and a title of some sort. In about a week he was going to have a significant windfall from the coal company's discovery of diamonds. He wanted to find a substantial piece of land with an old castle or manor house to invest in. Given the sad state of the economy, he was certain he could find the right estate.

And then from there he'd have to find a way to acquire some minor title. He wasn't sure how, yet, but first steps first: find an estate worthy of a noble. Still scanning the paper, he came across a Sotheby's advertisement listing high-end real-estate. He noted the address of the Sotheby's office in London and circled that as well.

Proteus packed his things in his suitcase, shouldered the satchel, and left his hotel room for the last time.

10

The watchmaker paused in the repair of the timepiece at his workbench. His assistant had taken care of closing the store for the evening, and so he worked undisturbed — other than by his thoughts. The piece of junk on the workbench was a cheap Italian copy of a Swiss masterpiece, and the idiots had substituted inferior metal for some of the critical components. *Copper gears intermeshing with stainless steel! What were they thinking?*

Grinding his teeth, he set down his tools.

The meeting in Battersea Park this morning regarding the American, had set him on edge. Ever since the meeting two weeks ago, Red-Bear had been tailing the target, and the watchmaker had keenly listened to his reports. And although he'd learned important details, significant pieces were missing. Ernest Rutherford's laboratories were the target of interest to the rich American, but his motives — and his name — remained a mystery. He went to the jazz bars and appeared like every other American fop, but there was too much absent from the picture; a fop wouldn't sneak into a physics lab at night.

Red-Bear was one of the sharpest tools at his disposal and usually quite efficient in acquiring information. The watchmaker had listened to the explanation that the American was unusually wary and difficult to track. It'd taken several assets almost a fortnight even to piece this much together.

The American must be trying to elude them. Using the logic of Occam's Razor, the American must be a spy. *But for whom?* That was where the watchmaker kept running into sticky gears.

The British and the Americans were like Gemini twins, inseparable, sharing everything. It was pointless for an American to spy on the British in the UK. Thus, the conclusion was that the *American* was not truly an American. He must be an agent working for a different government as a chameleon or double agent. *But for whom?*

The watchmaker was also disturbed by his dreams last night. Usually, he couldn't remember much about his dreams, but these had been as clear as a pristine watch-crystal: he was hunted by a counterspy he could never escape.

The sequence of dreams, which had tortured him most of the night, were of different locations within the city — at places he frequented — but the end was always the same. Exposure. Capture. Execution.

He exhaled sharply and nearly blew a tiny, wafer-thin gear off the table. Retrieving it, he chided himself and took in a slow breath to calm his agitation. *Fix what's in front of your face. Worry later.*

The watchmaker pushed the conundrum away, picked up his tools, and returned to the repairs. He adjusted the magnification of the loupes, and the tips of his tweezers approached the watch — but then began to shake.

He put the instruments down, removed his lenses, and pushed himself away from the workbench in disgust. He could work no more until he had a solution to the problem. Supposition and circular arguments would trap him in futile waste of energy. He needed proof.

Conjecture will not fell the tree, his father had been fond of saying.

He stood and turned to the correspondence chess game, the second one against the Dutchman. In the first, he'd gotten ahead, forced piece exchanges, and then driven a fast checkmate.

But this game was different; his opponent's level of play had jumped. The watchmaker circled around the board, evaluating it from different perspectives. The clocks in the workshop ticked, and pendulums swung; the familiar rhythms helped order his thoughts. The watchmaker suspected the Dutchman was getting outside help on the game, assistance that was forbidden by the rules.

And then, as he continued to stare at the board, a solution began to form. If he could play the Dutchman directly, in this room, the external assistance would be rendered void. Likewise, if he could capture the American, the considerable forces aiding him — which, although still hidden, must indeed be significant — would also be rendered void.

The American possessed a wealth of information, the watchmaker was certain, and the Soviets should gain this knowledge and then dump the American's body in the Thames. *We will learn his secrets and send a powerful message to the forces behind him.*

The thought pleased the watchmaker considerably, and he began drawing up plans in his mind. He would alert his boss at the embassy and recommend abduction of the American. They were well placed in the Savoy to carry out such work, and the American was ripe for the picking. The embassy had an efficient team, skilled in the wet-work of kidnapping and information extraction. Of course, bits of an unidentifiable body might later be found in the Thames, but this was of no concern to him. His colleagues in the embassy knew how to keep their noses clean.

He imagined the forces behind the American would scour London, looking for him or leads to his whereabouts, and this diversion would enable the watchmaker to accelerate Red-Bear's work at Cavendish. Allowing Red-Bear to become more aggressive would undoubtedly come as a surprise; it was the perfect feint-and-thrust of a well-planned chess trap.

11

The summer solstice was only a few days away, and Conrad and Proteus were on the outskirts of London, driving west toward Reading. Conrad hadn't stopped grinning since he sat in the driver's seat of the red Vauxhall OE Velox Tourer they'd picked up earlier in the day. He also hadn't stopped talking about the engine, the acceleration, and the handling. Proteus zoned out from the chatter for a moment, and thought about the property they were driving out to see near a town named Nympsfield, in the Cotswolds.

He'd evaluated numerous candidates during his several trips to Sotheby's, and this one seemed the best fit for his needs. The estate was called Woodchester, and the Sotheby's representative had remarked on its solitude and value. When he'd discussed it with Conrad, his assistant had said that meant it was remote and run-down.

The brochure described the mansion as Gothic revival — construction had begun in the mid-1800s, but was never finished. The property sat within four hundred acres of rolling woodland nestled in a steep valley. To Proteus, it sounded marvelous.

He turned his attention to Conrad, who was still going on about the Vauxhall.

"...you see, this engine here, packs one-hundred-fifteen

horsepower," said Conrad, raising his voice to be heard over the road noise. "It's got quite a punch." He stopped talking for a moment, and gave a wry grin. "Much more than the one horsepower that knocked you down." He shot a brief glance sideways at Proteus and then returned his eyes to the road.

Proteus touched his hand to the wound, which had nearly healed, and said, "I would imagine so, but perhaps you'd like to return to driving motor taxis."

The smirk disappeared from Conrad's face. "No, sir. Sorry. Just havin' a bit of fun."

Then he smiled again, and Proteus laughed.

"How's the new flat?" asked Conrad.

"Fine," said Proteus. "It's much quieter than the hotel."

They drove in silence for the next thirty miles, until just past Swindon, when Conrad asked for help with directions. Proteus pulled the map out from the glove box and tried to keep it still on his lap as the wind tried to rip it apart in the open-air cab. He looked up from the map and craned his neck to peer at a road sign. "Next right, north," he said.

"Aye, sir."

The surface changed to a much rougher mix of dirt and crushed stone as the vehicle turned off the main road and began heading north. Ruts jostled and bounced the car, and Conrad downshifted.

Rolling verdant hills and short stone fences flowed by the motorcar on the gently winding road. The sun approached its zenith; the bright rays warmed Proteus's shoulders and neck. Lulled by the car's swaying rhythm, Proteus was lost in thought. *Is Time aware? Is there a consciousness with deliberate intent? Did it take possession of the carriage driver or the horse? Or is it a force like gravity, pulling otherwise random events in a certain direction, such as flipping a coin twenty times in a row and always getting heads?* He didn't have the answers, and the warnings he'd received in the twenty-fifth century to proceed slowly and watch for anomalies now seemed of no practical use, if he didn't know what to look for. The uncertainty that he may or may not be a target — and that Time may simply flow around him to keep events on track to ensure the discovery of nuclear fission — was a deep hole to contemplate, and further digging wasn't helping him right now.

The car bumped, jostling Proteus from his calculations. "We're in the Cotswolds proper now, I reckon," said Conrad. Dust swirled up from underneath the vehicle and blew inside; he pulled down his goggles.

"We can stop and raise the drop top if you'd like."

Proteus shook his head.

After several more nauseating miles of being battered by the bumps in the road — and the terror of nearly colliding with bleating sheep — Proteus called out, "Stop!"

Conrad applied the brakes, and the vehicle fishtailed to a halt. Dust billowed up and surrounded them like a cloak.

"What's wrong, sir?"

"I want to drive."

"But ... but ... you don't know how to drive."

"I've been watching you," said Proteus. "It looks fun. Teach me."

Better to drive my fate than be a passenger.

Ψ

They got out and exchanged seats, and then a herd of sheep began crossing the road in front of them. Proteus listened to Conrad as he described the vehicle's controls over the background noise of hoofs and small bells. Proteus watched the sheep as each followed the one in front to hop over a low gap in the stone fencing. Herd seemed an appropriate term for the plodding group.

Then one fell, and several others stepped on it; a tussling, bleating argument erupted.

Proteus turned his attention back to Conrad, who seemed to be fussing entirely too much with his explanations of how to drive. Proteus was certain he'd memorized everything about driving the vehicle hours ago and cut Conrad off. "I think I've got this."

Conrad, looking somewhat sullen in his dirt rimmed goggles and cap, provided a weak smile in return.

The sheep finished crossing the road, and Proteus laughed, depressed the clutch, and shifted into gear.

The car bucked and halted — and then repeated the dance a few more times, like a jumping sheep — before stalling.

Proteus panicked, fearful the motorcar might explode; he jumped out of the Vauxhall's driver's seat and dove over the wall. Executing a cat-roll upon landing in the long grass, he ducked behind the stone barrier.

He panted and his pulse hammered as he crouched and scanned for threats. *Is Time striking out at me again?*

Proteus heard a two-toned whistle from the direction of the car. "Oi! You can come back now if you'd like," said Conrad from over the wall. "Sir."

Proteus stood and swiveled uncertainly on the spot. He climbed over the wall and padded slowly toward the car, watching Conrad, who looked somewhere between bored and irritated.

"Kangaroo petrol, I reckon," said Conrad. The corners of his mouth turned upward, and his facial creases deepened, highlighted by the road dirt caked on his face. He watched Proteus.

"Really?" asked Proteus. "Does that exist?"

"No," said Conrad. He giggled and then thumped the seat between his knees with his hand. "Had you going there for a bit, eh?"

He smiled the smile that had made Proteus trust him in the first place, and then Conrad resumed his teacher demeanor. "Easy on the clutch release. As you feel the engine engage, ease on the accelerator. It's never like turning on a light switch. You need to *feel*." He spread his fingers apart and rotated his forearms so that his palms faced upwards. "Like with music or a woman."

"Do these motorcars ever … um … catch on fire?"

Conrad chortled, then looked at his boss, his eyes searching. He appeared thoughtful for a moment, then said, "People who get hurt or killed — it's 'cause most've done something stupid."

Proteus exhaled to cover his nervousness. He parsed Conrad's meaning: *most people.*

"But some don't do something stupid," said Proteus. "Correct?"

"Aye, true. Sometimes innocent lives are lost," said Conrad. "And I've seen my share of people mangled in crashes on the streets of London — including children."

Proteus reached over to the electric starter, depressed the clutch — and paused. Here in the lovely English countryside, talk of death seemed abstract and out of place. It was easy to forget that Time might be stalking him. He shifted into first gear and eased off the clutch as he pressed the accelerator pedal. The Vauxhall powered forward with only a small hiccup, and he grinned.

Several hundred yards later, Conrad suggested he change gears and then talked him through a successful shift into second. The feedback of the road through the steering wheel and the rumble of the engine gave Proteus goosebumps. He depressed the accelerator and felt a growling surge of power in the seat of his trousers. The wind tossed his hair, and he shifted into third.

"Good show!" said Conrad. "You've got it."

Proteus laughed as the vehicle picked up speed. He glanced between the road and the horizon. The rolling hills, green pastures, and low stone walls repeated in patterns like a quilt, with a brilliant blue sky hung above it all. Proteus exhaled, then shivered, then inhaled a deep breath of the summer air. *Natural and clean.*

A tickling sensation built in his nose. He sniffed and then sneezed, then sneezed again. Mucus dripped from his nose. Another sneeze erupted; his nasal passages began to burn.

"You all right, sir?" said Conrad.

Proteus nodded. He braked to a halt and shifted into neutral. He retrieved his handkerchief and blew his nose.

"London air ain't good for you. Much better out 'ere, me mum always said, and it's true, natural things are best," said Conrad and smiled. After a moment, his expression changed and he looked away.

Proteus tried to see what Conrad was looking at but then sneezed again.

Conrad turned back toward Proteus. "Thank you. I've never driven anything like this. It's *bloody* marvelous!" He looked surprised, and his posture stiffened. "Sorry about the language, sir."

Proteus gave a thumbs-up sign and then sneezed into his handkerchief.

"Bit of hay fever, perhaps. You'll adapt soon and be right as rain," said Conrad. His face brightened some more. "Until then, perhaps I should drive. Yes?"

Proteus blew his nose and shook his head.

The coughing growl of the engine roared as he shifted into first and powered forward, halting further conversation.

Ψ

Proteus timidly engaged the car into gear, and a short while later they entered the hamlet of Nympsfield. The Vauxhall slowed as Proteus looked over the collection of small stone buildings. In front of one of them hung a painted wooden sign announcing it as *The Rose and Crown*. Wood smoke spilled from the chimney, along with the aroma of cooking. Proteus's belly growled.

"I'm starving," said Conrad.

"After we've finished with our errand."

Minutes later, the town was in the rear-view mirror. Proteus looked at the petrol gauge, which read half-full. He upshifted and grinned at Conrad. After a few miles, Conrad, whose attention had been divided between a map and milestones, pointed up the road.

"Turnoff's just up ahead," he said.

Rain began to fall; fat drops splattered big circles on the dusty windshield and hood. Proteus found himself mesmerized by the pattern and —

"Oi!" said Conrad. "Slow down. And turn right."

Proteus downshifted and turned onto a road marked by a vine-choked sign reading *Woodchester Mansion*. He straightened the wheel, and the car growled in response to his pressure on the accelerator. Conrad looked at him from the corner of his eyes and tried to hide a smile.

As they rumbled along the road, which was actually more of an overgrown path, Proteus caught glimpses, through the clusters of trees lining the approach, of a three-story stone structure with a tall, angled roof. He drove around a bend and was greeted by his first full view of the front of the manor house.

Conrad whistled. "Blimey, looks a little worse for the wear."

Proteus slowed as they approached; gravel crunched under the tires. He had been expecting a warm welcome, given what he'd learned about the family's eagerness to meet with him about the property. He scanned the empty, weed-choked expanse of crushed stone in front of the mansion.

Hopefully they have some food prepared.

He stopped several car lengths from the entrance. The place was dark and looked deserted; there was no one visible, despite the fact they were on time and expected. Proteus turned off the engine and applied the handbrake, following Conrad's instruction.

Conrad nodded his approval at the shutdown routine and then looked at the mansion. "Looks like they've forgotten about taking care of the place," he said.

They both got out of the Vauxhall. After closing the driver's door, Proteus stepped back to marvel at the vehicle. His mind was still buzzing from the residual connection to driving — the side-to-side, up-and-down motion — like a sailor newly on land.

As he walked towards the mansion with Conrad right behind him, he saw that Conrad was correct: it had been left to the elements. Wooden storm shutters, with paint peeling, hung askew above bushes that were overgrown and misshapen. The massive rectangular windows of the first floor were clouded with dirt, their panes rimmed with algae. Some were broken and missing, yielding glimpses into a dark interior. Woodchester Mansion was a derelict. Neglected. A child forgotten.

Proteus's eyes drifted up to the steeply slanted roof, where chimneys jutted out at irregular intervals. Craning his neck to look around a gable, he saw the top of a square tower, which appeared to be in the center of the structure.

Dotting the edge of the roof were hunched figures perched on corners and columns, staring down at him."What are those?" he asked Conrad. "They look like monkeys with wings."

"Gargoyles, sir," said Conrad. "Demons. They carry rainwater away from the roof … and ward off evil."

Proteus turned his head to look at Conrad, trying to gauge whether he was teasing him again. Seeing no sign of a smile, he resumed walking toward the mansion, and Conrad caught up and then overtook him. Their boots crunched on the crushed stone.

A low growl sounded from behind Proteus, and he spun to see a man and a large black dog scarcely twenty paces away; the latter was showing the whites of its eyes, and snarling. The former had a shotgun pointed at Proteus's chest.

"Who're you?" said the man in a deep voice. "You're not from around here."

Proteus looked at the shotgun's muzzle — its twin tubes stared at him like cold, metal eyes — and then over it and into the man's green eyes. He wondered if they'd driven onto the wrong property and thought through his reply — but then he heard Conrad step forward.

The gun shifted to point at Conrad as he approached slowly to stand in front of Proteus and opened his arms wide. He stopped and said, "I apologize. It's a misunderstanding. You see, I'm his chauffeur, and I must've taken a wrong turn."

The man continued aiming the gun at Conrad and then pivoted it slightly to point back at Proteus. "He was driving," he said.

"Yes, I was," said Proteus. "My name is A.J.B. Proteus, and I'm here to meet the Leigh family about the acquisition of Woodchester Mansion as my residence. Are you the representative of the family? Or are we in the wrong place?"

"Oh! Beggin' your pardon, Mr. Proteus," said the man. He pointed the gun at the ground then broke open the breach. The dog stopped growling. "My apologies. I've had problems with trespassers. Forgot you were coming today." He folded the weapon over his left arm and stepped forward, his right arm extended. "I'm Gareth, caretaker of the estate."

Proteus accepted the proffered hand.

Gareth was tall and broad-shouldered and wore a scarlet wool coat with leather patches at the elbows and shoulders. His scarred face smiled under a tweed cap as they shook hands; his grip was powerful.

Gareth whistled softly, and the dog stood and trotted over, tail wagging. "So you're the Mr. Proteus we've been expecting. Who's your chauffeur who's not a driver?"

"This is my assistant, Conrad."

"Pleased to meet you both," said Gareth. The black dog sat next to its master, its long tongue lolling out. "This here's Lucy. A gentler soul you'll never find, but she'll tear a wolf apart if the need arises." There was a rolling, almost musical, lilt to his bass voice. Lucy looked up at the sound of her name, and Gareth reached down to scratch behind her ear.

"Shall we tour the estate, then?" he said, his green eyes twinkling in the sunlight. "I was instructed to be at your disposal for the afternoon."

"Lead on, Gareth," said Proteus. He and Conrad followed in the big man's footsteps; Lucy trotted alongside.

The large, double-door entrance was framed by an even larger, triangular stone lip jutting out from the face of the building. Gareth said to Lucy, "Wait here," and she sat down. He inserted a dull brass key into the lock and twisted it. The door groaned as he pushed it inward.

Gareth stepped inside and unloaded two shells from the breach of the shotgun. Proteus followed him and saw him snap the gun closed and prop it behind the door. The shells went into his breast pocket. Conrad crossed the threshold and Proteus turned to marvel at the doors, which were almost half a foot thick.

The bright daylight only penetrated a short distance into the hall, and Proteus couldn't see much in the darkness beyond the rectangular splash of sunlight on the dusty stone floor. Gareth reached into an alcove in the wall and removed an electric lantern, which he turned on. As he played the yellow beam across the room, Conrad whistled. Proteus shot him a look.

"No one's lived in here for a quarter of a century," said Gareth. "I

live in the cottage up the hill, behind the mansion. Servants' quarters."
The light beam rotated to land upon Proteus and Conrad. "But as you
can see, there ain't been servants here for quite some time. Townsfolk
volunteer to help keep her up as best they can, but she needs a lot of
care. There's good history here. I hope you keep that in mind, Mr.
Proteus." Gareth paused, took a breath, and seemed on the verge of
saying more, but then he muttered something under his breath and
walked out of the room. "This way," he called back.

As they toured the mansion, Proteus became immersed in the
layout. Gareth pointed out the rooms, their functions, and the date
they'd been completed — or started, in the case of the unfinished ones.
The largest spaces were on the ground level: the billiard hall; a library
containing warped wooden shelves, populated with several hundred
books; a dining hall with a candelabra high above a shuffleboard-sized
mahogany table; a cavernous drawing room with huge, dirty windows
that must have at one time provided a lovely view of the gardens
outside (when there *were* gardens); a chapel with an enormous, peaked
window; and three kitchens.

Although he had grown up in an underground colony, Proteus
found the design claustrophobic and unnecessarily complicated. The
underused space and, in particular, the gratuitous use of wood struck
him as odd and wasteful. Dingy light filtered through the windows,
but in places the interior was so dark that only Gareth's lantern
showed the way. Empty candle sconces were distributed at regular
intervals, and Proteus tried to imagine what it must look like at night,
since there didn't seem to be any electric lights.

Conrad was strangely subdued during their tour. A few times,
Proteus experienced a strange, prickling sensation on his neck, but
each time he turned around there was nothing — only a stone wall or a
glimpse of a gargoyle through a smudged window.

When they finished and returned to the front, they found Lucy
guarding the door just as they'd left her. Gareth's shotgun was
undisturbed; he bent over to retrieve it. Suddenly, Lucy rose and
trotted over to Proteus. She stood on her rear legs and planted her
large front paws on his chest, her brown eyes latched onto his. It
seemed she was just about to speak, so intense was the intelligence in
that stare.

Gareth turned and saw what was happening, "Lucy. Down!"
She ignored the command and began licking Proteus's face.
"Lucy!"

She looked at her master briefly, then returned to her mission of washing Proteus's face with her huge tongue. It was one of the strangest things Proteus had ever experienced. He began to laugh.

"Lucy!"

After half a minute, Lucy decided she was finished and returned to the exact position and posture she'd occupied earlier when she had been waiting for her master.

Gareth appeared flummoxed. "I'm sorry. I don't know what's come over her. Never seen her do that, nor disobey me." He looked at Lucy and then back at Proteus. "Never."

He removed his cap and scratched his head, his fingertips brushing close-cropped stubble over the scarred scalp.

Up close, in the sunlight, Proteus was able to better see Gareth's head: the disfigurement was not a single scar, or a series of them, but rather looked as if the flesh had been burned and melted over a large area. It made it difficult to determine his age, but Gareth seemed fit and lithe. Proteus had observed his balance and quiet movement within the dark mansion — and was still bothered by the sudden, silent appearance of both Gareth and Lucy behind them on the gravel drive earlier. *I can't afford to be surprised like that. And I'm also responsible for Conrad's life.*

Gareth's green eyes locked on Proteus, as if reading his thoughts. The flesh was smooth and unscarred around his eyes, but the penetrating gaze told of a different pain. He replaced his cap and without breaking eye contact with Proteus said, "Lucy, home!" She stood and noisily galloped off across the drive toward the edge of the woods.

Gareth stood motionless, still studying Proteus. Finally, he said, "She saw something she liked in you."

"Shall we be going, sir?" said Conrad, interrupting them. "It's half past four, and we're to meet the family barrister in town at the public house, by five."

Proteus broke off eye contact with Gareth and looked at Conrad. "Yes ... of course."

Turning back to Gareth, he said, "Thank you for your time and the tour of the estate."

Gareth grimaced — or smiled, Proteus couldn't tell — and said, "You've barely scratched the surface of the estate. Perhaps next time, if there is one, I'll show you more." He touched his fingers to his cap, turned, and walked off after Lucy.

On the way back to the car, Conrad whispered, "That was bloody peculiar, if you ask me. I'm half starving. Let's get some pub grub for our meeting."

"Good idea."

"Can I drive?" asked Conrad, smiling and raising his eyebrows.

"No."

$$\Psi$$

After meeting the barrister over food and drinks, Conrad and Proteus left the pub with full bellies and an unsigned copy of the deed to the estate. It was six and would be light for several more hours.

Proteus paused to study the sky. A large black cloud blocked the sun, but a ray of gold penetrated at one edge. His eyes followed the beam to the ground, where it illuminated a patch of forest. *After never having seen it until I came here, I could look at the sky every day for hours on end, for a thousand years, and never tire of the beauty.*

"You all right, sir?"

"Um … fine." He turned away from the view and caught up with Conrad. As they walked to the car, Proteus headed off the inevitable question. "Yes. You can drive this time."

He sat in the passenger seat, and Conrad hopped in the driver's seat. Proteus thought about the transactional discussion with the barrister representing the family, a corpulent man in a suit who was definitely hiding something. His language had been couched in confusing clauses and vague assurances as to the exact repair status of the property. He spoke often about the family's reluctance to part with such a gem, but his body language had said the exact opposite.

Regardless, Proteus knew he was buying an estate that needed money to fix, but he needed an estate to build the social clout to be accepted into the Royal Society.

At present, there were two steps remaining before the estate could be purchased: approval of Proteus's character by the citizenry of the hamlet; and a transfer of funds in London, at Lloyd's Bank. The latter made sense to Proteus, but the former was puzzling.

"Did he say we have to meet with a religious person?"

"Two," answered Conrad. "The vicar at St. Bartholomew's, which is Church of England, and then the priest at St. Joseph's, which is Roman Catholic."

"Wait … what?"

"Well, we need both their blessings."

"Why? Aren't they the same … um … religion?"

"Sort of," said Conrad. "Without getting into too many details, they aren't always on the best of terms." Proteus looked at him, and Conrad continued, "Apparently, the Catholic Church had blessed the construction of the mansion quite early on, and Cardinal what's-his-name personally paid a visit at the turn of the century. But the Protestants have claimed the surrounding flock, so to speak. So we must meet with both."

"I don't understand the intersection of religion and real estate," said Proteus.

"Me neither, sir. But you just follow my lead and it'll be fine."

Conrad started the car.

It was a short drive to St. Bartholomew's. The small church had a squat, square crenelated turret attached to three mismatched one-story buildings with tall, peaked roofs. Moss smothered the northern flanks of the roofs, and ivy gripped the stone walls as if trying to drag the whole structure underground. The thought chilled Proteus's bones.

The church was a curious stone montage, and he wondered how long ago the original structure had been built, and when the additions had appeared; clearly, there had been several different architects and masons over a long period of time.

Proteus gazed at the cemetery with its stained tombstones erupting from the green grass like teeth, some tilted askew. He wondered about the funerary rites of this time period and the times before. The ways that different religions dealt with death had been part of his instructions, but right now he couldn't recall many of the details. It hadn't seemed important back then, and he hadn't truly paid attention. It wasn't as if any of their religions could bring back the dead.

"Shall we go inside?" said Conrad, interrupting Proteus's musings.

They walked up the steps to the door, and Proteus raised his hand to knock, but Conrad stepped in front of him and pushed the heavy wooden door inward. "The flock are always welcome in God's house," he said as he strolled inside.

Proteus followed him into the dimly lit foyer. It smelled of candles, dust, bird droppings, and another odor; his nose wrinkled.

They crossed the threshold into the main chamber, where rows of wooden pews sat silent before a stone pulpit. A swath of bright colors caught Proteus's eye; a large stained-glass window was transforming the early evening sunlight into a colorful mosaic on the stone floor.

Dust motes danced in the rays at the far end of the church. He studied the picture on the window: a man with robes and a hat, clutching an open book in one hand and a long stick tipped with a big plus-sign in the other.

Proteus looked for other mathematical symbols but could see none. He decided to ask Conrad about it later.

"How may I be of service?" said a voice from the darkness.

Proteus's eyes shot to the source of the sound; he saw a black shadow in an archway. The figure stepped into the light spilling from the stained-glass window, and Proteus identified a short man in dark clothes. Greens, blues, and purples from the window played across a balding head, long sideburns, and a fleshy face as the man stepped forward.

"My name is Archibald Bartholomew Joseph Proteus," said Proteus. "And this is Conrad. I'm here to meet with the ... um ..."

"Vicar," whispered Conrad in his ear.

"... with the vicar of St. Bartholomew. I intend to purchase Woodchester Mansion, and I'd like to seek his blessing."

"I'm the vicar of St. Bartholomew," said the man, and hiccupped. "All are welcome in this house of God."

"Thank you, Vicar," said Conrad, and with his right hand he pointed in turn to his forehead, chest, then his left and right shoulders.

The vicar shook his head slightly and looked down his nose. "Wrong church," he said.

"Sorry," said Conrad.

"We're all God's children," said the vicar. He squinted at them and then belched. "So you're the two Londoners. But I must say your accent is not British, Mr. Proteus."

"No," said Proteus. "I'm American, but I trace my ancestral lineage back to the original estate."

"The Leigh family," said the vicar.

"No, before them, the Duckies."

A puzzled look crossed the vicar's face. After a moment, his face brightened and he said, "Ah, you mean the Ducies."

"Yes, the *Ducies*," said Proteus. "I'm descended from a second cousin twice removed. I've only recently discovered the relationship, after being contacted by the executor of the will. An uncle I never knew left me a sizable inheritance, with instructions to take good care of Woodchester Mansion and to contribute a substantial amount of money to your parish."

"Well, then, I ... um ... where are my manners? Oh dear," said the vicar. His cheeks flushed. "We simply must toast with a bit of sherry! Follow me, gentlemen." He shuffled back through the dim stone archway. Conrad looked at Proteus and winked. They both followed the vicar.

"How much of a *donation* did you say?" asked the vicar as they joined him in his chambers.

Three sherries later, Proteus walked out of the church a bit tipsy. He was glad he'd had the foresight to limit Conrad to only one and send him on an errand to rent them rooms at the inn for the night. They had one last stop before heading there: St. Joseph's Church.

Conrad started up the Vauxhall, and they drove off. It was getting cool as the last rays of the sun yielded to early twilight. "Archibald Bartholomew Joseph Proteus," said Conrad, letting it roll off his tongue. "Is that your full name, sir?"

"Um ... yes. It's a long story, but yes," said Proteus. "Although I may switch the order of the middle names for our next meeting."

"Crafty," said Conrad, and nodded. He negotiated a curve in the road. "Are you going to switch the story and tell the next one that his church is your favorite of the two as well? Aren't you worried they'll catch on?"

"It doesn't sound like they're on speaking terms, nor were their predecessors. You heard some of what the vicar said, and I suspect we'll find the same at the Catholic church. In the end, each'll be happy with the funds they've received. They won't compare notes."

"Oh, I see. They'll be like two cats, each thinking they've eaten the only mouse in the house."

After processing the metaphor, Proteus said, "Yes. Something like that."

Conrad turned onto the drive leading to St. Joseph's Church.

Ψ

"It was just as you said, sir," said Conrad as he climbed into the Vauxhall. "Once he heard the words *estate* and *donation*, it was smooth as silk."

Proteus was giddy and carefree. "What did he say that wine was? Christ's ... um ... something?" he asked. "And what were those stale crackers?"

"That was a private mass, sir," said Conrad. "It was all blessed. Quite an honor, I'd say." He started the engine and eased the car into gear. The Vauxhall left the church and headed back to Nympsfield.

"Afterwards, the wine tasted the same, but the snacks were much better," said Proteus.

"I wouldn't know," said Conrad and fell silent. The car headlights picked up a bend in the road, and he steered around it smoothly. A moment later, the tires bumped over an uneven segment, jostling them both. "There's one thing that bothers me, though. You just lied to two holy men."

Proteus felt the jab of the words: it was deceitful and immoral. He knew that Conrad was right. *But how do I explain it to him? There's a pressing reality. Humanity is dying and will become extinct if I fail. The ends justify the means.*

They rode in silence.

When they parked at the inn, Proteus said, "Everything I do is for a greater good. You must trust me."

"If you say so, sir, but I'll have you know I'm not keen on dishonesty."

"Thank you, Conrad," said Proteus. "I know you're a righteous soul. And I'll tell you the truth, whenever I can, but there are some things I'm not allowed to say, and the less you know the better."

"I'll ask again," said Conrad. "Are you a spy?"

"No," said Proteus. "I don't work for any government. Now let's get some sleep. We drive back in the morning." He got out of the car and walked toward the inn. After a moment, he heard Conrad follow him.

12

In a small stone cottage tucked within the forest on a hill above Woodchester Mansion, Gareth hung an iron kettle over the hearth, tended the fire, and went back to his sketchpad and charcoal. From the candlelit table, he looked over at Lucy asleep in front of the fire and thought about the day's encounter. *What did you sense, girl? You're seldom wrong — and never about people. And you've never disobeyed me. What was it?*

Gareth became lost in thought, mumbling to himself.

The kettle whistled, rousing him from his musings. He looked at his drawing, frowned, and put down the stick of charcoal. The flesh on his head, neck, arms, and chest began to tingle, heralding the onset of the burning pain yet to come, as it did every night. He rose, grasped the kettle with an oven glove, and stepped into the kitchen, ducking to avoid the thick wooden beam over the threshold. He poured the hot water into a teapot and added three Earl Grey teabags, along with the medicinal herbs he'd picked and chopped up earlier in the day.

Gareth returned to his table. From her prone position, head between outstretched front paws, Lucy's eyes followed him.

"Oh, so you're awake now, are you?"

Lucy stood and came over to Gareth. Her large head rested on the table as she looked at him and wagged her tail. Her eyes and the slow, side-to-side wag spoke of her contentment and happiness at being with him. He scratched her behind the ears and then handed over a bit of jerky from his shirt pocket.

"You're a good girl," he said. "But what did you see in the American?"

Lucy tilted her head and continued to look deep into his eyes.

"Not saying much, hmm?" Gareth chuckled. "Well, how about another question: who is he?" He stood and paced in front of the hearth. "I've no idea of his business, but I think he's not who he says."

He stopped to look at the only decoration hung above the mantle, a dull-grey metal cross, bearing the lion and brown, on a red ribbon. It was something he'd gazed at a thousand times before. Lucy went back to the rug in front of the fire and lay down.

Their medals won't bring any of my men back, Gareth thought. Bile rose in his throat. He looked at Lucy and said, "I distrust the wealthy, the royalty, and the elite. They got us into the *war to end all wars,* but where were they? Not in the trenches, that's for bloody sure!

"I'm not sure about this Mr. Proteus. Not sure at all. But there's something odd. I've met many a man, and ... far too many have I observed in their last moments. I've seen the look in their eyes, and I've witnessed their actions. Some cowered and pissed themselves. Some went insane. Some sacrificed their last breath to save another when they could've escaped and lived. I know men, and I know Lady Death.

"I saw the look in his eyes as he looked back at me over the barrel. 'Twas as if I didn't have a shotgun aimed at his chest. There was no fear. Or perhaps he *wanted* me to shoot him. I've seen that a few times before, too, in the faces of soldiers dying in agony. But I've never seen that look in the eyes of the so-called aristocracy.

"Nay, there's something amiss here, but I can't quite put my finger on it, Lucy."

Lucy had watched her master impassively during this soliloquy, but at the sound of her name she raised her head from its resting place on her paws.

"You're a good girl," Gareth said and handed her another treat from his pocket. Then he sat down again at the table and looked at what he'd been drawing.

A few moments later, the page he'd ripped from the sketchpad began to blacken and curl as the hearth's flames consumed it.

Ψ

Gareth looked up from his book at the sound of the cottage door opening. Lucy jumped up and trotted over, wagging her tail, to join the woman who'd entered.

"Hello, Papa!"

"Hello love," said Gareth and rose to greet his daughter, who had bent to ruffle the fur on Lucy's head.

Carys straightened and flicked her auburn hair, cut in a bob, away from her eyes. It shone in the hearth fire as she stepped forward to give Gareth a hug and a kiss on the cheek. "How've you been?" she asked. Her green eyes were exact copies of her father's, and they searched his face.

"Good, love, good," he said. "How're your studies?"

"Trying," said Carys, and her smile faded. She released her embrace and stepped back. She took off her long wool coat and hung it on a peg near the door. Her trousers and riding boots were dusty from travel. "I'll need to go back earlier this weekend, Papa. Sunday morning, I'm afraid. I've a biology exam to prepare for."

"Oh, that's quite all right, love. I understand." Gareth felt a pang in his chest. "As long as it's not a rich Oxford brat you're running back to." His tone sounded harsher than he had intended.

"Papa!" said Carys. "They're not all snobs. Besides, most think me a country bumpkin."

"I know, lass. I'm sorry," said Gareth and was about to quip a reply but changed his mind. He stepped into the kitchen, ducking under the beam, and said, "Supper'll be ready soon. Can you put the kettle on for tea?"

"Yes," came the reply from the den. He heard her boots, and then a soft question from the doorway: "Papa, is everything all right?"

"Yes," said Gareth. He turned to look at Carys, then continued, "I met a strange American. He's buying the estate."

Carys's eyes widened in surprise. "What?"

"Aye."

"What'll happen to you?" she asked, her voice rising in pitch and her forehead creasing into a frown. "Must you move?"

"Nay, I don't think so. He wants to fix it up, and I made sure he understood that no one knows the mansion and grounds better than

91

I."

Carys was still frowning. She looked down at the floor in silence, then back up at Gareth. "An American? Why? What would he want here? Who is he?"

"So many questions," chuckled Gareth. "Put the tea on, and then we'll sit down. I'll tell you everything I know over supper."

13

"What the devil is this?" said Rutherford. "A collection of different sized ellipses and circles?"

"It's what I recorded through the microscope, Professor," said Marco.

"You know I don't permit drinking of spirits in the laboratory."

"I wasn't drinking."

"You should repeat the scatter experiment then. Did you consider the foil may be contaminated?"

"Yes," said Marco. "I've tested and retested using multiple foil samples."

"And?"

Marco reached into his shoulder bag and extracted several dozen hand-drawn scintigrams and plopped them on his boss's desk. "All the metal foils we've tested — gold, lithium, silver — the pattern's on all of them."

Rutherford shuffled through several of the scintigram-plots, then dumped them back on the desk. "Blast. There must be an explanation," he said and stood to pace about his office; glass fragments crunched under his boots. "Marsden and Geiger did the original work almost a decade ago, and there was nothing like this then. Why are we getting different results now?"

"Perhaps it's the lowered error rate that we worked so hard to achieve. With lower vacuum pressures, better glass, and purer materials, we're most likely seeing things previously hidden in the noise, Professor."

Rutherford stopped pacing, thought for a moment, and then said, "That's an excellent hypothesis." He resumed his pacing. "Hmm, this complicates matters quite a bit. You know what's needed? Results. More results." He spun to face Marco. "Why are you standing there looking like a frightened mouse when there's so much more work to do? Let's go!"

Rutherford turned and stormed out of the office. As he swept through the hallway, he cut a swathe through the academics milling about like a highly-charged particle in one of his cloud chambers.

14

Proteus woke up before dawn, arms and legs twitching, and waited impatiently for the symptoms to resolve.

When they'd passed, he rolled out of the small, sagging bed and stood. Still groggy, he went to the window and opened the curtains. The undersides of the clouds on the horizon glowed red, and he thought through the events of the previous days.

He had a headache from the sherry and the wine and was sick to his stomach. *Maybe some food will help.*

He looked down at the gravel drive of the inn and had a sudden sinking feeling: the Vauxhall was gone! Hurriedly, he dressed and left his room; he knocked on Conrad's door but got no answer.

Proteus hurried down the creaking wooden staircase two steps at a time. The common room was empty, but he could smell wood smoke and fresh bread wafting in from the kitchen. He strode out of the inn just as the sun's rays crested the hills in the distance. Birds chirped and flitted in the trees and a far-off rooster crowed, but there was no sign of the Vauxhall — *his* car — or Conrad.

He trotted out to the road and looked in both directions. Proteus ground his teeth. *Why would he leave me like this? How could I have misplaced my trust in someone so badly?*

Then he heard the noise of an engine. It grew louder, and soon he spotted a dust cloud on the road. As it came closer, he saw a red glint in the sunlight: the Vauxhall.

The dust cloud blossomed. Soon he was able to see Conrad's grinning, goggled face bouncing up and down with the car's suspension as the vehicle roared toward the inn.

Conrad was chatting enthusiastically even before he pulled to a complete stop. He leapt out, and said, "Sorry, sir — went off to fetch petrol and also something for the missus. Was hoping to make it back before you woke. I noticed last night that it was below half a tank." He ran his hand in a caressing manner over the hood, then looked at his palm and frowned at the dirt. "Such a pleasure to drive. I'll make sure she's cleaned and polished after we get back to London, sir."

Proteus studied him. Conrad seemed to have recovered from his downbeat mood of last night. *But he's right; I did lie. I'll need to be careful to keep him at a distance from my dishonesty in the future.* He saw a worried look flash across Conrad's face.

"What'd you get your wife?" asked Proteus and managed a smile. "I didn't know you were married."

Conrad grinned and reached into the passenger seat. "These, sir," he said as he produced a bouquet of flowers. "A dozen tiger lilies."

"They're beautiful," said Proteus and bent closer to inspect them. He inhaled the sweet esters and then examined the complex structure of one of the flowers: six petals pointing out like a star, broad at the base where they formed a cup, and bending back in a gentle arc that tapered to a point; long, thin pollen-tipped stamen reached upward from the deep center. Despite the apparent symmetry, there were beautiful imperfections in the structures and the swirl of colors, unlike the perfectly machined uniformity of the Colony.

His nose tingled, and then he sneezed. The pounding in his head increased, and he backed away from the flowers.

A sour, burning sensation built in his stomach, and his mouth was as dry as cotton. His appetite evaporated, and he swallowed dusty saliva. Conrad watched him with a strange look in his eyes. Proteus's headache intensified, and he held onto the car for support. After several heartbeats, the pain lessened, and he could speak again. "Where'd you go?" he asked in a ragged voice.

"Up toward Stroud. I asked our host at the inn where I could get petrol, and I happened upon a roadside flower stand. I left you a note on your door. I meant no offense."

"I didn't see it."

"I'm sorry." Conrad's eyes searched his face. "Are you all right, sir?"

"Go get some breakfast. I'm going to my room," said Proteus. "Be ready to go in an hour."

"Yes, sir."

Ψ

In his room at the inn, Proteus got out the SDU from his satchel and recorded a personal log:

"I feel dreadful, and I don't know what's making me ill. Is it too much wine, the hay fever that Conrad mentioned, or something else? My head and bones hurt, and I'm nauseated. Could it be Time-sickness? I just don't know." He reached out with a trembling hand to end the recording. *Perhaps the drive back will clear out whatever it is.*

He packed up and went downstairs. Conrad was waiting for him in the Vauxhall.

"Didn't mean to alarm you," said Conrad after he'd started the engine. In the distance, dew on the fields refracted the sun's rays like small diamonds. White clouds hung in front of a red horizon.

"It's okay," said Proteus. "I ... just don't feel well."

Conrad put the car in gear and they left the inn, emerging onto the open road and heading southeast. The top was up and the windows were too, and Proteus appreciated the relative security of the enclosure. *Maybe it's simply the pollen,* he thought.

They drove along in silence. Behind them in the mirror, the clouds built; the undersides turned to smudged charcoal.

Shivers shook Proteus's body, and he reached back to the rear seat for his overcoat. Wrapping himself in it, he retreated into misery. Pounding built at the base of his skull.

"My jumper's back there too, sir, if you need it," said Conrad.

Proteus nodded and reached for it as another trembling wave shook him. Teeth chattering, he rearranged his clothing, adjusting the layers for warmth. He began the mind-centering discipline to alleviate his suffering. His breathing and pulse slowed.

After an hour, they came to an intersection, and Conrad turned to head directly east. The vehicle picked up speed again. The improved road surface lessened the forces transmitted into the chassis, for which Proteus was grateful; the incessant vibrations had burrowed into the marrow of his bones, and each jarring pothole hit his abdomen like a punch.

He began to recover enough to extend his awareness beyond the immediate confines of the car. In front of them, the sun was halfway to midday, but the sky hadn't brightened much and the light had taken on a greenish tinge.

A blast of wind rocked the Vauxhall. Conrad manipulated the steering wheel to counter. "Looks like we're in for a bit of rough weather, sir," he said.

Proteus rolled down his window and stuck his head out to look behind them. Wind blasted the back of his head as he looked at the black array of stratocumulus clouds looming large. A sickly sea green radiated from the grey swirls in the leading edge of the storm.

He watched in silence, air currents rippling the hair on his scalp, studying the scale of the storm front as it swallowed the terrain. Silver dendritic lines suddenly flashed and danced against the black clouds. The dark wall was gaining on them.

Proteus retreated into the cabin, wound up the window, and curled back up in the overcoat. Thunder rolled over the car, and the first drops of rain tapped the roof and windshield — before long, it was drumming down.

"I can outrun it," said Conrad.

Proteus nodded. Nausea rose in his throat, and he balled up in the swaying cabin, sinking deeper into the seat. His joints and muscles ached; his skin hurt. *What is happening to me?*

It's worse than you think came the unbidden reply.

Once that thought had bubbled up, it became hard to dispel. *It's Time-sickness. You're dying.*

Despite knowing it wouldn't help, he couldn't stop himself from thinking of the medical reports he'd read as part of his training of the time travelers who'd returned — and then succumbed to the sickness. Flu-like symptoms first as the immune system went into overdrive, and then their organ systems began to fail, one by one. Liver, kidneys, heart, lungs, brain, and bone marrow all shut down.

Proteus closed his eyes and began another breathing technique, prolonging each cycle of air — *slow in, slow out, count* — and tried to rebalance the thoughts assaulting his mind.

The Vauxhall accelerated.

Exhaustion overtook Proteus, and he fell into a hard sleep—

—and jerked awake, bathed in sweat, burning hot with fever.

Proteus reoriented himself. He was in the cab of the Vauxhall. Conrad looked at him from the driver's seat, and said, "You all right? You shouted in your sleep."

"I'm ... okay," said Proteus and pulled off the overcoat and sweater. He mopped his forehead and studied his surroundings. The terror of the dream began to fade. "How long was I asleep?"

"About an hour. We're almost to London. Drop you off at your new flat, I presume?"

"Yes."

"Can I—"

"Yes. Please take the car," said Proteus. "Just help me up to my flat." *I need to search the Cube.*

A short time later, Conrad stood by his side as he sat on the sofa in his flat. "You don't look so good. Can I fetch a doctor?"

"No!" said Proteus; the force of his voice pounded his temples and he winced. He sank back into the cushions.

"You sure? I know a good nurse."

"Leave, please. I'll contact you when I need you."

The door closed behind Conrad, and Proteus rolled over in pain and began to pull off his clothes. He looked over at the satchel. *I need to consult the diagnostic algorithms in the Cube ... check my symptoms ... but I'm too tired to think...*

Ψ

Proteus fell asleep and dreamt.

He was being chased by something; he heard its claws on the cobblestones as he stumbled, running in a dark city, trying to escape. It gained on him, and Proteus willed himself to move faster, but it was as if he was struggling through cold molasses, sweating to stay ahead of the beast pursuing him. The alley suddenly tilted up to forty-five degrees, and he bent over to move on all fours, pulling himself along with his hands as he pushed with his legs. But he was moving too slowly ...

Its hot, sulfurous breath baked his back; a shadow rose and blotted out all light. Proteus tried to scream but could make no sound. He fell —

—into a bonfire surrounded by people with masks, dancing.

Burning. Burning. Burning.

He woke up to find his sheets soaked in sweat, smelling like stale onions. The room spun, and Proteus's stomach contents decided they were storming north. He got up and lurched toward the bathroom as his mouth flushed with saliva. He tripped, fell to the floor, and vomited. Violent shivers coursed through him, and he curled into a ball, hugging himself to ward off the frigid cold racking his body. "P-p-plea..." he begged as his facial muscles spasmed.

I don't want to die.

The wave of chills passed, and he crawled on all fours to the bathroom, where he heaved into the toilet. And then heaved again and again—

—until he collapsed, quivering in the corner, and blacked out.

He dreamt of snow, mountains, and freezing to death.

Ψ

His shivering woke him up. He smelled the sour vomit on the floor and on his skin as he crawled over the lip of the clawfoot tub and into it. He fumbled with one of the taps and yelled as a cold jet of water splashed over his back. He began to shake again. He reached up and turned on the other tap, the one for hot water.

It's Time-sickness, an internal voice whispered again. Chills rolled through his limbs.

His heels drummed against the thick porcelain tub as the water rained down; he hugged his shoulders in a fetal position. He tried to speak through the paralyzing spasms wracking his body. "K–kill me ... now," he whimpered.

And passed out again.

Waves crashed onto the shore under a leaden sky as charcoal clouds scurried by, harassed by the gale. White gulls cried and wheeled above. Farther out, beyond the break, white caps frothed and churned, whipped by the approaching storm. Long grasses bowed and waved in the stiff breeze on the edge of the dune upon which he stood. Sand stung his face, and he shielded his eyes.

Under pewter skies, torrential rain soaked his skin. In the distance, lightning strobed, revealing a massive anvil cloud. Closer to shore, midnight clouds hung like dark bulbs above the churning ocean. A long tongue grew from one of them, elongating, slowly rotating, and reaching downward toward the roiling steel-grey surface of the water.

Hail fell, leaving marble-sized impact craters in the sand. The black cone narrowed as it neared the surface, and began twisting. A milky haze rose from the ocean's surface to touch the tip of the descending vortex, which rotated faster and faster.

The waterspout howled as it grew in size and intensity and moved in the direction of the shore, straight at him.

Ψ

A warm, rhythmic pulsation on his face and chest woke him, and Proteus blinked up into the steaming stream from the showerhead. His shivering had stopped. He sat up to put the rubber stopper into the plughole and then lay back.

When his arms began to float, Proteus shut off the faucet. His vision began to fade as he sank into the embryonic warmth of the water. He drifted off—

—and then woke in tepid water, uncertain of how long he'd been asleep.

He pulled the plug and then rose from the tub and reached for a towel. He stepped over the lip, gripping it firmly lest he slip. And as he toweled off, he looked in the mirror. A sallow face with yellow eyes looked back.

I need to urinate — and I need to consult the Cube.

Not certain that he could continue to stand upright unaided, he braced himself against the sink. He urinated into the toilet, and a dark brown stream splashed against the eggshell-colored porcelain. Proteus shuddered and then began to sob.

He staggered back to the bed, picking up his satchel on the way.

He powered on the SDU and queried his symptoms. The Data-Cube indicated that his liver had shut down, cause unknown. But it speculated that his body was in flux from an immune storm, perhaps from a pathogen, or perhaps from Time-sickness.

It gave dietary and hydration recommendations, along with avoidance of known hepatotoxins of the time — especially alcohol. Beyond that, only time would tell if he lived or died. It warned about the medical capabilities of the time period and recommended against seeking health care at all costs; the doctors were still too early in the transition from anecdotes to scientific method to be of much help. They had no antibiotics or antivirals for infectious diseases, and Time-sickness couldn't even be cured in the twenty-fifth century, let alone the twentieth. He fell asleep reading the report.

And dreamt of storms and death.

15

The watchmaker sat at his workbench, his tools untouched for hours. He wondered in disbelief at the news that the American had vanished. His boss had sent a team to the Savoy, and they'd stormed into the room but found it empty; the American had checked out of the hotel that morning and hadn't been seen since. They'd lost all trace of him.

One moment they'd been a hair's breadth away from hauling the counterspy into the Soviet embassy and torturing the information out of him — literally on the cusp of obtaining his secrets — but then the operation had gone astray. The watchmaker knew there'd be hell to pay and was thankful he wasn't in the cross-hairs, or Red-Bear and his team. Whoever had led the kidnapping group from the embassy would be reassigned; most likely into the Thames.

But what has happened to the American? Where has he gone?

He knew the answer the moment he posed the questions: *I am the prey, and he's gone silent to hunt me.*

The watchmaker recoiled at the intrusive thought, and then laughed at himself. *Paranoia. Dreams are always anchored in reality, and the ones you've had simply reflect your fear of being caught. No one is hunting you.*

Ψ

Borya Volkov steepled his fingers together and rested his elbows on the polished surface of the massive oak desk in the top-floor room of the Soviet embassy in Chesham Place, Belgravia. He gazed at the man perched upon a small stool in the center of the office.

From outside the window, which was flanked by heavy scarlet drapes, arose the noise of the street: motorcar horns, clomps and whinnies of horses, and the rumblings of double-decker buses.

Borya pointed an index finger at the window. His assistant, Pyotr, a muscular man with a square head, arose from a low couch like a serpent uncoiling, glided to the window, and released the sashes holding back the drapes; the room dimmed as it was cut off from daylight. Borya's eyes adjusted to the sallow electric light leaching from the sconces and desk lamp, which lent the office the pleasing appeal of a gentlemen's smoking parlor where one could relax with a fine cigar and a stiff drink. But there was nothing pleasant in Borya's mind.

"Relax. You did the best you could," he said in Russian. He reached into a mahogany wood box on his desk and held up a cigar. "The American is elusive. You lost him."

"Yes," said the man on the stool, straightening his posture and nodding.

Pyotr removed a cigar-cutter from his coat and approached his boss. The man on the stool watched every move as Pyotr took the cigar, chopped off the end, and handed it back to Borya. The chopper disappeared into Pyotr's coat, and he produced a large silver lighter, which he struck. Then he leaned forward to light the cigar as his boss puffed.

Borya exhaled slowly, letting the smoke roll across his tongue, enjoying the taste of the Cuban cigar. "I know you will not fail again," he said.

"No. Never again, Commissar Chief."

"Good," said Borya and inhaled. "Good." He exhaled and nodded at Pyotr, who stepped forward and grasped the man; one large hand cupped the chin and the other the top of the head.

A crunch echoed off the office walls as Pyotr forcefully rotated his hips and twisted the man's head, snapping his neck.

Pyotr let his victim slide to the floor, moved the small chair, and rolled up the dead body in a large rectangle of red carpet that had been placed there earlier for just this purpose. He opened the office door, and a bearded man dressed in a black wool sweater and cap entered. The man then helped Pyotr carry out the corpse.

Failure must always have consequences, Borya thought and looked at the picture of Joseph Stalin hanging on the wall. *Always.*

Presently, Pyotr returned and looked expectantly at his master.

"The American is hard to trap," said Borya. "But as the proverb says, *you may never leave your fate.* His time will come, and we will get from him what we need."

Pyotr stood motionless and nodded slowly. The yellow light from the desk lamp glinted in his eyes as he waited, hands clasped behind his back like a soldier.

"Pass a message to the man with many watches. I want the information from Cavendish that the American was trying to steal. We will have those secrets." He looked away from Pyotr to gaze at the picture of Stalin.

Pyotr snapped to attention; his square jaw and fleshy lips twitched into a smile, showing brown teeth. "It will be done," he said and bowed. "May the capitalists drown in greed."

After Pyotr left the room and closed the door, Borya allowed himself a smile, the first and perhaps the only one of the day. Something very unusual was going on, and he would get to the bottom of it.

16

The tempest abated. The anvil cloud moved eastward; bright silvery dendrites flashed against the jet-black underside. A thin horizon appeared as the grey of the sky and the sea pulled apart. Wind flowed from behind Proteus, carrying the smell of wet evergreen. A broad shaft of sunlight penetrated the retreating storm. An arced spectrum — from red through green, yellow, blue, and violet — appeared above the waves.

Proteus awoke thinking of water, his mouth bone dry.

He staggered to the bathroom and looked at his reflection: hooded, jaundiced eyes peered above a jaundiced face with a week's stubble. He looked like a rotting pumpkin that had grown furry with mold.

Proteus filled a glass with water from the faucet and gulped it down; then another, and another. The clear, cold water soothed his insides with each swallow, bringing him back to life. He filled another. Halfway through the glass, he coughed and choked.

Slow down, he chided himself. But each swallow was bliss.

As he filled his glass again and drank, a tingling built along his spine. Proteus trembled and held on to the sink. After a few moments, he staggered back to the bed and crawled under the covers. He rolled over and looked at the window, its grey light barely brightening the room. The stale biscuits on the nightstand attracted his eyes as another sensation burrowed into his awareness: hunger.

He reached over and grabbed one of the biscuits. Breaking it apart, he put a small piece onto his tongue. The stale, salty morsel was the best thing he had ever tasted. He sobbed.

I'm not going to die.

Proteus broke off another piece of the biscuit. Soon there were only a few crumbs left. He fell asleep, and his dreams were tormented by the Colony and his sterile life underground.

Ψ

Proteus awoke ravenous and parched. He sat up cautiously, expecting a wave of vertigo, but it didn't materialize. Rising slowly to his feet, he found that his balance was stable, and he was stronger. In the bathroom he drank several glasses of water. The reflection watching him was less sallow — more like a living human and less like a corpse. Pressure in his bladder built and he relieved himself in the toilet. The stream was much lighter in color than the last time he remembered peeing.

He checked his pocket watch: seven in the evening.

Proteus busied himself getting ready, then came back to look in the mirror. His skin color was more of a flax yellow and less full-on bright pumpkin, but he thought it might still put people off, so he wrapped a scarf around his face and pulled his bowler hat low. His stomach growled as he left in search of food.

Near his flat he found a restaurant and gorged himself on steak, potatoes, and Yorkshire pudding. He ate too quickly, and his bloated stomach pressed uncomfortably against his trousers. As he slid the empty plate away, a deep yawn welled up within, and he leaned back to let it loose and stretch his arms. Fatigue pulled on his eyelids, and he settled his bill and left.

Ψ

After several days, Proteus's skin color had returned to normal.

What happened to me?

He looked down, clenching and unclenching his fists. *My appetite has*

been relentless. I didn't eat or drink for almost seventy-two hours. But now ...
Why am I alive?

His eyes flicked back up to the reflection in the mirror. Small black pupils awash in pools of brown looked back. He stood motionless for thirty heartbeats. A vibration tickled his fingertips, then moved over the backs of his hands, flowing up his arms. The buzzing continued up through his neck, into the base of his skull, where it drilled away.

Proteus put his hands over his ears and gasped. Pain throbbed in his head with each heartbeat, like blows from a maul.

He bent over — and cried out.

And then the thunderclap headache vanished.

He gasped and held on to the counter, breathing heavily, feeling nothing but emptiness. He slowed his breathing and waited in confusion.

Warmth glowed along the backs of his arms and neck, and then his scalp. The tingling warmth intensified and washed over him in waves — and then built into a crescendo. Pleasurable, visceral sensations flooded into the void left by days of bone-wracking pain and sickness.

A low growl sounded in his abdomen, and the familiar yearning for food plucked at basal instincts. It was time to eat again.

Ψ

After dinner, Proteus climbed into bed, and his head had barely made contact with the pillow before he drifted off.

He dreamt of walking in a park, over the grass, barefoot.

His hand reached out and touched the trunk of a living tree. The rough bark of the scarlet oak shimmered under his fingertips — pulsing. Aromatic oils wafted into his nostrils, and Proteus sensed the flow of water within the vascular system of the tree.

The dream shifted.

He witnessed the birth of the Earth and the formation of the primordial soup from which the first single-celled organism sprang.

Images of evolution: multicelled organisms; plants; animals.

Then empty darkness. Proteus trembled.

A pure white light flared like a candle in the black void. It grew, now a bonfire. He shielded his eyes. Brighter. Now a star. Blinding him.

ACT 2

17

Autumn 1921

I survived, but I don't fully understand why.

Proteus looked at the rain tapping on the window of his flat and the dark skies beyond as dusk descended on London. He thought of the first surviving time traveler, the man who had the same nature-dream disease as Proteus.

The genomic changes — the segments within his dark DNA that had come alive — were responsible for the man's survival. But what else had happened to him?

And now me?

My morning tremors are gone! The numb patches on my skin are gone! Gone! Even my dreams, ceaseless from childhood, have changed.

Has my genetic death sentence been commuted?

His eyes unfocused, and he listened to the storm outside as he pondered.

Ψ

In the morning, Proteus awoke before dawn, refreshed. He marveled again at the absence of the tremors that had been a daily occurrence for the past several years and dared to hope that he was cured.

He called up the mission objectives up on the Data-Cube. It had been a month since he'd last snuck into Cavendish and adulterated the experiments — and whether the minds there had been thrown off, and how far, was hard to know. Would Rutherford stop at the electron and proton, and his perfectly balanced atomic model, or would he pursue the heavy particle he suspected existed?

But the neutron must remain hidden for as long as possible. When it's discovered, and then split, that's when the real race for fissile weapons begins.

He needed to look at Rutherford's data, so after lunch he began prepping for another foray to Cambridge. Conrad had been given the month off and was away on holiday with his wife and daughter. Proteus had lent him the Vauxhall as well, so Proteus would have to make his own way to the train station.

For tonight's work, he selected black coveralls, leather gloves, and a black wool cap. He'd purchased an army surplus backpack and had a seamstress alter it to make it smaller and more compact. Then he had dyed it black.

Proteus placed his tools and SDU into the main compartment of the pack. On the way out of his flat, he paused to look at himself in the mirror. Most people would probably assume he was a workman of some sort, if he was even noticed at all. He flipped off the lights and headed out.

Carefully crossing the street — mindful of any lurking horses or motorcars that might run him over — he took in the different modes of street transportation. For several years, the horse-drawn hansom cabs had been disappearing, steadily supplanted by the evolutionary pressure of the motor taxis. He watched one blare its horn and swerve around a hansom; the motor-taxi driver waved his arm, taunting the slower carriage.

At the first major intersection he came to, traffic was backed up behind several double-decker busses waiting for a white-gloved policeman to stop the cross traffic. Drivers behind the buses soon began honking their horns at the delay. A few of the buses were of the newest design, with an enclosed top. Proteus chuckled. Transportation engineers had apparently only recently discovered that in rainy London an enclosed roof was a good idea; now, ridership was soaring.

The policeman blew his whistle, waved a white hand, and stepped out of the way. The buses lurched forward, looking like big red buffalos, farting sooty exhaust.

Walking would take him longer to get to the train station than would the Underground, but it was a pleasant afternoon and he preferred the open sky to the tunnels and tombs below.

18

"The energy produced by the breaking down of the atom is a very poor kind of thing. Anyone who expects a source of power from transformation of these atoms is talking moonshine."
~ Ernest Rutherford

Well after dark, Proteus was prowling across the Cambridge campus toward Cavendish when he heard voices and stopped. He determined they were headed toward him, located a tree, and quickly climbed up.

Striding across the lawn were two men in dark trench coats and fedoras. Initially, he thought that one of the men was quite short, but as they approached his tree, he realized one was normal-sized and the other was huge.

They spoke a language that Proteus recognized as Russian. As they passed almost directly under his tree, he could have hit either one in the head with the apple in his coat pocket. He smiled as he thought of Sir Isaac Newton.

He saw they were headed for the back entrance of Cavendish, and waited until they were halfway between his tree and Cavendish before swinging down to a soft landing on the wet turf. Proteus looked at the pair sneaking toward the building, silhouetted against the lights within Cavendish.

Best steer clear but see what they're up to.

The pair disappeared around the corner of the building, and Proteus sped up to close the distance. He peered around the corner and saw the large man wrap a towel around his hand and punch out one of the small window panes of the door. He reached in, while the smaller man looked in all directions.

The big man popped the door lock and they entered the building.

Proteus stayed close to the edge of the back of the building and followed them in, careful to avoid the broken glass. Inside, he heard them in the stairwell and followed cautiously.

Silently, he opened the door to the third floor and peered along the corridor to the right, in time to see the large oaf smash the glass on an interior half-light door.

The two Russians were soon inside.

Proteus crept forward; then motion caught his eye, and he spun to the left. Ten feet away, a janitor stared at him.

"There are foreign thieves inside the building," said Proteus urgently. "Summon help. Quickly!" He stepped back and opened the stairwell door. "Go!"

The man's eyes went wide, and he stared at Proteus. Loud thumps and crunches sounded down the hallway, and the janitor jumped and then scurried through the door. Proteus heard him clomping down the stairs as he turned back toward the office.

What are they doing?

Proteus approached the office. A placard on the wall read *Professor Ernest T. Rutherford, Chair.*

His boots crunched on the glass on the floor as he crossed the threshold and rapped his knuckles on the door frame. "What are you doing?" he said. "You gentlemen have made quite the mess."

He ducked as a small knife thunked into the wall above his head. The smaller man recoiled from his throw and reached into his trench coat to withdraw another, larger knife.

He pointed the tip at Proteus and then switched the knife to a reverse grip, and rounded the corner of an enormous, cluttered desk, coming for Proteus.

The larger man dropped a desk drawer, and clutched a large flat object against his chest with one arm. In the other he wielded a short, thick club.

"Gentlemen! Please, I implore you to cease and desist," said Proteus. Then he switched to Russian. "Go home. Drop your stuff." Or something close to that, he hoped.

Both men hesitated. Then their expressions changed; they advanced toward him around opposite sides of the desk.

Proteus didn't want to fight both of them simultaneously in this confined space. And he especially didn't want to allow the large one to get his big hands on him.

He turned, pulled the knife from the wall — judged its balance — and threw it at the wrestler.

The knife struck the big man in the chest, and he stumbled backward, dropping the object he was clutching. He crashed into a wall.

The other one closed in with his knife, and Proteus ducked to avoid a roundhouse slash aimed at the left side of his neck; then he blocked the man's elbow, halting the follow-up reverse direction stab aimed at Proteus's chest.

He snaked his left arm over his assailant's weapon arm and grabbed the wrist; at the same time, he leveraged an arm bar with his right. Then he stepped behind his now off-balance opponent and used a leg reap to flip him. While the man was in the air, Proteus folded the knife arm behind him like a chicken wing. The man landed on his back and screamed as the tip of the long blade burst from his abdomen.

Proteus stood and turned—

—and the left side of his head exploded in pain, and he spun and hit the floor.

His vision swirled vertiginously, and a loud ringing assaulted his ears. His mind struggled to process what was happening.

Get up! an internal voice screamed, but his limbs were slow to move.

His vision cleared enough to show a tilted view of dirty floorboards under a sideways desk; a large boot stomped down, blocking his view of the debris and dust underneath. *Get up*, Proteus pleaded with himself.

He was hauled up to a sitting position, and two massive, tattooed arms coiled like pythons around his head and neck. Full awareness returned to Proteus in time to feel the pressure against his carotid arteries and the back of his skull as he was locked into a choke hold.

Oh no—

The wrestler's arms bulged as he squeezed his elbows together.

A pressure wave exploded upward into Proteus's head; his eyes bulged. Grey, flickering, jagged lines burst along the edges of his field of vision and swarmed inward.

He clutched at his assailant, reaching desperately backward over his shoulders.

His thoughts tripped, slowed, and stumbled.

Dying.

Grey filled everything.

Right hand.

Handle.

Proteus pulled the knife from the wrestler's chest; he stabbed blindly over his left shoulder.

The pythons flinched, spasmed — and then withdrew.

Proteus twisted the knife, then collapsed to the floor.

Heaving in lungfuls of air, he rolled onto hands and knees, still unable to see. He heard and felt two loud stomps on the floorboards. He shook his head and tried to concentrate; the flickering symbols retreated.

He saw the boots come for him again, and he rolled to the right — but then the wrestler crashed to the floor.

Proteus gasped for breath as he crawled backward, away from the giant. Stars flashed in his vision, and he braced himself against a wall as his vision cleared. The large man was quivering in a seizure on the floor, and a crimson pool was growing under his head. The knife projected from his left eye socket.

Proteus slid farther back and panted. His eyes scanned the room, looking for threats and a means of escape.

Slow your breathing.

Proteus leaned against the wall and stood slowly. His head throbbed and his teeth felt as though they no longer fit together. He looked about the bloody mess in the office; then he remembered the janitor. *How long until he returns with help?*

He staggered toward the desk, the surface of which was invisible beneath a mess of papers, odd-shaped glass vessels, and books. He grabbed the edge for support and, bracing himself, he saw a huge tome resting on top of the chaotic desk.

That's what the wrestler had in his grasp. Is that what he hit me with?

He picked it up to examine it. The heavy volume had the dimensions of a chessboard, but it was seven inches thick. Proteus opened and leafed through the pages.

It was Rutherford's experimental compendium — full of data, diagrams, and equations. *Not a good thing for the Soviets to have*, he thought. *Should I take it? How will my theft change things?*

A distant bang sounded within the building. *I need to get out.*

Proteus jammed the notebook into his pack and then stepped over to the wrestler and extracted the knife from his eye socket. He used the man's overcoat to wipe some of the blood off his boots. The other man moaned in the corner, and the clock in Proteus's head ticked off several more seconds.

He approached the door, then stopped and looked at the mangled, splintered remains of the desk drawers on the floor. A small, dark lump caught his eye, and he picked it up. He recognized the faceted black mineral as pitchblende, the raw radioactive ore that yielded the elements for the experiments, and tossed it into his pack.

A door banged open at the end of the hallway, and he heard voices and footsteps. *Time to go.*

He went to a window, opened it, and looked down. It was too high to jump.

The voices and footsteps came closer.

Proteus braced himself inside the stone window frame, then squeezed around the edge of the casement window. He crept out to stand on a lip of stone, then explored with his hands and boot-tips to hug and move along the side of the building.

The footsteps halted inside the office.

Proteus circled around to the dark side of the column to which he was clinging, his fingers and toes guiding the way. He held on to the stone, concealed in the shadows, and peered back into the office. The janitor and a man wearing a tweed sweater were looking around the room. The two men stood frozen for several heartbeats and then began shouting for help.

Proteus's heart drummed.

He looked down, pressed his chest against the column, and then extended the reach of both arms until his fingers found the juncture of stone and brick wall on opposite sides of the column. Hugging it, he climbed down using his boot-tips to find nubbins of holds. The raging adrenalin dump that still flowed through him shook his arms and legs. His fingertips squeezed hard on each hold as his toes probed downward for each new bump.

Another ten feet.

He leapt off the building — but landed off-center and fell on his side. Something sharp stabbed his abdomen. He rolled away from the pain, groaning. Patting his right lower abdomen with his hands, his right fingers found a wound — and he jerked wet fingertips back in pain and alarm.

He looked around on the ground and saw the end of a stick in the flattened grass where he'd landed. Trembling, he moved closer to the building and into the shadows. As he looked up at Rutherford's office window, his fingertips explored the wound — and he gritted his teeth to avoid crying out.

Thankfully, the wound was shallow and not bleeding much. He'd have to take care of it later, back at his flat, after he'd escaped Cambridge. Voices echoed from above, and he heard answering shouts from across the lawn.

Proteus limped along the edge of the building and into the darkness.

19

Lying on his back on his bed, Proteus held his breath — and winced as he yanked the tape off the wound. After trying different methods with previous dressing changes, he'd concluded that ripping the adhesive tape off in one fell swoop was preferable to the slow process of trying to tease it away gingerly from the skin, which resulted in micro-bursts of agony.

Two days after the event, he was still processing *why* he'd intervened at Cavendish.

He propped himself up on the bed to inspect the wound as he removed the blood-tinged gauze. The edges of the skin around the puncture wound were red, but there was no pus, and it didn't seem infected.

He grimaced as he stuffed fresh gauze over the wound and taped it in place.

Proteus looked toward the table, where Rutherford's notebook lay next to the lump of pitchblende he'd taken from the office. He'd confirmed the radioactivity of it with the SDU. Pitchblende — otherwise known as *uraninite* — was the ore that Marie Curie laboriously processed to extract radium and thorium for the experimentalists of the world. Later, it would be mined for its rich uranium content to create nuclear bombs. But at present, Marie Curie ground it up, eventually cooking tons of it in acid baths in her laboratories in Paris to produce gram amounts of radium and thorium that Rutherford and others relied on for their experiments. All of them were oblivious to the dangers of radioactivity.

Proteus had read the biographies of Rutherford and knew the man liked to squirrel away pitchblende in his desk, as well as in his pockets. Decades hence, it would cost a king's ransom to decontaminate that office. Proteus thought of the smashed desk and dead Russians — and the fallout that might result from that — and then began flipping through the notebook.

Most of the data was from before 1920, but a small and more recently written section contained a reference to new particle-scattering experiments resulting in "strange circles". His heart sped up as he read. Proteus's grueling work was finally having an impact!

He lingered on the section, and then flipped through the pages before and after. Unfortunately, there weren't any experimental records for these new findings, so Proteus was still in the dark as to the magnitude of the influence on Rutherford's atomic model.

He needed more information about Rutherford's thoughts. Proteus looked at the ore again. He should find a safe way to dispose of it where it couldn't harm anyone.

Ψ

The watchmaker sat on the bench in Battersea Park and checked the time. Red-Bear was never late. He tossed a few seeds to a pigeon and fantasized about strangling it; then he checked the time again. Something was wrong.

He sensed a large presence sitting down behind him and breathed a sigh of relief. But then he caught a glimpse in his peripheral vision of the shape behind him. It was too large for Red-Bear. The watchmaker stood to leave.

The figure spoke the code word to him in Russian, and the watchmaker risked a glance at the side of the man's face. He flinched when he recognized Pyotr from the embassy.

It was never good to see Borya's errand-boy-cum-assassin; it always meant something bad.

"Sit," said Pyotr in a rumbling bass voice.

The watchmaker hesitated a fraction of a second before complying. His skin crawled as he eased himself back down on the bench. The last thing he wanted was to have his back to the behemoth. However, the logical conclusion was that if Borya had wanted him dead, Pyotr would have just snapped his neck without first saying hello. But logic did little to calm the tremors in his hands.

"Red-Bear is dead," said Pyotr. "And Sasha."

"What?" said the watchmaker. His pulse pounded in his ears, and a familiar, squeezing pain began in his chest. He'd expected to receive the experimental data pilfered from Cavendish by Red-Bear, not the news of his death — and Sasha, too. "How?"

"Butchered in an office," said Pyotr. "In Cambridge. Boss suspects the American. Have you seen him?"

It felt like someone was stepping on the watchmaker's chest; with a shaking hand he reached into his coat pocket for the small, corked brown bottle he always carried. *Pyotr is here to deliver an ultimatum.*

"I've no ... idea ... where he is," said the watchmaker, gritting his teeth. Shaking in pain, he uncorked the bottle and shook out several tablets into his palm, spilling one onto the ground.

He popped two tablets under his tongue.

And panted. The pain intensified, and his ears buzzed with the thrum of his hammering pulse. He was too paralyzed to move and—

—then the pressure in his chest began to lift. He took in ragged breaths as he tasted the burning sweetness of the nitroglycerin in his mouth. A bitter reminder of his mortality.

"It's big deal," said Pyotr.

The pain eased further, and the watchmaker's heart backed away from the precipice.

"Yes, *it* ... is," he said.

The bulk behind him shifted. "Hey, you okay?" said Pyotr.

"Breathing and *thinking* about the American," answered the watchmaker. The pain retreated further, and he refocused his attention on what was at stake: his life.

He thought through the ramifications of his response and said, "Ever since your team botched the kidnapping, he's been a ghost. No one's seen him in London. And he hasn't been seen at Cambridge."

In the silence that followed, he wondered if he'd gone too far. Pyotr didn't think, he obeyed, and he wasn't here to talk.

Pyotr cracked his knuckles.

"I … I will find him," said the watchmaker. "Somehow, I will find him."

He felt the weight shift behind him again and held his breath.

Then he heard Pyotr thump away.

The watchmaker exhaled and looked down at his feet for the missing pill. After a minute of searching, he still couldn't find it, and he stopped the search. One of the pigeons must have scooped it up.

He imagined it flying when the tablet was fully absorbed and the lethal dose hit. When it plummeted from the skies, would it be crushed by a bus, trampled on the streets, or would it drown in the Thames or be eaten by a cat?

The probabilities of these outcomes branched out like the chess problems on his board, and a part of his mind ran through the pigeon calculations while a larger portion dove into the problem of finding the American.

20

"That man is an Euclidian point: position without substance."
~ Ernest Rutherford

"There're two detectives from Scotland Yard here to see you, Professor," said Charles, one of Rutherford's assistants.

"Well, show them in," said Rutherford. "Don't just stand there gawking."

Charles retreated. A few moments later, there was a knock on the door. "Detectives Marlowe and Billups," said the assistant.

"Which is which?" asked Rutherford.

"I'm Chief Inspector Marlowe," said a tall man with a handlebar moustache and a long, thin nose. "And this is Detective Billups." He nodded toward a shorter man with a barrel chest. "We're from Scotland Yard."

"Yes, I know that already," said Rutherford. "Why are you here? I've already spoken with the local constabulary. Have you found my notebook?"

"Not yet, but we're investigating, sir," said Marlowe. "As to your first question, the two dead men in your office have been identified."

"And?"

Billups's blue eyes locked on Rutherford as he reached into his jacket and retrieved a small notebook and pencil. He flipped open the cover and began writing. "Taking notes," he explained.

Marlowe said, "We reviewed the report from the local police. You said that you don't know the deceased, is that correct?"

"Yes," said Rutherford.

"Yes, you do know them? Or yes, he's correct in that you don't?" asked Billups. Marlowe scrunched his brow and looked out of the corner of his eye at Billups.

Rutherford exhaled a long breath, propped both elbows on his desk, and dug the knuckles of his index fingers into his temples. After a moment he said, "Look, I'm really quite busy at the moment. My primary data notebook has been stolen at a critical time. I *must* be able to compare the new findings with the original data, which I can't do if I don't have the original *bloody* data. Perhaps your time could be better spent solving this crime out there rather than blathering around here. I've already said I don't know the men. Is there some reason you're harassing me?"

"We don't mean to be a bother, Professor, it's just that the two blokes found … right here, was it?" said Marlowe, nodding at the two chalk outlines and bloodstains on the floor.

Rutherford put both hands back to his head and began to massage his temples. "Are you always this astute, Detective Marbury, or did I simply catch you on a good day?"

"Marlowe."

"What?"

"It's Marlowe, sir. Inspector Marlowe."

Rutherford exhaled slowly. Billups's pencil scribbled in the silence that followed, and the wall clock clicked its rhythm.

"Well, as I was saying," said Marlowe. "It turns out, these two blokes were from the Russian embassy—"

"And?"

Billups and Marlowe looked at each other, and then Billups scribbled in his notebook. "Have you had any dealings with the Russian embassy? Any reason they might come here?" asked Marlowe.

"No, and no," said Rutherford. "Where is my notebook?"

"We think these two blokes were here to steal scientific secrets and were after your notebook. But there was at least one other man. The caretaker on duty that evening spoke with him and has given us a description, and—"

"We think there were two competing groups vying for your secrets," said Billups, interrupting Marlowe. "And there was a fight, and the Russians lost."

Rutherford ground his teeth, and extracted his pitchblende ore from his pocket, and began rolling it around in his hand. "So where is my notebook?"

"We think the Germans have it," said Billups.

"The Germans!" said Rutherford. "Why would the *blasted* Germans have it?"

"There's an important piece of information, which I'll tell you, but it shouldn't be shared with anyone else outside this room," said Marlowe. When Rutherford nodded in agreement, he continued, "The bloke the caretaker encountered spoke with an American accent."

Rutherford looked at Billups and then back at Marlowe, wondering if they were truly as daft as they sounded. He had no time to waste with nonsense.

He shook his head and said, "Apart from the obvious logical fallacy of stating that the Germans have my notebook and providing evidence of an American, surely you must know that Cavendish is an international center of experimental and theoretical physics. There are Frenchmen, Germans, Russians, and Italians all working together *openly*. There are no secrets!"

"No need to shout, sir," said Marlowe.

"I'm not shouting," said Rutherford. "Your theory makes no sense."

"Have you heard of Carl Lody?" said Marlowe, holding up an index finger. Billups's pencil scratched in the silence.

"Who? He's not a physicist I've heard of."

"Carl *Hans* Lody was executed as a spy against His Majesty's government in the Tower in 1914. A German spy who spoke perfect English but with an American accent," said Marlowe.

Billups nodded and said, "And traveled with an American passport."

"Do you have another theory that you're working on?" said Rutherford. "Something … eh … intelligent? Perhaps you can spell it out for me, beyond the example of a dead spy from the Great War."

"MI5 is looking into this whole affair, and they'll soon be in touch," said Marlowe.

"MI5? What the blazes is that?"

"Military Intelligence Section Five, counterespionage. They look for foreign spies within His Majesty's territory."

"Yes, I know what counterespionage *means*," said Rutherford. "But good Lord, why?"

"International military and industrial espionage, of course."

"That's absurd."

"So says you, but according to my calculations, the maths say otherwise," said Marlowe. He looked at Billups, who nodded.

"Maths?" thundered Rutherford. "What maths?"

"First is subtraction," said Marlowe, holding up a finger. "Your scientific notebook, containing your research. Gone." He paused to look at Billups, then continued, "Second is the addition of two dead Soviet embassy attachés, found brutally murdered. Add in a mysterious American, who's likely German."

"—and all in your office in one evening," added Billups.

"Put it all together, and it sums up to something bloody suspicious!" concluded Marlowe. "Smells like international military industrial espionage to me!"

"It does indeed," said Billups.

Rutherford shook his head. He took a deep breath and closed his eyes.

"The caretaker said he'd never before seen the man who told him to fetch help," said Marlowe. "Do you have a list of every worker, student, and professor within the building's laboratories?"

"No, I do not," said Rutherford.

"Aren't you the chair of the department?"

"Yes, but that doesn't mean I'm the babysitter of the blasted building. One of my assistants can put something together for you, I suppose. Why haven't you talked to administration?"

"They sent us to you."

Rutherford looked at the chalk outlines on his floor and exhaled. "I understand. Can you leave me, now?"

"Yes, of course, sir — sorry to be a bother. If you think of anything else, please telephone. Here's my number." Marlowe offered a small piece of paper. "Meanwhile, you should expect a visit from MI5. And it's best if you keep mum about this, if you know what I mean?"

"No. I don't."

Billups coughed and rolled his eyes. He looked briefly at Marlowe and then said, "Sir … MI5 is part of His Majesty's special service against foreign spies. They don't much like people to know about them or their dealings."

"So I shouldn't talk to them?" said Rutherford.

"I think it would be wise to tell them everything you know and then forget they were ever here. Am I clear, Professor?"

"Yes, of course. Thank you," said Rutherford and accepted the piece of paper.

Marlowe nodded, touched two fingers to his forehead, and said, "We'll show ourselves out, then. Thank you for your time, Professor."

Billups snapped his notepad shut and opened the office door. Marlowe left — but Billups hung back and fixed his pale blue eyes briefly on Rutherford. He appeared to be on the verge of saying something but then cleared his throat and left the office.

Rutherford took a sheet of paper from his desk, swept a clear space, and looked for his pen. After a vain search, he extracted a pencil nub from his pocket and began to write:

Dear Professor Curie,

Thank you for your correspondence. Your words are most kind, but without your pioneering efforts I would not have been able to achieve the results I have. The insight you provide is invaluable, and I wish to convey my deepest appreciation for your work.

I am intrigued by your usage of concentrated sources of radium to treat tumors in the faces of the poor souls who have been afflicted by these maladies and look forward to ...

21

"Are you sure?" asked Conrad. "It seems like you've been getting the runaround for the past year. Every time you agree on a price, the family backs out, and then the negotiations start again." He wondered at Proteus's seemingly endless patience, as well as his deep pockets.

"Yes," said Proteus. "My barrister said that all parties have signed, and the sale of Woodchester is now final."

"Well, cheers then," said Conrad and raised his glass of beer.

"Cheers," said Proteus, and they clinked glasses.

"I still think they played you, and you overpaid," said Conrad. He sipped his lager; the cold beverage was quite welcome on this hot June day. It'd been his idea to come to the Badger and Boar. The cellar of this eighteenth-century building near the Thames provided welcome relief from the sweltering heat on the streets above.

"Perhaps you're right."

Of course I'm right, thought Conrad. *Does money mean nothing to him? He's so naive at times.* But instead of pressing his boss further, he said, "So what was it you wanted to talk to me about? You mentioned a further business proposition."

"Yes. Several, actually," said Proteus and then took a drink.

"Yeah?" Conrad set his beer on the table and leaned forward. His heart beat faster as he waited for Proteus to swallow.

He heard his name called out from the bar and turned to see the publican point a finger at him and set two plates down; the pies were ready. "Food's ready. Be right back," said Conrad, and stood to retrieve them, then returned to their table and set the plates down.

Proteus looked at his food with a puzzled expression. "Steak and kidney pie. Is that what you called this?"

"Yes," said Conrad.

"But kidneys make urine."

Conrad laughed.

"Seems a bit barbaric."

"Well, if you're going to kill an animal, why not make use of as much as you can?" said Conrad and thought, *Americans can be so squeamish at times.* "Mind if I tuck in? I'm starving."

Without waiting for an answer, he began eating. The pie wasn't as good as his mum's, but it wasn't bad. Proteus lifted his fork and took a bite. Conrad watched Proteus's face as he chewed: first, his eyebrows went up; and then he nodded; swallowed, and smiled. He looked like a child enjoying adult food for the first time.

"See? Just forget what it's called and enjoy it," said Conrad, and took another bite. *He really is good chap*, he thought. *He asks me what I think and never talks down to me.*

Conrad soon finished his food. He took a sip of beer and looked at Proteus, who was only just halfway through his meal — and waited impatiently for his boss to finish.

The work's fun and the pay's grand. But what's next?

Finally, Proteus finished eating and put his fork down.

"So ... business propositions?" said Conrad.

"Yes," said Proteus. "First, I wish to promote you to office manager. There will be an increase in your salary and responsibilities. You'll supervise staff, oversee the day-to-day operations of the business, and begin organizing the renovations on Woodchester."

"But sir," said Conrad, wondering if his boss was pulling his leg, "you don't have an office, and there are just the two of us."

"True," said Proteus. "Finding office space to lease will be your first task, followed by hiring suitable staff. Here are the specifications and budget for the office and the renovations." Proteus passed across a sheet of paper.

Conrad took in a sharp breath when he read the total amount. "Blimey, that's a lot of money!" He looked around to see if he'd been overheard.

"Yes, it is."

Conrad looked at the line item details, and then his breath caught again when he saw what his new salary would be. He took a big swallow of his lager. "That's quite a generous amount you're offering me."

"Yes, but I know you'll earn it," said Proteus. "Do you accept the terms?"

"I do indeed, sir. When do we start?"

"Now."

22

Autumn 1922

Proteus walked along the hallway, groggy from last night's fitful sleep — following another Cambridge sabotage run — toward his new offices he'd not yet seen. The building was not far from the financial district and his flat.

Earlier this morning, Conrad had called on the telephone from the office and told him that everything was *bloody marvelous*, and he needed to come as soon as possible. The phone call also signified that the telecommunications gear was operational.

Proteus smiled when he came to the placard outside the main door: *Providence, Ltd.*

He knocked on the door and was greeted by a cheerful Conrad, who grabbed his hand and shook it several times. "Welcome. Welcome!" he said. "Please come inside and let me show you around. You're really going to like it, I think."

As Proteus stepped inside, Conrad said, "This is the reception area. These offices once belonged to a solicitor firm, J. Pinkley Barrett, Esq. & Sons. Apparently, the playboy sons drove J. Pinkley Barrett deep into debt. I was able to acquire them at a discount," said Conrad. "Here, follow me."

Conrad pointed out the communications room, which had telegraph machines, telephones, and a stock ticker, then he took Proteus through several other rooms.

"Let me show you the last one," he said. "Your office."

He led Proteus to a bright room in a corner location, with windows on two walls. Proteus went to the windows and looked out to see beautiful vistas of the horizon and the Thames below. His throat tightened.

"I know how much you like the sky, sir."

"It's lovely."

"The first two employees start tomorrow. Per your recommendations, I advertised for librarians, academics, and students. I think you'll like them," said Conrad. He hadn't stopped smiling since he'd greeted Proteus at the door.

Proteus opened his mouth to speak, but Conrad was already talking again. "I've got a dozen more interviews to conduct this afternoon. So the tour's over. I'll telephone you tomorrow morning with an update. You can see yourself out. Ta-ta for now."

"Okay," said Proteus and chuckled. "Bye."

23

February 1923

In the twilight, a cold mist fell. Proteus shivered as he walked along a sidewalk filled with people returning home from work. Their stooped shoulders and slate-grey silhouettes told their tale, just as the dandies and flappers already out in their motorcars and fancy clothes seeking the next party told theirs.

He adjusted his black overcoat against the drizzle and then continued on until he reached Burlington House, where he stopped to look at the bill posted outside: *The Structure of the Atom — Lecture by Prof. Ernest J. Rutherford*. It was a Royal Society invitation event, open only to members, rich elites, and select members of the press. Despite his tremendous monetary growth in the past year and a half, Proteus hadn't yet acquired the status needed for an invite.

He looked at his watch: five o'clock. The doors would open in one hour, and the lecture would start in two. He turned and walked down the street, looking for the alley that led to the back of the building. Under his black greatcloak was a newly tailored suit, and over his shoulder he carried his satchel containing his SDU and tools.

After circling around to the rear of the building, he found a back door and used his tools to pick the lock. Soon he was inside and creeping down a hallway as he listened.

A scraping noise echoed from ahead. He padded in that direction, then peered around the corner of a backstage curtain. Workers were arranging chairs and finishing the set-up for this evening's event. Proteus hung back in the shadows and looked at his watch. He had about twenty minutes until the front doors opened and guests were admitted. He looked at the podium and the row of five chalkboards lined up behind it, then looked for the best seat. He wanted to be close enough to see Rutherford's face — mostly because he'd never actually seen the man in the flesh — but not so close that he drew scrutiny.

The workers finished and left. Proteus brought out the SDU and used the infrared to scan for anyone he might not have seen. There were several people in the lobby, but the hall itself was empty. He removed his greatcloak and found his seat.

Soon the doors opened and ushers escorted invitees into the hall. Proteus busied himself with a copy of the *Times*, doing his best to appear engrossed. As he'd hoped, no one paid any attention to a sharply dressed gentleman reading a paper.

The wait stretched on, and Proteus was ready for the lecture to begin. Historically, he knew that the lecture was supposed to be about the proton, but he didn't know exactly what Rutherford would say. The more that Proteus was able to waylay the research into the atom, the less reliable the historical data contained in the SDU would be.

Would Rutherford open up about the confusing new findings his team had been getting or perhaps even present a new hypothesis about the atom? Or would he skip any new controversy and simply rehash old research? The proof would be in the pudding, and Proteus would just have to wait to see if his activities over the past eighteen months had achieved traction — or were for nothing. Right now, he would be content with even a small deviation in the lecture.

After the long-winded introductions and pomp had concluded, the floor was turned over to the Master of Ceremonies, whose name and title Proteus promptly forgot. As the MC spoke of science and discovery, Proteus looked around the room. The attendees were all important people. There were theoreticians, experimentalists, industry moguls, business financiers, government statesmen, and probably a few spies.

The MC continued talking, peppering his monologue with bad metaphors and the names of bigwigs. Proteus noted a group of people off to one side, twenty rows back from the front. He thought he spotted Niels Bohr, one of Rutherford's protégés. He knew the other names of

Rutherford's lab group from memory: Marsden, Geiger, Kapitsa, Chadwick, and a half-dozen more, although it wasn't possible to identify each one of them from where Proteus sat.

"... and it is my distinct privilege and honor to introduce to you the director of Cavendish, Professor Ernest Rutherford," concluded the MC, prompting applause from the audience. Rutherford stood, smiled, and strode on stage with a clump of papers in his hand. Stubbing his toe, he stumbled — but then recovered his balance — and stepped carefully toward the wooden lectern.

He cleared his throat and looked about the room. Proteus studied his face: a thick moustache entirely hid his upper lip, his thinning salt-and-pepper hair was combed neatly to one side, and his eyes held a penetrating glare as he looked at the different sections of the audience. Even from ten rows back, Proteus could feel the man's intensity. Rutherford was not unlike the radioactive elements he worked with in Cavendish.

The clapping faded, and the remaining few burbles of conversation died out as the audience waited for Rutherford to begin.

"Good day!" he said; wood panels lining the hall vibrated, and several people in the front row flinched at the volume of his voice. "The content of my address this evening about the structure of the atom has become transformed by inexplicable developments. These startling new discoveries are the focal point of my address this evening. And they have completely changed my view of the atom."

A wave of gasps fluttered through the audience, followed by silence.

Proteus held his breath. His heart pounded. *Can it be true that I've steered him away?*

Rutherford took a deep breath and raised his chin. He held up a piece of chalk and said, "If I may!"

As he approached the blackboard, a murmur flowed through the hall like a breeze on a meadow. Proteus watched him draw x- and y-axes, and then he began pecking the board with the chalk, leaving small dots. As he moved about the board, he paused periodically to consult one of the papers in his hand. Rutherford's large frame, black ceremonial robe, and tapping chalk brought to mind one of the clever ravens Proteus had seen at the Tower of London.

Before long, Proteus understood that Rutherford was plotting an experimental scintigram on the chalkboard. He knew the dots on the paper were a summation of thousands of hours of work. Each scintigram had been recorded by a bleary-eyed graduate student in the basement of Cavendish, in the dark of the lightless *Box*, where one sat staring into a microscope for hours on end, looking for faint, pinpoint flashes of radiation on a small phosphorescent screen — and then stabbing a pencil-tip onto graph paper.

The pecking chalk echoed, and the people in the packed lecture hall watched in rapt attention. The chalk snapped. Rutherford paused to retrieve the longer piece from the floor, tossing away the nub in his hand, and went back to plotting.

As the drawing unfolded, Proteus gasped and put his hand over his mouth: *Oh, no!*

His heart pounded. There were ovals and circles — subtly different from the pattern he'd etched with the SDU — but in far more detail than he'd expected.

How could my trainers have been so wrong?

Perhaps the resolution of Rutherford's equipment was greater than the twenty-fifth-century scientists had anticipated. But there was nothing he could do now but watch and await what came next. The drawing tickled at a memory, but he couldn't quite recall it.

Rutherford finished the scintigram, then stepped away from the board and brushed chalk dust off his clothing. Proteus sank lower in his seat and covered his nose with his handkerchief.

"We're not certain what these new data reveal, but we seem to be getting results that differ from our ... er ... earlier experiments from over a decade ago," announced Rutherford in his loud New Zealand accent. "We've now done this experiment over and over. I've personally verified the equipment, radiation source, and foil samples. I have a few thoughts on what this might mean, but first I'd like to open the floor for discussion and questions."

An older man raised his hand. After being acknowledged, he stood and pivoted to look around the room. He had a long white beard and was dressed in formal black attire.

"Lord Kelvin," said Rutherford. "I am honored by your presence. I await your question, sir."

Lord Kelvin cleared his throat. After a few more moments of staring around the room, he said, "From here, the scintigram looks like a drawing of a rodent's face."

Several members of the audience tittered, and a few nodded. Proteus pressed the handkerchief tighter over his nose and mouth and wished he could disappear.

"Ah yes," said Rutherford and slapped his large hands together.

"That's just what I thought as well." He went back to the chalkboard and pointed as he said, "These two bits I'm calling the *ears*. And these others look like a nose and eyes, don't they? I bet you can even imagine a mouth if you squint hard enough."

"What is you explanation?" asked Kelvin.

"I believe what this indicates is that the gravitational force within the atom, with its electrons spinning around, is more similar to the solar system than we expected. And—"

"We look forward to the retractions and corrections to your previous papers."

"—as I was saying, magnetic forces also influence the behavior of the alpha particles near the nucleus, and—"

"Perhaps one of our esteemed theorists can assist," said Kelvin. "Einstein?"

Silence.

"Is Albert Einstein in attendance?" called out the steward for the Royal Society and looked around the hall.

"He's not here," said an audience member. "Declined the invitation."

Another answered, "I believe he's visiting Erwin Schrödinger at the University at Zürich."

"What about Werner Heisenberg? Wasn't he invited?"

"I'm not certain," said the steward.

Kelvin looked around the room, waiting for others to speak. He noticed a raised arm and said, "I think this gentleman might have something to say."

A slouched man with large eyebrows and a mouth like a bass stood up. Even before he was introduced, Proteus recognized Rutherford's protégé from Copenhagen.

"Ah, Niels. Good to have you here. Please proceed."

"I," said Bohr, and then continued in slow syllables. "Think. That. Things. Are missing."

"Hear, hear!" came a call from a member of the audience.

A quivering arm shot up in the air. The man appeared to be practically vibrating at the chance to speak. Lord Kelvin pointed to him and said, "Professor de Broglie."

The man stood up and turned to look around the room. He had the largest forehead Proteus had ever seen. "What's the frequency of the alpha particles in this system?"

"We haven't yet measured that," replied Rutherford.

"All matter has a frequency, *vous savez!*"

"Yes, I've read your papers," said Rutherford.

Another frowning scientist stood and began questioning the reproducibility of Rutherford's experiments: "How can we be certain of anything now?"

"What if the universe isn't as we think ..." said another.

Proteus had heard enough; he looked for the way out. He hastily stepped over and around people as he headed toward the aisle and then to the exit. Behind him, more discussions erupted — and then shouting.

Once outside, Proteus breathed in the cold evening air and smiled at the success he had already achieved — then he brushed his hand at a speck of dirt on his lapel.

Ψ

Back in his flat, Proteus reflected upon the evening's lecture with mixed emotions. Success was success, and he'd been taught that that was the only thing that mattered. The research into the atom absolutely had to be bent away from the recorded course of history. The future depended on it. He should be overjoyed at the evidence of traction — but mostly he was drained.

Perhaps I just need an early bed.

He prepared for sleep and slid under the covers. He reached over and turned off the bedside lamp.

His thoughts drifted to the work ahead. Contrary to almost every other aspect of 1920s society, the physicists and theorists were not secluded in autocratic or nationalistic silos. They openly published and shared across borders. Thus, if Rutherford and his laboratories disappeared overnight, someone else in another country could potentially carry the torch of nuclear discovery forward. Resistance from Time might simply bypass Proteus's work by having another research group discover fission.

This terrible thought prevented him from falling asleep. He envisioned the National Socialists, Imperial Japan, or the Soviets dropping the first nuclear bomb.

It was well after midnight before he drifted off.

Ψ

The next morning Proteus walked into the communications hub, as he'd taken to calling it, and paused to absorb the activity. Providence, Ltd. was bustling.

A telegrapher was tapping on her key, sending the telegram to the mayor of Oxford that Proteus had composed earlier, inquiring about available office space. Conrad was already overseeing the set-up of a satellite office in Cambridge, and soon Proteus hoped to have a second in Oxford.

He stepped to the stock-ticker machine and held up the tape it was punching and unrolling onto the floor. He tore it off and put it in his jacket pocket. The song on the radio ended, and the BBC announcer launched into the news in a deadpan, clipped monotone, as if he were reciting a shopping list, of the fallout from the failed Beer Hall Putsch in Munich by the leader of the National Socialist Party, Adolf Hitler, and his accomplices. Hitler was now in prison, and the announcer read quotes from several British politicians who were hopeful that the street fighting in Germany would settle down and not continue to threaten the stability of the fledgling Weimar Republic.

Proteus took the news with a grain of salt and left to go to his personal office. The other rooms in Providence, Ltd. were occupied by people collecting and collating information, which was the principal business of the organization. Whether newsprint, scientific journals, monographs, or books, everything related to advancement in the fields of physics, mathematics, and chemistry was put into reports for Proteus to scan.

In total, Providence, Ltd. employed twenty-nine men and women — and was growing. When the satellite offices were up and running, he'd have access to academic libraries and lectures and could keep tabs on the goings-on (and occasional drama) at the universities.

Proteus closed and locked the door to his office, removed the SDU from its biblical cover, and then accessed the Data-Cube. He pulled up the list of researchers he tracked, including Bohr, Heisenberg, Hahn, Rutherford, and Curie, among others. Although they were located in different countries, the funding models were similar; the scientist decided the direction of research, but the institution or government provided the cash. It was a tension Proteus planned to use to his advantage, but right now he needed to update the database with the information in the summary reports on his desk.

Turning his attention to the reports, Proteus picked up the one on the latest scientific advances in experimental physics. His data group was becoming increasingly thorough. Since Rutherford's lecture, there had been a flurry of activity, which wasn't surprising given Rutherford's stature as a Nobel Prize winner. And when a Nobel Prize winner discovers something new in their previous research, people take note. Several groups in Europe were following Rutherford's lead and were trying to build upon the new finding of the mysterious *mouse circles*, as he'd taken to calling them.

Although Proteus had no practical, direct means of interfering with experiments in different nations, there seemed to be an erosion of trust developing between the experimentalists. Some thought Rutherford was pulling the wool over their eyes to cater to British nationalist interests while he went in a different direction, whereas others sought desperately to replicate his findings.

Most found nothing unusual. Some thought that Rutherford's reputedly precise instrumentation was off, or that he'd become addled — or maybe he was years ahead. The French claimed to have found triangles in their scatter experiments — some reporter had dubbed them *eiffels*, and the label had stuck.

The sniping within the ranks of the experimentalists had deteriorated into a fracas, and they'd become as mistrustful of each other as they were of the theorists. Some of the feuds seemed personal, but others were theoretical. Although this seemed a positive development, whenever laboratory results clashed with the theory, all bets were off as to the outcome. This in turn highlighted Proteus's next problem. He put down the report on the experimental physicists and picked up the one relating to the theorists.

Pure theorists such as Einstein and Schrödinger developed equations to explain how the universe worked and then left it to others, such as Rutherford, to experiment and confirm.

As Proteus read through the report, it was difficult to draw any conclusions. Certainly, they were arguing, poking holes, and trying to torpedo each others' theories, which seemed like a good thing, except that *groupthink* was anathema in the scientific realm. Their brooding, ridicule, and fighting were necessary to advance their understanding of the mysteries of the universe.

The theorists hadn't been specified in his mission objectives, but it seemed to Proteus that he should do something on this front to aid his overall success.

Another pair of butterfly wings to gently push the air and steer the scientists off course.

24

The two MI5 men drove out of London headed northeast. "Do you really think he's an agent for the Soviets, sir?" asked Morris as he depressed the clutch and shifted gears in the black Crossley.

"Who, Rutherford?" asked the captain. "I suppose he could be, but it's more likely he is being led about by the nose and hasn't a clue. You know those Cambridge types. All smart in their field, head in the clouds, but apt to fall down a flight of stairs after not paying attention to what's in front of their face."

Morris chuckled but kept his eyes on the road. Rain began falling, and he turned on the wipers. The shower intensified, interrupting the conversation.

After several minutes, Morris said, "What interest would the Soviets have in the director of the physics department, or Cambridge in general, sir?"

"Change in tactics," replied the captain. "With your recent commission, you weren't exposed to the old ways of the NKVD. Right after the war, they used to hang out in pubs near our army bases, in their *ushanka* fur hats, drinking and asking patrons for military information. They'd walk right up to some bloke and say in a heavy accent, '*Please to be giving secrets, da?*' Needless to say, they were easy to spot, and the longevity of their spycraft amounted to that of balloons in a pin factory."

Morris laughed.

"We rounded up quite a few in those days, but we were too successful. The crafty buggers shifted gears and went underground. And our daft post-war government keeps cutting our funding. Slashing us to the core. There's no more spies, they said, you've got 'em all, good show. In the meantime, the NKVD melted into the darkness and began infiltrating universities, arts, entertainment, and other areas with international exposure. They learned from our successes, as well as their own failures. Instead of trying to ferret out where a cavalry division was stationed, they're now angling to learn about the direction of our technologies. And to recruit."

"Ah … I see," said Morris.

"Their shadowy presence puts them in a good position to influence minds. And this is an integral component of their *political* war. A part that so many in Parliament are blind to. The Soviets aim to start a revolution in our backyard and win the next war without ever firing a shot. Clever bastards. And Parliament can't see it because they only think of spies as depicted in cloak-and-dagger fiction."

The rain intensified and winds gusted the Crossley. "Miserable bloody weather. How much farther, sir?"

"We're coming upon Bishop's Stortford, so about halfway there."

They rode in silence for ten minutes, rain splattering on the windshield and the wipers tapping out their pendulum rhythm.

"So, how do you want to play this, sir?" asked Morris. "Scotland Yard said he's an irascible sort."

"Well, he's a bigwig, so kid gloves," replied the Captain. "He's not likely to be impressed by our credentials, but by the time we leave, he must understand that we don't abide spies on British soil, or those who help them, wittingly or not.

"As I said, he may not have a clue that there's more going on than his atoms. So we'll play out the line, let him swim whichever way he wishes, but make sure he knows there's a hook on the end. A hook that we control."

Morris smiled and said, "Aye, sir."

"We can always take him back to Thames House for questioning at a later date, but I'd prefer to go soft and to be discreet," said the captain. "I want you to pay careful attention to his body language and facial expressions when I speak with him. That'll be much more important than what he says. And remember to follow my lead."

"Aye, sir," said Morris and took one hand off the wheel to adjust the small semi-automatic pistol in his waistband to a more comfortable position.

25

Secluded in his office, it'd taken Proteus the better part of three hours to prepare all of the final official hereditary documents for the afternoon's meeting for his claim to a peerage. Titles weren't handed out, nor could they be bought, and so William, his chief barrister, had been working through the tedious layers of bureaucracy for well on six months, driving teams of junior attorneys like the invading ships of the Norman Conquest.

And — at considerable expense — it was beginning to pay off. Tomorrow, Proteus would present the original lineage documents defining his relationship to one of the first nobles in the Woodchester area.

The forgeries had involved altering digital copies of old records in the Data-Cube, which Proteus had flashed onto sheets of vellum and then weathered with UV light.

He smiled at the insertion of his name in a box on the genealogy chart and carefully placed the *aged* documents in their leather binders. Radiocarbon dating didn't exist in the 1920s, and he was confident these would pass inspection.

Next, he turned to the stack of scientific reports waiting for his attention.

Ψ

When Proteus finished reading through the stack, he rubbed his eyes. He hadn't had quite enough sleep last night and had been concentrating without stopping all day. It'd taken his organization half a day to pull together all the information in the two reports, and then it had taken Proteus a full day to process just one of them.

The problem was that there were no electronic systems to search for specific phrases or keywords; his SDU was of no help, and Proteus couldn't clone himself. He needed more eyes to sort and filter at the fine level of detail that, currently, only he understood. But some of the atomic research topics hadn't yet happened — and might never.

He needed help with the reports, and Conrad was the only one he could trust. *It will be tricky, though.* Conrad didn't know the science like Proteus did, and he certainly didn't know the future. But if Proteus was careful, he could present topics to Conrad and explain that some of them were secrets and not to be discussed.

Proteus decided the simplest approach was to give Conrad a written list of words, and let him ask any questions he wished, which Proteus would answer directly or indirectly. There was a good chance the questions wouldn't involve enough depth to risk Proteus inadvertently revealing the future or trapping him in a circular web of lies.

His mind made up, he spent fifteen minutes composing the list of words and phrases, and then summoned Conrad — who'd returned from Cambridge last week — into his office. After he'd finished explaining, he asked Conrad if he had any questions.

"Yes, sir," said Conrad. "How does this work turn a profit for Providence?"

"Well ... I, um, look for certain types of scientific research and evaluate them to see if there are any industrial applications."

"And then help develop them with funding and the like, right?" said Conrad. "And help patent the ideas. For profit. I get it."

"Yes. It's along those lines," said Proteus. "But I also want to help develop technologies that will benefit society and the Earth. Was that your only question?"

"About the big picture? Yes," said Conrad. "However, I've got quite a few questions about this here list." He paused and looked down at the paper. "For example, *atomic and subatomic collisions, quantum mechanics, Heisenberg's uncertainty principle, Schrödinger's cat box* ... did I pronounce that last one right? I'm not too certain with umlauts."

"Pretty close, yes."

"Is it a spelling error, though? Did you perhaps mean, *hat box?*"

"No. It's correct."

"Well, I'm going to need more information, then. I won't be a party to cruel experiments on animals."

"No cats have been hurt. It's a mental exercise related to theories of the atom."

Conrad sat unmoving, waiting, and Proteus realized he'd have to provide more information. *But how do I even begin to explain quantum mechanics and the atom?* He looked at his watch: 5:00 p.m. "Previously, you offered to teach me snooker. How about we go and play, and I'll answer questions as best I can?

"That sounds hunky-dory."

"What?"

"Sounds fine."

"Okay," said Proteus. "But keep in mind the atom is not well understood and can be a confusing subject."

By way of answer, Conrad winked and then stood and opened the door. "Shall we? I know just the place."

$$\Psi$$

After walking for several blocks, they arrived at Thurston's Hall in Leicester Square.

"We're in luck," said Conrad as they entered. "There's no tournament tonight, so it's open play."

Inside, the air was thick with tobacco smoke, and the staccato clacks of billiard balls colliding echoed off the polished wood flooring. There were three connected rooms, and Proteus counted twenty-odd snooker tables, with roughly half occupied. The central room had a bar along one end, and a gramophone was warbling out the latest jazz tunes. The voices of men — dressed in sports blazers, tweed suits, suspenders, vests, herringbone suits, and pinstripes — rose and fell, along with the clinking of pint glasses.

Conrad paid for the two of them and was handed a ticket for table thirteen. As he led the way, he described the game of snooker. They stopped at a table along the way, and Conrad pointed out some important aspects of play. Proteus watched balls colliding after one of them was propelled forward by a long stick. Players used angles and momentum to achieve the outcomes they desired. It was a game of pure Newtonian physics, and he was eager to demonstrate his knowledge of science.

Conrad set everything up at their table and showed him the best way to start the game.

On his first break, Proteus dug the tip of the cue underneath the white ball, launching it into the air and off the table, where it bounced and rolled along the wooden floor and under the other snooker tables — to the laughter of the patrons.

Conrad jogged off, returned with the ball, and said, "It's all right, you'll get it. But here's an idea: I'll show you a shot and teach you, and you answer a question about the *atomic list*."

Proteus looked around the hall, worried about being overheard, but decided it was too loud to be a concern. Unless Einstein and Schrödinger were playing at an adjacent table, he and Conrad were free to talk.

Conrad reset the table and explained the opening break shot as he lined it up; then he pushed the stick smoothly, and the balls smacked and rebounded. Then he startled Proteus by diving right in. "The first thing I'm curious about are *atomic and subatomic collisions*. Since I've been working for you and given our focus on physics, I've been reading a lot about Newton's laws. But atoms are too tiny to see, so are atomic collisions like that? Like this game we're playing?"

"Not exactly. Objects we can see follow classical mechanics, but atoms and subatomic structures follow—"

"—quantum mechanics, right?" interrupted Conrad.

Proteus clenched his cue to prevent it from falling over, and he looked at Conrad, wondering at the speed at which he'd pieced things together. He breathed slowly and said, "Quantum mechanics is a new science that concerns the strange behavior of atoms, which are unlike the physical objects we can see. Newton's laws don't apply."

"Okay. Watch this," said Conrad. The ball left the tip of the cue with a strong spin and curved around one ball to strike another, knocking it into a corner pocket. "Newton called that shot. Your turn."

One muffed shot later, Proteus yielded.

"Looks like classical mechanics is better for this game than the quantum mechanics," said Conrad. "My next question is about the *cat box*."

Proteus considered how to explain then said, "Schrödinger's Cat is a thought experiment. It's a little bit like the chicken crossing the road."

"What?"

"Imagine this. You're observing a chicken standing on one side of the road. You're then blindfolded and told that the chicken may or may not cross the road, randomly, at some point in the future. Quantum mechanics says the chicken is on both sides of the road at the same time until you take your blindfold off, and then your observation forces the chicken into one resolution."

"Well, that's daft!" said Conrad.

"Yes, it is, and that's why Schrödinger thought up the cat box, to make fun of the theoretical physicists in Copenhagen," said Proteus. "In the box is an unstable trigger containing a tiny amount of radioactive material, along with a cat and a vial of poison gas. It is then sealed. The trigger follows a time probability governed by radioactive decay, and will emit radiation somewhere between a few seconds to a few hours. And when the gamma ray jumps out, the vial breaks and the cat dies."

"That is disgusting," said Conrad.

Proteus continued. "So, after you seal the cat box, it's just like the chicken and the road, in that two states exist simultaneously. The cat is both dead and alive at the same time until you, the observer, open the box — and then the cat resolves into a dead kitty or a live one."

"That's just absurd."

"Exactly. Einstein and Schrödinger hate the fuzziness of quantum mechanics. They think the Copenhagen group is a few variables short of a full equation," said Proteus.

"Ah, I see," said Conrad. He pointed to his head. "The lift doesn't go all the way to the top floor of the building." He chuckled and sank another shot. "But he didn't really do the experiment, right? It's a bit sick."

"No, he didn't do the experiment. But the point was to show that if you probability-fudge an equation to explain how atoms work, and everything we see is built of atoms, then cats can be alive and dead at the same time. Einstein and Schrödinger want to explain how the universe works, and you can't do that by hedging probabilities. For example, are you going to make that shot, or—"

Conrad hit the white ball with his stick; it ricocheted off another, then collided with a third one, which fell lightly into a side pocket.

He grinned. "Game."

"I don't think I got any balls in any pockets."

"No," said Conrad. "But you had some solid shots, and I'm sure you'll pick it up with practice."

But after two more games, it was apparent that Proteus wasn't picking it up. He'd scored one point in the second game, and two in the third, to Conrad's fifty and sixty, respectively. Proteus signaled his surrender for the evening.

On their way out, Conrad said, "You know what I think? We should make this a regular gig. Once a week, you and I."

"Yes. I'd like that," said Proteus. He imagined how much easier full honesty would be. To tell Conrad that he was from the twenty-fifth century, and about the Earth and humanity dying, and the nuclear war he was trying to prevent.

Schrödinger's cat box letter to Einstein was still several years away, but Proteus knew had to scan for these, and other keywords regardless of the recorded history, for two reasons: history was notoriously hazy on proto-ideas, which were often bandied about years or decades before becoming solidified; and now that Proteus had altered the timeline for atomic research, would Schrödinger write about the cat box sooner, later, or never?

26

Proteus walked home toward his flat after presenting his case for peerage, recalling the tepid reception he'd received. His route took him westward along the northern edge of the Thames. This was one of his favorite walking routes, though it was slightly longer than other options.

A scream erupted from the alleyway he'd just passed.

Darting back, he rounded the corner to see a woman engaged in a struggle with a man in dark clothes. They were fighting over something, yanking it back and forth.

She yelled, "Let go!"

Proteus ran to help.

The man looked up at Proteus, and then shoved the woman toward him. She tripped and stumbled, and Proteus caught her — then he scanned for her assailant but heard only retreating footsteps echoing in the alleyway.

She held on to him. "Thank you," she said and sobbed. "He almost got my purse."

"Are you injured?" asked Proteus.

"No," she said. "But I'm lost. Can you please walk me back to my hotel, the Ritz?"

"Yes, of course."

"Thank you for saving me. The world needs more gentlemen willing to help."

"Yes, indeed," agreed Proteus.

"My name is Svetlana."

"I'm Proteus."

"Nice to meet you," she said. "If you hadn't arrived when you did … well, I shudder to think what the beast might've done to me."

As they walked back to the Ritz, Proteus heard the faintest lilt in her voice, which reminded him of the accented English he'd heard from central and eastern Europeans. But more importantly, during their chatter he had a growing awareness that something was wrong.

He frowned when he realized that she held no fear.

"I'm feeling a bit faint," she said. "I think a smoke and a strong drink will help shore me up. Will you accompany me?"

"Umm …"

"It's my treat, and I insist," she said. "You rescued me, and a lady honors her savior."

Proteus nodded his agreement but cautioned himself to be wary. *Things are not as they appear.*

Soon they were sitting at a table in the lounge at the Ritz. It was early in the evening, and the theaters had not yet disgorged the rich on their quest for the next party. It would still be a few more hours until the onslaught on the Ritz began in earnest.

"You have a faint accent," he said. "Where are you from?"

She snapped her fingers and then raised an index finger.

A waiter approached, and she leaned over to him and whispered. The waiter nodded and walked off. Svetlana turned back to Proteus and said, "Kiev."

"Ah. Kiev."

"Have you been there?"

"Not yet," said Proteus, and images of the nuclear plant meltdown at Chernobyl filled his head. "Perhaps one day."

The waiter returned with a tray. Perched upon its cork surface was a clear glass bottle and two shot glasses.

"This is better than anything you can get anywhere in Europe," said Svetlana. The waiter opened a bottle with Cyrillic lettering on its label and poured out two glasses of the clear liquid. He served them their drinks, set the bottle down, and left.

Svetlana raised her glass to eye level and said, *"Salut."*

Proteus repeated the word and returned the gesture. He took a small swallow — and his throat caught fire, followed by his chest and abdomen. Shuddering, he let out a small gasp, wondering if his esophagus had just been stripped of its lining, and coughed.

Svetlana laughed and refilled her glass. She fit a cigarette into a long black holder, lit it from the candle on the table, and inhaled.

Proteus was still blinking back tears as Svetlana exhaled and launched into a description of the cultural icons of Russia: Red Square; Saint Basil's Cathedral with its onion-topped towers; the Bolshoi Theatre; the Tretyakov Gallery.

She raised her glass again.

Proteus's stomach still burned from the first swallow of the Smirnov, and he didn't want a second, but he needed to learn more about those who were pursuing him. Then a thought shook him: *is she an agent of Time?*

He grimaced and banged down the rest of the turpentine — then blinked back more tears and coughed again. *Best listen and learn.*

Svetlana was still talking, and he replayed her words in his mind to catch up.

"—has also rewarded the peoples of Russia with high-quality vodka," said Svetlana, and smiled. "Their hard work in building the workers' paradise has ended the prohibition. No longer will our comrades have to drink swill from a bathtub still." She poured another round and set the bottle down: Lenin stared somberly from the label.

Proteus watched her full red lips as he listened. She had a slight lisp, rolling Rs, and a musical lilt.

"Much better than English gin, don't you agree?" she said, her pale blue eyes studying him through long lashes.

"Absolutely," said Proteus. He thought of the murderous tyrant, Stalin.

"The English can be such stodgy bores at times," she said. "But you are not English."

"No."

"American?"

"Yes."

"Then we are comrades," she said. She smiled and poured another glassful, then once again studied him over the glass. "What do Americans say?"

"Bottoms up."

"Yes! I like that expression. *Bottoms up*," she said, mimicking his voice, and laughed. "You Americans are the cat's meow."

She drained her glass.

Two men wearing blazers and two flappers in short black dresses entered the lounge. Then more people arrived, and a gramophone began playing a raucous jazz tune. The smell of pipe tobacco and cigarette smoke wafted over from the bar.

In a corner of the room, a man in a dark suit held up a newspaper and looked over the top of it at Proteus.

Proteus decided that staying longer was too risky. "Well, I really must be going," he said. "Thank you for the drink. I'm glad you're safely back in your hotel."

"Aww, but you're spoiling the party," she said and pouted. "Let's go and have some fun."

"Perhaps another time," said Proteus.

He stood, bowed, and turned to look around the lounge, but he had lost sight of the man in the dark suit.

"You can find me by asking at Frolics," said Svetlana.

Proteus looked at the patrons again before turning back to her. "Thank you."

More partygoers streamed in through the door, and Proteus slipped past them to leave.

27

April 1925

The crump of artillery fire sounded from distant guns.

Gareth's adjutant appeared at his side. "Orders, Colonel?"

Explosions erupted all around and men yelled; horses bolted.

"Gas!" yelled a soldier.

"Masks!"

"You must go, sir." His adjutant held a horse, a dappled gelding. His horse, Mercury.

Gareth said, "No. You go to headquarters, and report. Ride. Now."

The adjutant mounted and rode off, and Gareth prayed for wind and rain as he ran to his men.

Even in the fog of the dream, the acute smell of fresh hay penetrated his nostrils as he recalled the yellow-green mist flowing over the ground, then down into the sandbagged dugouts and deeply-buried trenches. Part of his mind knew this was a dream — the same one he'd had a hundred times before — but he was powerless to change it. Or wake up.

Phosgene!

He extracted his gas mask, sealed it to his face, and lunged toward his men, clawing at the dream. He urged himself to run faster

Men contorted and convulsed. Screaming.

The rubber of his gas mask crumbled. Pain seared his flesh as the gas penetrated through his clothing and disintegrating mask.

A new gas weapon! Acid was eating the rubber.

"This way," he yelled. "Follow me!"

He led his men to the latrine pits.

Quickly!

"Dive in! Go under and hold your breath. Do it!" Ammonia in the urine, to neutralize the gas.

Stragglers came towards him. "Hurry up, save your lives!"

Gareth pushed and shoved them in. His hands burned, and he pulled off his cavalry gloves. The skin on his hands came away with them. "Gods above! Save us."

Tying his neckerchief over his eyes, he staggered into the pit and went under.

Gareth awoke, panting and sweating, his chest in a vice grip.

He sat bolt upright and saw the familiar surroundings of his cottage. Slowing his breathing, he told himself that it was only a dream.

The same bloody dream. Tears welled up. *Always the same one. So many died. So much pain. Will it ever leave me alone?*

The bed rocked as his dog, Lucy, landed from her leap. She licked his face and then sat, studying him with her intense brown eyes.

"You're a good girl," he said. "Always here for me … after the dreams."

Gareth smiled as he rubbed her ears with both hands. *She senses so much.* He looked at the twin brown pools studying him. Something tickled his mind.

"Well, we'd best be starting our day," said Gareth. "Ready for an early walk and then breakfast?"

Lucy jumped down off the bed and trotted to the front door.

"We've a long day ahead." He thought about the chores he needed to do. Mr. Proteus had been true to his commitments so far, and the work on the mansion was half complete, but it seemed a never-ending task. New power lines had been strung, and Woodchester now had electricity, although lights had thus far only been fitted on the ground level. The interior was still a bit of a mess, but the windows had been replaced and the leaks in the roof fixed. It had a long way to go, but at least it was now sealed off from the elements.

Carys had just finished her third year at Oxford and would be home soon. Thinking of her made him smile. As he dressed, he thought about Woodchester's new owner and his arrival later in the week —

and sighed.

Ψ

Proteus downshifted and accelerated around the curve. The Vauxhall's power rumbled through his bottom. He couldn't imagine driving another vehicle but had to admit he had no other frame of reference.

Driving on an open road in the countryside under blue skies was especially fun now that he was familiar with the route. This was his seventh trip to Woodchester, and he'd been able to relax and appreciate the countryside more with each visit.

It was frustrating that the repairs and renovations were still only half-complete, despite three years of effort. The first year had been consumed with architectural and engineering assessments, drawings, and permits. After that, Conrad had to hire and coordinate the various teams of skilled laborers: foundation workers, stonemasons, roofers, carpenters, and painters.

Proteus had definitely learned more than he really cared to about the process. The laborer teams necessarily had to work in a certain sequence and couldn't all attack the mansion at once. A delay in completion of a task by one group cascaded to the others, delaying them. Thankfully, Gareth had turned out to be a remarkably resourceful project manager-cum-foreman, and without his daily oversight the work achieved thus far would have taken even longer.

The road surface changed, and the vibrations rattled Proteus's teeth. It wouldn't be long now until he arrived. This trip would be a little different from the others, though. Proteus was due to stay the night at Gareth's cottage, which he'd not yet seen.

Ψ

Carys stopped her horse, Valiant, on the ridge trail overlooking Woodchester to take in the changes. It was the morning of her third day home, and it was still strange to see so many changes. The dappled grey mare shifted its stance in a way that spoke of impatience.

Carys patted Valiant's neck as her eyes followed the electric lines snaking along the long, winding drive to the mansion: workers' trucks were parked on the gravel; piles of stone and bags of concrete mix were stacked next to the mansion; and scaffolding ascended to the roof, where stonemasons were repairing weathered gargoyles. The echoes of their calls and shouts to each as they worked were carried uphill by the wind.

She couldn't see her father but knew he was down there somewhere, immersed in the renovations. Carys smiled at the thought of his happiness.

This morning, they'd hugged in the kitchen at the news on the radio that a Geneva Protocol prohibiting chemical and biological weapons in warfare had just been signed. But there was bitterness; it had taken seven years, after so many had been maimed, for a ban to be agreed upon.

Never again.

Carys pushed the thought aside as she gazed at the mansion. There were so many changes. Her favorite room was on the southwest corner of the third floor. It was the warmest and the brightest, and she'd read many a book there as a teenager. Her father always made sure it was kept up — and now he'd prioritized it in Woodchester's renovations. She didn't anticipate being able to spend time there after the new owner moved in, but it was sweet gesture by her father regardless.

She looked back to the top of the hill and wondered for the hundredth time why it hadn't been chosen for the site of the mansion. The spot where she sat upon Valiant offered a beautiful vista of the surrounding countryside and would have a been a lovely location. But for reasons unknown to her, the builders had chosen the bottom of the dark valley. It wasn't so bad in the summer months, but in winter the sun only graced the upper floors for a few hours each day.

Her horse nickered in impatience. Carys leaned over and whispered, "Oh, Valiant, is someone hungry?"

After gazing for a moment more at the mansion's limestone walls glowing pink in the morning sunlight, she allowed the animal to resume its steady clomp along the trail, down into the valley. The horse's movement swayed her from side to side in the saddle, and she lost herself in the motion.

Her thoughts turned to the rich American who'd purchased the estate, and her mood darkened. *The American who's flaunted his wealth to buy this estate must be a self-righteous twit. Like some of the man-boys at Oxford. So full of themselves. He'll probably discard my father at the drop of a hat.*

Valiant, sensing the change in mood, picked up the pace.

Roaring up the driveway below was a red motorcar; its driver waved and honked as he approached the mansion.

Carys sighed and guided Valiant toward the stable.

Ψ

Proteus pulled up to the mansion, stopped the engine, and got out.

"Lucy, *no!*" yelled Gareth, and Proteus spun to see the large black Labrador retriever running at full tilt toward him, tongue and ears flapping as she galloped. He prepared himself for the onslaught, and a tingling touched his neck.

Lucy jumped and almost knocked him over. She licked his face excitedly, spun in a circle, then jumped up to lick his face again.

"Lucy!"

Proteus looked up to see Gareth laughing and jogging over the crushed stone toward them. At her master's approach, Lucy stopped jumping up at Proteus.

Gareth said, "All these years of training..." He looked at Lucy, who was now sitting obediently midway between them.

"It's quite all right, she's lovely," said Proteus. "Every time."

A smile creased Gareth's facial scars. "Would you like to head up the cottage first, or take a look at how the repairs and renovations are going?"

"I'd love to see the work you've been overseeing."

"I've been here, looking after this place, since the war ended. It's been through some rough times, but now it's finally becoming what it was meant to be. Let's go inside, shall we?"

Proteus heard boots crunching on the gravel and turned to see a woman walking toward them. Tall and broad-shouldered, she resembled Gareth.

"Ah, Carys," said Gareth. "Let me introduce you to Mr. Proteus."

Carys had bobbed auburn hair and wore a short red wool jacket, tan jodhpurs, and calf-high brown leather boots. "Hello," she said and extended her hand.

"I'm Proteus." He shook her hand, noting the firmness of the grip. "It's nice to meet you."

"Father has told me about you," she said, and her green eyes studied him

"Well, I hope some of it was good," said Proteus, and smiled.

Carys stared at him with the same intensity he'd seen in Gareth on his first trip here. "Well, mostly that you have a lot of money," she said. "But we don't really know much about your line of work. What do you do?"

Proteus stopped smiling. "I'm in the information business."

"And what does that mean, exactly?"

"I evaluate new research for potential applications and further development."

"What kind of research?"

"Carys," said Gareth, interrupting her, "we'll have time for questions after supper." Then he turned to Proteus. "You are still staying the night?"

"Yes."

"Good. I have a rabbit stew that's been slow-cooking since this morning We'll head up to the cottage after the inspection."

"Well, I'd best get cleaned up," said Carys. She kissed her father on the cheek. "See you in a few hours, Mr. Proteus." She turned and walked away.

After she'd left, Gareth said, "She's still a bit tense since the end of her exams at Oxford, but I'm sure she'll warm to you." He inclined his head toward the mansion. "Shall we go inside? They've fixed all the leaks in the roof, and the wiring's mostly completed." He looked down. "Lucy, go and find Carys." The Labrador trotted off after her.

Proteus looked in the direction that Carys had gone, wondering what she studied at Oxford — and why he had goosebumps on his arms.

As Gareth approached the mansion, Proteus retrieved his satchel from the front seat of his car, then caught up with him.

Gareth pulled open the door and flicked on the lights. "Much nicer inside than the last time you were here. Come, you'll see."

28

The watchmaker looked at the message again and smiled.

He fed it into the coal fire. She'd found the American, and she'd learned his name — Proteus — although whether that was his first name or last was unknown. The final part of her message was a request for orders: how should she proceed?

It's him. The cause of so much misery. But should Svetlana try to lure him closer and entangle him in a relationship? Or keep her distance and try to learn his comings and goings and contacts?

He looked in disgust at the chessboard. The middle squares were evenly controlled by black and white, but his opponent had a palisade of interlocking pawns making further advancement tedious and difficult. The watchmaker had missed an opportunity earlier, and now the game was mired in trench warfare. He preferred an open, fluid game.

He considered a bold sacrificial move to break things up but hesitated. Impatience was a liability in chess — and espionage — and unless the probability was very high, calculated steps almost always won over a blitz. The watchmaker sat down to study the game, and after several minutes, a strategy began to emerge. He turned away from the board to let the plan mature and went back to his workbench.

Repair tickets were stacked high in the in-box — but the elusive spy needed the watchmaker's full attention. He thought of his message to Svetlana: *Observe from distance.*

The American had eyes in the back of his head and had murdered two of his assets already. Not that he would mind sacrificing Svetlana, of course. But he'd lost the American once, and Pyotr had been clear, despite his brutish language: there would be no additional failures.

The watchmaker thought of the assassin he must hunt, and his mind wandered.

After a moment, he stood and said, "Paul, I need fresh air." He gathered his coat. "Mind the shop."

Ψ

His doctor had advised walking for his health, and the London Zoo had always provided a better understanding of those he wished dead. The behavior of animals contrasted with the orderliness of clock-workings and chess; he'd also learned that a change of scenery could aid in problem-solving.

The summer sky darkened, threatening rain, as the watchmaker crossed the street and entered the gate to the zoo.

Killing at night and slipping away. Not even my sources within Scotland Yard have a clue.

He stopped at the aviary, but the sounds of flapping and screeching were soon too bothersome for him to think properly; he headed to the monkey house, which was always a treasure trove of insight into base human behavior: fear, anger, jealously, and scheming.

He came upon a series of barred pits for large carnivorous cats and glanced at the placards. Lions. Bengal tigers. Pumas. The stone-walled pits were below the pedestrian pavement by about ten feet, with a double layer of bars, and some had elevated concrete platforms for the cats to sleep on.

The lions appeared bored, and the tigers paced.

Thunder rolled and echoed from the stone pits, and the first fat spots of rain splatted onto the pavement. Cursing his failure to bring an umbrella, the watchmaker picked up his pace until he came to a sheltered area. There were more pits here, but these were in the shadow of the enclosure overhead.

The rain became torrential. He sighed and sat on a bench. The bars of the empty pit, six feet away in front of him, had a placard: *Leopard (Panthera pardus) — found in Africa and Asia, leopards are solitary and hunt mostly after dusk. The leopards' spots provide excellent camouflage in their natural environments. Silent in movement and excellent climbers, leopards have been known to drop from tree limbs onto unsuspecting prey below.*

There was more information about the preferred diet and behavior of leopards, but the watchmaker found his gaze attracted to a second sign mounted on a sandwich board. It described the *Leopard of Rudraprayag*, a man-eater that had been terrorizing villagers in Uttarakhand, in northern India, since 1918. Brave British and Gurkha soldiers were pictured on the sign, and, at this very moment, they were hunting the beast — which had been known to break down doors and drag villagers off into the night.

The watchmaker laughed at the imagery. One had to admire a cat that knew where the food was stored and how to gain access to it. He imagined the sign was put up so that British parents could frighten their children into behaving properly lest the fearsome leopard burst into their rooms at night or creep out from underneath their beds.

The drumming of the rain lessened, and the watchmaker glanced at the end of the covered walkway. Soon he'd be able to continue to the monkey house without being drenched.

He heard the sound of a saw cutting slowly through wood and turned back to the pit.

Large yellow eyes stared at him from ten feet away; he flinched backward from the snarling face and fangs of the leopard and almost toppled from the bench.

Bloody hell — this is why I hate animals. They're bloody chaos.

The watchmaker reassured himself that there were two sets of bars and he was in no danger, but he wished he had his pistol nonetheless. He slowly stood and backed away.

Deciding he'd had enough of the zoo, he walked out into the drizzle and headed back to his shop. The watchmaker had no further interest in trying to capture the American: he would be tracked down and shot.

29

Dear Herr Professor Schrödinger,

I write to thank you for your hospitality while I visited Zürich. It's a delightful town and the people are quite friendly. It seems you and I are two birds of the same feather, and I thoroughly enjoyed your company and insightful conversation.

Unfortunately, upon my return to Berlin I learned of a fractious international meeting during which some very unkind things were said about your wave equation. Bohr, of course. Frankly, I find that Dane tiresome. His slow mumblings about random probabilities are quite difficult to decipher, which I suppose is in keeping with his equations.

Even that Prussian Heisenberg has leapt on board. The young pups are so insistent that random quantum jumps are part of the nature of the atom that they've given up all pretense of predicting the electron's momentum and location. What good is trying to develop any theory if, in the end, you're going to describe the inner workings of the atom as a magic box of randomness that does spooky stuff? If the universe has no causality, then we may as well push physics off the edge of the flat Earth.

Imagine if Newton had shrugged and said, "I don't know, it all looks random to me," and then cloaked his equations in arbitrary uncertainty to allow for the possibility of apples falling up.

It's nonsense, and I fear for the future of physics.
I look forward to your next letter and hope you are in good spirits.
Sincerely,
Albert Einstein

30

"All my life through, the new sights of Nature made me rejoice like a child."
~ Marie Curie

After they'd finished inspecting the mansion, Proteus walked with Gareth up the hill toward his cottage. It was a sunny afternoon, and it had grown warmer in the several hours they'd spent inside the mansion.

The forest began almost at the point where the mansion and stables stopped. As they passed under the canopies of large trees, the shadows were dense and cool. Gareth explained that these were beeches.

"The forest is beautiful," said Proteus as he stopped to inspect a cluster of large ferns. The green spiral tips of new growth were unfurling like scrolls. He touched the feather-like fronds and closed his eyes for a moment to enjoy the sensation.

"True," said Gareth. "It's a special place."

As they continued uphill, Proteus heard the sound of running water and through the trees caught a glimpse of a pond. Gareth saw the direction that Proteus was looking and said, "There's five ponds in all. That one is the Kiln Pond."

Woodsmoke drifted down the trail.

There was a rustling in the dense underbrush—

—and Lucy burst out from the bushes, darting and dancing around them both.

175

"You're a silly girl," said Gareth and laughed. He lunged for her playfully; Lucy ran off a few paces and then jumped back. She then sprinted away, only to change course and come back full speed and leapt at Proteus's chest — knocking him into Gareth. The three of them collapsed in a pile off the trail.

Lucy squirmed away, danced in a circle, and then ran off in the direction of the cottage.

Gareth laughed and stood. As he held out a hand to help Proteus up, he said, "I think she likes you."

Proteus gripped the offered hand, and Gareth hauled him upright.

"You're not hurt, are you?" asked Gareth.

"No. I'm fine." He picked up his satchel from the ground, looked into Gareth's green eyes, and smiled. By now Proteus had had enough encounters with Gareth that he hardly took notice of the scars anymore, but the eyes held pain and sadness, despite the smiles and laughter.

Ψ

After a switchback in the trail, Proteus spotted the cottage. As they got closer, he saw it was bigger than he'd first imagined. The two-story limestone structure was nestled under the interlocking green cover of tall trees, making it appear like a toy.

Dappled gold spots danced on the slate roof as the wind sighed through the leaves. A cool breeze flowed up through the forest. Proteus kept a wary eye on the bushes and undergrowth lest a playful Lucy spring out again as they approached the cottage.

The four rectangular windows looked out toward the valley; Proteus stopped to look back in that direction but couldn't see much through the dense vegetation.

"Built a century ago as the family's summer home in the forest," said Gareth. "And then forgotten. The forest kept growing, as they're wont to do." Proteus turned to see a smile crease the scars and then disappear. "The cottage, nestled here, is the most natural and peaceful place I've ever been."

Proteus nodded and said, "It's beautiful." He thought about the pain he'd sensed in Gareth and noted that although he knew of the man's military experience in general terms, he didn't know the details of how he'd come to be disfigured. *Burn scars from fire or chemical*

176

weapons — but what other horrors has he been through?

"Well, here we are," said Gareth and opened the thick wooden door.

Lucy came bouncing over to greet them, and Proteus squatted down on his haunches to ruffle her head and ears, as he'd seen Gareth do. Lucy wagged her tail. Proteus stared into her chestnut eyes; there was a connection as palpable as the beautiful fur he was rubbing.

Ten thousand years ago, we bonded. The thought jarred him — and as he pulled his hand away, he wondered if other humans experience a strong connection with dogs.

"Carys. We're home," announced Gareth. His voice echoed off the stone walls, and then he turned to Proteus. "Let me show you to your room. Supper's in half an hour."

He led Proteus up the stairs to a stone-walled room with a bed, a small table, and a chair by the window. After Gareth had left, Proteus set down his satchel and went to the window to gaze into the forest.

Every minute, the light shifted, mesmerizing him. Something flashed red in the bushes. Proteus shifted his focus and spotted a fox, paused with a front paw in the air. He watched the animal sniff and then disappear into the undergrowth.

His stomach growled. From the moment he'd stepped into the cottage, his stomach had been on a mission to remind him how hungry he was. The aroma of the stew permeated the house and had changed as if some sort of spice had been added to the mix. Proteus checked his watch and, although he had only been alone for a quarter of an hour, he left to go downstairs.

"Would you like some tea?" asked Gareth as Proteus stepped into the living room.

"Yes, please."

Gareth motioned for him to sit on the couch, then served him a cup of tea before joining him. Lucy had been fed and was snoring in her bed near the hearth. Footsteps sounded on the stairs, and Proteus looked up to see Carys descending. She had changed clothes and was wearing a red cardigan, black wool trousers, and leather slippers.

She walked toward them, and Gareth rose to greet her. Proteus stood as well.

"Hello, love," said Gareth.

"Hello, Papa," said Carys and kissed him on the cheek.

Should I say something to her?

Carys turned to Proteus and nodded a greeting. Proteus executed a short, awkward bow.

Gareth said, "We're all set to eat, if everyone's ready." He ushered them into the dining room. Carys and Proteus sat at the round wooden table while Gareth went into the kitchen.

Filtered sunlight lit up the roses in a vase on the table. Proteus looked at Carys, trying to think of something to say.

Gareth returned with three wine glasses and a bottle. "From Burgundy," he said. "A Pinot Noir of which I'm fond." He poured out three glasses and then held his up in a toast. "To our guest, the new owner of Woodchester. Thank you for breathing new life into the estate."

"To nature and the beauty of the Earth," said Proteus.

Carys studied him across the rim of her glass. "To the bond and love of family," she said, looking at her father. She took a sip of her wine.

"Cheers, love," said Gareth and returned the toast.

Proteus raised his glass and drank.

Gareth disappeared into the kitchen and returned with the bowls of stew. He sat down, folded his arms into his lap, and looked down with eyes closed. Carys did the same thing. Unsure of the etiquette, Proteus emulated them.

"God, bless this meal, and watch over us," said Gareth.

Proteus waited in silence. He heard a clink and opened his eyes to see Gareth holding a steaming spoon in the air. Proteus picked up his utensil and began eating.

The tender rabbit meat in the stew was spiced with pepper and balanced by sliced potatoes, celery, and carrots. They ate in silence for a few minutes, only momentarily disturbed by Lucy taking up guard position under the table.

"Carys," said Gareth. "Tell Mr. Proteus about your studies this semester."

Carys swallowed and took a sip of water. "Well," she said, "I'm most keen about biology, and especially botany. I also learned about nutrition and health and the new discoveries of two vitamins." She paused to eat and then said, "What are your academic interests, Mr. Proteus?"

"Physics, mostly. And some mathematics, but the topics are a little dry."

"Yes. I've found them that way," said Carys and sipped her wine. "I prefer living, growing complex organisms."

"I do, too," said Proteus. He smiled and thought of what to say next.

"Then why aren't you studying biology?" Carys put down her

spoon and looked at him.

The bluntness of the question caught him off guard, and he struggled to answer it. By the time he opened his mouth, Carys was already speaking again.

"The name Proteus is odd," she said. "Brings to mind the bacterium."

"Or Homer's *Odyssey*," added Gareth.

Proteus opened his mouth again but had no words, so he scooped up a large spoonful of stew and began chewing. He swallowed and reached with a trembling hand for another mouthful.

"Perhaps we can address you by your first name?" said Carys and smiled.

"Um … sure," said Proteus. "It's Archibald."

"Well, Archibald, I believe I interrupted you. You were about to tell us why you chose your career path."

"I didn't have the opportunity to study biology when I was growing up. My training led me elsewhere, but now that I'm here …" said Proteus, and stopped to select his words carefully: "… in England, I mean … I find nature to be a good teacher."

He waited. The silence seemed to stretch for years.

"Shakespeare said that," said Gareth. "From *As You Like It*. Let me quote:

And this our life, exempt from public haunt,
Finds tongues in trees, books in the running brooks,
Sermons in stones, and good in everything."

Carys smiled. "I remember your quoting that to me as a young girl," she said. "I think that's one of the reasons I love nature so much."

"What I appreciate about science is that things are in balance," Proteus said. "Everything has a role and is interconnected." He hoped it sounded better to her ears than it did to his.

Carys's spoon clinked as she put it down. Her eyes searched Proteus. "You know," she said. "I recently had the most thought-provoking discussion with professor Arthur Tansley. He's new to Oxford and is working on a theory that bacteria, plants, and animals are in balance with the Earth. He believes that all the different systems are related and depend upon each other. A change in one can hurt another. He's gathered together published reports from across Europe and America. And I think it's quite a marvelous concept."

Proteus nodded in agreement as he chewed his food. Intelligent words again refused to form themselves.

"Do you read outside of physics, then?" said Carys.

"Yes," he said — and resolved on the spot to scrutinize the SDU for information on Tansley, Homer, and Shakespeare.

Ψ

As the after-dinner conversation dwindled, Gareth stood and said, "I'll clean up. Carys, do you mind taking Lucy out for her evening patrol?"

"Of course, Papa."

"May I come along?" said Proteus.

"Certainly," said Carys. "I'll show you one of the ponds."

A moment later, the three of them were walking along a trail. Proteus asked about the flora and fauna they saw and memorized every detail of what Carys told him. He learned about the yew tree, holly, heather, lavender, shrews, field mice, kestrels, and merlins.

The sun was a hand's height above the horizon when they sat down on a cluster of large rocks at the edge of a pond as still as glass — or, at least, it was until Lucy launched in the air and landed with a loud splash.

"Lucy!" said Carys, laughing. "Always showing off." The Labrador paddled off after a few ducks, which protested and moved away.

Carys looked toward the horizon, her face unreadable.

Proteus counted his heartbeats, and wondered what she was thinking about. He was about to speak when he heard her take in a breath.

"I love sunsets," she said. The light glinted on her cheeks

"I love sunrises," said Proteus. He wondered why he'd said it so fast or whether he should have said something else entirely.

"Why?" she asked.

"Hmm?"

Goosebumps played over his arms, and he was at a loss for words as he looked at the contours of her face in the waning light.

She laughed and turned to look at him. "Why do you love sunrises?"

"Oh," said Proteus. He searched for the right words. "I think because of the way it struck me the first time I saw it."

Carys laughed and said, "And you remember that?"

"Yes."

"Archie! You Americans are so full of bluster," said Carys. She frowned. "Always trying to impress."

Proteus replayed the conversation in his mind, trying to understand why her expression had shifted from laughter to scorn. *Why did she call me Archie?* His saliva dried, and he swallowed, then tried to speak, but ended up coughing.

"Are you feeling all right?" said Carys.

"Fine," said Proteus.

"You never did describe your work in London."

"No," he said. "You're right." He struggled to formulate an explanation before giving up and saying, "You should come visit my offices, and I can show you."

"I'll give it some thought," said Carys. Proteus's heart sank. Then she asked, "What's the name of your firm?" and Proteus's heart climbed up a rung from the depths.

"Providence," said Proteus. "Limited."

"Odd name for a company interested in physics."

"Yes, but it goes beyond physics," he said. "I'm also interested in how industrial technologies developed through physics, and other disciplines, affect biological organisms, and the Earth as well." Proteus wanted to say more, to tell her everything.

Carys turned to look at him, and her green eyes watched him for several heartbeats. "It sounds most interesting," she said. "I think I will visit."

"That'd be grand," said Proteus, and his heart grew wings.

Lucy plodded out of the pond and shook herself. The sun was below the horizon, and the light was fast fading.

Carys said, "We'd best head back."

When they arrived at the cottage, Gareth had a pot of tea ready, and the three of them sat in the living room and chatted into the evening as Lucy snored in her bed.

Ψ

Carys couldn't sleep and lay awake in her room, thinking about the day. She sat up and looked at the wall, which was bathed in tree-filtered moonlight, and she crossed her legs underneath her. The wind rose and fell outside, shifting the shadows on the wall.

She replayed the conversations with Archibald Proteus. He was

181

obviously formally educated — but she'd seen his eyes as he'd asked about the plants, insects, water, and wildlife, and then listened to her explanations. It was the look she'd seen in children touring the estate. Curious wonderment.

He's odd. Yet my father and Lucy trust him.

31

"The task is not to see what has never been seen before, but to think what has never been thought before about what you see everyday."
~ Erwin Schrödinger

Dear Albert,

I, too, immensely enjoyed our visit together. We share much in culture, philosophy, and theoretical approach. And I'm in agreement: to achieve full understanding of time, gravity, electromagnetism, and nuclear forces, we must have a fully developed unified field theory.

This back and forth with the wave-particle stuff is getting tedious. I've just returned from a miserable several months in Copenhagen as Niels Bohr's guest. He kept insisting that it's the act of observing a subatomic system that changes it. I tried to reason with him, but of course, it's futile.

And then his new protégé, Heisenberg, jumped in. I had no idea he was even in Copenhagen, but apparently Bohr's new institute is attracting all of them like a magnet for chaos.

What uncertain nonsense.

If I don't see the sun rise tomorrow morning, has it not risen? Have I snuffed it out by not looking, or is it still deciding until somebody looks?

What if no one looks?

And Bohr speaks so slowly, it's excruciating. We went on walks in the park to debate our theories, and I counted twenty steps for each syllable he uttered. I grew frustrated and then sick. But he kept boring into me with the same *argument over and over.*

And now that I'm back home, away from Bohr and Heisenberg's torments, I read the papers. Mein Gott, I have grave concerns about these National Socialists. Nothing good will come from their machinations, I'm certain.

These are ill times, Albert. Ill times!

Until our next communication,

Erwin

32

She'd lost Proteus.

Lost him!

The watchmaker decrypted the message again, to be certain. But it remained unchanged, and he reached for the bottle of nitroglycerin tablets in his waistcoat pocket to head off the encroaching wave building in his chest. The tightness increased and breathing became difficult.

He opened the bottle and popped one under his tongue.

How could she lose him? Sweet burning flooded his mouth, and the pressure wave ebbed.

As the constriction in his chest left and he breathed deeper, he realized he needed more oxygen to think clearly. He fed the message he had decoded to the hearth and walked past his game in progress without looking at it. He told Paul he'd be back soon and left the shop to go to the park. The fresh air would clear the cobwebs.

He had no arranged meeting and thus went to a different park from his routine so he wouldn't have to worry about running into Pyotr. The semiliterate dreadnought was the last person he wished to see right now.

The watchmaker thought about the message again as he walked.

Proteus had last been seen three days ago in a sporty red motorcar, heading west out of London. Up to this point his attention had been seemingly fixated on Cambridge to the northeast, but what was of interest to the west? There were the shipping ports in Bristol, several aeroplane manufacturers in the Cotswolds (the watchmaker had agents there), Stonehenge, and then farther west, a bunch of sheep in Wales.

But closer to London was the university at Oxford. And unless Proteus was going on holiday or communing with long-dead druids at Stonehenge, the watchmaker had found his answer. *But why? What does he want there?*

Having deduced roughly where Proteus was, he was less concerned that he'd truly been lost. The killer of his assets would be back. Like the Leopard of Rudraprayag, the hunter had tasted blood.

He would trap this creature in its own habits. And kill it.

The watchmaker entered the park feeling better than when he'd left the shop. He stopped at a bench to breathe and ponder his next steps.

A squirrel darted toward him and then stopped: it twitched as it sat up on its haunches and looked at him, begging for a morsel.

The watchmaker thought about tossing it a nitroglycerin tablet. He laughed.

33

"Stop telling God what to do with his dice."
~ Niels Bohr

After breakfast, Proteus spent the morning with Gareth reviewing blueprints, logistics, and priorities for the renovations. They reviewed details about the next phase of the work, which involved interior stonework, setting up Proteus's offices on the second floor, and stringing telecommunications lines to the estate. At noon, they took a break for tea and sandwiches, and then Proteus got ready to leave.

Carys had gone riding, and they'd said their goodbyes earlier. Proteus had given her the address and telephone number for Providence, Ltd., and she'd promised to contact him to arrange a visit. Even now, hours later, he could feel the tingle as they'd shaken hands.

He placed his satchel in the car and then turned to ruffle Lucy's ears. There was a threat of rain, and so he kept the soft-top of the Vauxhall up. Turning to Gareth, he said, "Thank you for everything. I've had a splendid time."

"Our pleasure," said Gareth.

"And thank you for the excellent work on the estate."

"Thank you for paying for it," said Gareth. "She's coming along."

As he drove off, there was a pang in his chest, and he longed to turn the Vauxhall around and drive back for just one more conversation with Carys. But he needed to get to Oxford by late afternoon to meet about leasing office space, and then — after a quick side trip to the Mathematics department — it would be back to London in the evening.

As he got closer to Oxford, the clouds darkened, and soon the rain began pelting down.

$$\Psi$$

After dusk, Proteus walked in gentle rain toward the Mathematics building of the University of Oxford. The meeting had gone well, and he now had a second set of offices in a university town. He flipped up the collar of his black overcoat and studied the pedestrian traffic. The light from the gas lanterns mounted on the front of the building looked like dim candles in the haze of precipitation, and there was scarcely anyone about.

He stopped, bent to tie his bootlaces — and scanned for lights still on in the building, trying to ascertain how many people might still be present, and which areas to avoid. Ninety percent of the building was dark, which surprised him. He extracted from under his greatcoat the paper he'd picked up in town to reread the section on Einstein's brief visit to Oxford and the schedule of events. Tonight there would be an early-evening reception, and tomorrow at noon would be Einstein's keynote address at Rhodes House. He checked his watch: 10 p.m. He was certain the reception was being held here, but perhaps they'd already finished for the night. His frame of reference was the party crowd in London, but maybe mathematicians were different.

He shifted his backpack, which was light, with only the SDU inside. His knife and multitool were attached to his belt, and the rest of his gear was secured in the boot of the Vauxhall.

Primarily, Proteus wanted to snoop to see what he could discover about Einstein's forthcoming presentation. Through Providence, he'd learned that Einstein was becoming mistrustful of some of the quantum theories being developed, and he knew that historically this would grow. *And if I can catalyze this suspicion and accelerate the impending war with Niels Bohr, all the better.*

Einstein had already quipped one of his famous lines, *God does not play dice with the universe,* to criticize the randomness upon which quantum mechanics theories depended to describe subatomic particles. In his view, if your theory couldn't predict the behavior of a system, your theory needed more work. Waving one's hands, shrugging, and throwing in a random number into an equation in order to make it fit the data — most of the time —drove him crazy. After all, it wasn't $E = mc^2 + fuzzy\ probability\ stuff$. He was concerned with natural laws that could explain the universe.

Proteus walked directly toward the building for a short distance before setting off at an angle. His eyes flicked between the doors, the windows, and the deep shadows beyond the lights. Everything seemed quiet, deserted.

He crept along in the darkness toward the corner of the building and reached for the multitool. Beads of water dripped from the brim of his black cap. As he breathed in the heavy, moist air and looked for the easiest access point, he shivered.

A loud bang split the evening's silence; Proteus spun toward the front of the building and froze.

Two men in sweaters stumbled down the front steps, and the doors swung closed behind them. Their laughing voices pierced the heavy dampness. A few steps away from the building, they put their arms around each other's shoulders and began singing. Proteus remained motionless.

Suddenly, one of the men stopped, put his hands on his knees, and vomited.

Mathematicians, thought Proteus. *Alcohol and equations don't mix.*

He resumed stalking toward the building, confident the men would remain oblivious to his presence. As he reached the edge of the structure, Proteus heard the singing resume and saw the pair were halfway to the street, arm in arm once again.

Proteus put his hand on the wet stone of the building and watched the front entrance for half a minute before deciding a back way in was likely a better option. He didn't want to encounter more of the intoxicated symbol-scrawlers.

He made his way to the rear of the building, then extracted his multitool and approached the back door … and found it unlocked.

He slipped inside and eased it closed behind him.

Moving along a corridor, Proteus heard someone singing, and he stopped. All the doors along the hallway were closed except for one, which was where the singing was coming from. He waited for what seemed like an eternity before a man in an oversized suit shuffled out through the door, closed it behind him, and went along the hallway.

Five seconds later, the lock clicked and Proteus slipped inside quietly to find a mess: papers were scattered; textbooks lay askew; ashtrays were overflowing; and beer bottles were thrown willy-nilly. The chalkboards lining one wall were covered in scribbled symbols and equations, along with a few cartoon stick figures with dialog boxes, which presumably represented mathematician humor.

There was chalk dust everywhere.

Proteus took out the SDU and captured several images, then left the room.

Farther along the corridor, he came to a placard identifying a lecture hall and stopped to let himself in. Not wishing to risk turning on the lights, he brought up the infrared on the SDU and scanned the hall.

No one was home, so he switched to a low-lumen visible light and looked about the hall.

There were at least twenty chalkboards. He stepped to one of them and studied the equations, then stood back and brightened the light. All of the boards, precisely arranged, were neatly scripted with equations. This was what he'd hoped to find; all of the work for tomorrow's presentation was laid out cleanly.

He spent half an hour capturing images of all of the boards. He didn't fully grasp the formulae or derivations, but later he could compare this work with the historical data contained in the SDU to try to glean where Einstein might be going as the result of Proteus's machinations.

Einstein was set to give an announcement in his latest theorem, and Proteus suspected photographers would be due in to shoot all the chalkboards. The reception attendees must have been catching up on old times and relaxing in the other room he'd visited. He looked around the hall again and noticed that seven of the boards were bisected across the long axis with a large spindle, enabling each board to be rotated to display either side. There were also tidy stacks of paper and several large notebooks. Proteus collected up as many of these as he could and piled them in a corner.

Then he erased every single chalkboard with a wet towel. He went back to the notebooks and papers and stuffed them into his backpack, which he set by the door.

Proteus grinned as an idea popped into his head, inspired by the cartoon figures in the mathematics party room and Rutherford's mouse circles.

He peered out into the hallway and, seeing no one around, stepped out. It took several dead-end attempts, but eventually he found a janitorial closet and took out an upright electric vacuum cleaner.

Back in the lecture hall, he disassembled the vacuum and then mounted the motor on a heavy bench. He slid several of the chalkboards together to form a screen, then moved one of the rotating boards next to the heavy bench.

Proteus chalked an outline of a cartoon mouse on one side of the board. He then rotated the board to the other side and began sketching the same mouse in a different pose. As he worked, he rotated the board a few times to check the alignment of the images.

When he was finished, he stepped back and gave the board a good spin: the flipping images overlapped nicely. He then attached the motor's fan belt to the board's central spindle, which served as the axis. He tested it to make sure it rotated smoothly and that everything was securely fastened.

Proteus took two desk lamps over to the board he'd set up and plugged them in. After arranging the lighting just so, he turned on the electric motor and headed toward the door.

He heard the hum of the motor and the accelerating cadence of the rotating board as the set-up slowly picked up speed. Proteus thought of the stir this chalkboard might cause in the morning and hoped it would leave a lasting impression.

34

Einstein's head throbbed a bit from the party last night, and he wondered at the early summons he'd received. The messenger spoke no German, and Einstein only knew a little English, but after trying to send the man away several times, he understood that he was wanted, urgently.

When he arrived at the Mathematics building, he stopped briefly to light up his pipe and then went inside. A cluster of people stood outside the door to the lecture hall, where he'd supervised the careful reconstruction of his proofs yesterday. The burble of their voices stopped at his approach.

"Herr Professor Einstein, we don't know what happened," said a man with flushed cheeks. Einstein looked at him, puzzled, then stepped inside the hall. His idle curiosity was soon replaced by a gut-squeezing horror, and he dropped his pipe and stared in silence. The chalkboards had been erased.

A faint *whap-whap* noise echoed from deep in the hall. Einstein shuffled forward; every board he came upon had been wiped clean, and even the backs were erased.

Everything was blank.

The background rhythmic noise faded as the pounding in his

cranium rose. He ground his teeth and reached for a chair with cold, sweaty palms. *What is happening? This is not reality.*

The throbbing in his head retreated, but the background noise, which sounded like a large ceiling fan on high speed, persisted. *"Was ist das?"* he said.

He scratched his head and moved past his ravaged boards toward the noise. He rounded a wall of boards to stare at the source: a motor with a fan belt hooked up to a blackboard, which was spinning rapidly. Bright lights were focused on the board, and a white image flicked back and forth against the black, in a two-part rudimentary animation.

A thaumatrope, he thought and looked closer.

The flickering image resolved itself into a mouse, looking over its shoulder, repeatedly dropping its trousers.

Einstein gasped and exclaimed, *"Verdammt Maus!"*

35

"She calls you Archie?" said Conrad.

"Yes."

"And you're all right with that?"

"Yes," said Proteus. "Why shouldn't I be?"

Conrad laughed, set down his pint, and looked at his boss, wondering how he could be so dim.

"Why are you laughing?" said Proteus.

"You're hooked, mate!" said Conrad and chuckled at the flush creeping into Proteus's cheeks.

"What does that mean?"

Conrad picked up his beer and smiled. "It means you want to be with her, and she knows it. You're hooked like a fish on a line."

"Possibly, you're misinterpreting the situation. I don't think that's what's happening at all."

"Oh, yes?" said Conrad. "How many times have you been out to Woodchester or Oxford in the past four months?"

"Well ... there's work in both places to be done," said Proteus. "Important work."

"How many?"

"Eight," said Proteus.

"I see," said Conrad. "And of those eight trips, how many times did you see Carys?"

Proteus mumbled something as he raised his glass and finished off his beer.

"I didn't catch that, sir," said Conrad.

"All of them."

"You're in love."

"I don't know what you're talking about," said Proteus. "There wasn't any sort of love stuff. At Oxford, I simply went to classes with her and heard some interesting lectures. We talked. At Woodchester we went for walks. That's it."

"You carried her books, didn't you?" said Conrad, almost bouncing in his seat with mirth.

"Yes," said Proteus. "How did you know that?"

Conrad howled with laughter. The puzzled expression on Proteus's face was priceless, and it made him laugh even harder.

When Conrad's guffawing had settled down enough for him speak again, he said, "You're definitely in love, and you'd best listen to your wingman here if you want to navigate your way through this relationship."

"Well, I think—"

"It's not about thinking," interrupted Conrad. "It's about feeling." The lost-child look was back on Proteus's face, and Conrad shook his head slowly. *He's spent too much time with his head buried in books,* he thought. "I'll help you out, sir, don't you worry. Another pint?"

"Yes, please."

36

"The important thing is to not stop questioning. Curiosity has its own reason for existing."
~ Albert Einstein

Proteus sat in his office, gazed out the window, and thought through the problems he faced. *The curious scientific mind is difficult to throw off track for very long. Like a dog who's gotten a whiff of a meaty bone buried in the ground, he paces on the surface knowing it's immediacy and, even after losing the scent, the hound persists. He backtracks, prowls, and digs. He knows he is right, and the reward is there.*

Rutherford is proving to be a tenacious hound, despite my creative sabotage. For a period he's been chasing the Mus-ex-Atomos, the mouse in the atom, down what I thought was a deep hole. He's run after it enthusiastically, but now, intuitively, I sense he feels it's wrong.

I fear it's only a matter of time until he resumes his proper digging into the secrets of the atom. I think he senses discovery is almost within his grasp, and it's taunting him. Unraveling the intertwined mysteries of radioactive energies and the atom is his burning passion, and he will never rest until it's done.

Proteus opened the Data-Cube to reevaluate his mission objectives, which were all focused in England. The scientists in the twenty-fifth century had intentionally set his targets within a small geographic region, focusing primarily on Rutherford, because they didn't know the nature or extent of the Time-resistance he might experience in trying to change the past. They also didn't want to risk a broader campaign that might trigger secondary and tertiary effects farther down the timeline.

However, now that Proteus had been working for several years and had experienced Time-resistance, he knew he was in a better position to judge than those in the twenty-fifth century. In war, a rigid plan lost battles. He had to be flexible and adapt. There were too many scientists experimenting with Curie's radioactive elements for him to hold them off for any length of time. All of them used material painstakingly purified by hand in her lab.

Proteus knew he needed to go upstream to the source: Curie's Radium Institute.

He shut down the SDU, secured its cover, rose from his desk to fling open his office door, and said, "Freda, I need to get a round-trip flight to Paris."

"For when, sir, and how long?" asked his receptionist.

"As soon as possible, and a week, I guess."

"Very good, sir. I'll attend to it at once."

$$\Psi$$

Proteus rushed back into his office and began wrestling with the plans. He had to interrupt the sole supply from Marie Curie by disrupting the purification process and removing the accumulated stockpile.

He opened the Data-Cube, called up the history of the Curies and the Radium Institute, and began reading. Marie Curie shared the 1903 Nobel Prize with her husband, Pierre, and Henri Becquerel. She was the first woman to a win a Nobel Prize and the first person to win it twice. Proteus read further and flinched at Pierre's tragic trampling by a horse carriage in 1906. A chill passed along his spine as he thought of his own accident, and he skipped forward to the date-specific information on the floor plans of the institute — and tried to push away thoughts of mortality and extinction.

He read through the refining process and learned of the chemicals and equipment used. Sabotage seemed straightforward, and Proteus was optimistic he could cripple the lab, possibly for months. Along with the theft of the purified radioactive elements stored there, he hoped for a year or more of disruption.

Estimates were that the combined mass of the purified radium, thorium, polonium, and uranium stored on site was, at most, three kilograms.

Only three kilos. But who wanted to gather up all the intense radioactivity into their backpack and then walk out of the institute with it? It also left the question of what to do with it afterward.

Proteus mulled over the logistics and was deep in consultation with the Data-Cube when he heard a muffled squeal from the communication room outside his office. This was followed by footfalls and then a buzz of voices. He couldn't make out what they were saying — but something had happened.

"Off," he said to the Data-Cube and then secured the SDU away.

There were more footfalls, then three rapid knocks at his door.

He crossed his office to unlock it and then opened the door slowly to peer out.

Freda was beaming and practically dancing in place. She held out a transcript, and said, "Congratulations."

Proteus relaxed and let the door ease inward. He accepted the paper from Freda. In the background, the room swelled with people.

"To the earl," shouted someone.

"Jolly good!" shouted another. And this was followed by cheers: "Hip, hip, hooray!"

Proteus read the telegram from the Office of Standards about his new title: A.J.B. Proteus, Earl of Nympsfield. This opened the door for his membership to the Royal Society, which he needed to influence research funding away from the atom.

There was a lot of work to do, but he decided that Providence, Ltd. needed to celebrate, if only for a bit.

"Afternoon off, everyone," he said.

"What about a party?" asked Freda. It was more of a statement and was met by a chorus of cheers.

Proteus hesitated for a moment before agreeing. "Yes, let's set up something fun for after my trip to Paris. Freda, you're in charge. Not the Savoy, or the Ritz," he said. "Perhaps a park and a picnic."

Freda clapped her hands in excitement and bustled off.

37

Proteus stepped out of the motor taxi into a growling buzz. In between buildings of Croydon Aerodrome he caught a glimpse of two large, twin-engine biplanes waddling along a grass taxiway. He leaned back inside the motortaxi to grasp his leather satchel and paid the driver.

Gravel crunched under his boots as he walked toward the main building. He was soon able to see a large runway. At one end, a biplane was turning in place to line up for takeoff. Proteus slowed and then stopped as the rumbling increased, sounding like police motorboats he'd heard on the Thames. It sat motionless for a moment, engines snarling and propellers whining ever louder.

Then, with a full-throated roar, it crept forward, picking up speed, and began to bounce on the grass runway. Bursts of white mist appeared behind the engines as the bulbous wheels splashed through puddles on the runway. Sunlight glinted off several windows along the side of the white biplane as it shrieked down the runway, now halfway to the end.

It was still accelerating when it neared the end of the runway, and Proteus wondered if the bouncing biplane was going to go cartwheeling off the end when it ran out of real estate. He held his breath.

Then, wing tips rising first, the plane floated upward. Looking ungainly and uncertain, the thundering twelve-passenger beast from Imperial Air climbed, struggling for needed altitude. Higher it climbed, and then the plane banked; the sun flashed off the parallel white wings.

It continued upward, finally looking like it was going to stay airborne, and Proteus exhaled. The engine noise faded, and he returned his gaze to the main terminal building and continued walking.

Inside the hub, there was a subdued but excited tone. Well-dressed people moved different directions. Compared with the train and Underground stations, there weren't as many people smoking.

Proteus found the gate for his flight to Paris and showed his ticket to the agent. He glanced at his fellow passengers: five men in suits; two military men in khaki dress with officer epaulets; three flappers who were smoking and chatting away with two dandies.

He had the SDU in his satchel, secured in its Bible wrapping, and was confident that it wouldn't be inspected. Aerodrome customs staff were looking for contraband, guns, and explosives in passengers' luggage, not Bibles.

He and his fellow passengers boarded the plane via a hatch along the rear of the fuselage. Inside was a very narrow central aisle with a seat on each side, with a total of twelve seats in all, and a tiny lavatory aft. Proteus squeezed along the aisle and located an empty seat near the front. The chairs were made of wicker and were bolted to the floor. Just like in the motorcars, there were no lap belts.

The windows were rectangular, with rounded corners, and above each was a loop with instructions: *In case of emergency, pull ring sharply.* And above the windows, running the length of the passenger compartment was cargo netting for passengers to store small bags and briefcases.

The cockpit had no door or bulkhead and was open to the rest of the passenger compartment. One of the pilots was looking at gauges and writing something on a piece of paper on a clipboard. Proteus looked out of his window and saw a second pilot emerge from underneath the lower wing, along with a man in an oil-stained blue coverall. Both had clipboards and moved about, inspecting different parts of the exterior of the plane, sometimes tugging on a wire or a strut.

After about ten minutes, there was a rasping metallic whine, then a cough and a roar as one of the plane's three engines came to life. Acrid blue smoke drifted by Proteus's window and he smelled unburnt fuel. Another engine barked, and then a third. As the engines spooled up, a shuddering, low-harmonic frequency passed through the fuselage, rattling the windows and a few loose bolts.

The vibration built and went up through his feet and into his seat, then into the base of his skull. A titter buzzed through the cabin as his fellow passengers expressed themselves.

Within the next fifteen seconds, the engine noise drowned out almost all of the conversation. Proteus turned to look aft and saw the second pilot board the plane. He had large mutton-chop sideburns and wore a crisp blue uniform and a peaked aviator cap, which bore a silver-winged badge. He began moving forward, stopping at each pair of seats to shout introductions and pleasantries. When he arrived at Proteus's seat he beamed a grin, yelled something about it being a smashing day to fly, and slapped Proteus on the back of his shoulder. Proteus thought about the juxtaposition of *smashing* and *flying* and managed a weak grin as the exuberant pilot moved forward to the next pair of seats.

The other pilot, whom Proteus had not met, pulled out a wrench and began wrestling with something under the instrument panel.

The engines thrummed and then slowly began to increase in volume and pitch. Pilot Mutton-chops looked back down the aisle, flashed a thumbs-up, and then released the brakes. The enormous biplane rolled forward, picking up speed, bouncing along the grass runway. Proteus gripped the edge of his seat with white knuckles and stared at the emergency instruction above the window. Historically, there were no recorded plane crashes today (nor on the date of his scheduled return); he'd checked before confirming the reservation. This knowledge helped his anxiety — but didn't eliminate it.

The plane continued to pick up speed, and then Proteus was pressed down in his seat as the plane lurched skyward. A momentary disorientation passed through him and, although he knew it did no good, he gripped the seat harder. The interior rattled, and something heavy fell on the floor. Looking out the window, Proteus could see that the plane was continuing to gain altitude, and then he got a look down on the airport as the plane banked to starboard.

After having spent decades of his life underground, the view of the Earth's surface from above was exhilarating. He scanned from the ground to the horizon to the sun and above. The plane soon entered a layer of clouds, and Proteus lost sight of the both the ground and sky, which dampened his spirits.

Thirty minutes later, the clouds thinned and then vanished, and the plane cruised above a large body of water: the English Channel.

When they reached the French coastline, clouds were again visible below. Proteus looked down on the white and grey wisps, mesmerized by their shifting forms. His thoughts drifted to the forthcoming raid on Madame Curie's radium stash. *She is far too generous with it and provides it to experimenters such as Rutherford without charge. A few grams of pure radium equal the cost of a modest estate in the English countryside, and she just gives it away.*

Proteus half-convinced himself that his reasons extended beyond saving humanity in the future and that his planned theft was justified on an altruistic level. Madame Curie and Rutherford had little knowledge of the dangers of exposure to radiation. She had slaved over bubbling cauldrons of crushed pitchblende ore, with toxic alkalis and acids, extracting and purifying minute amounts of radium from tons of ore through a series of chemical reactions. All in her poorly ventilated and heavily contaminated laboratory.

Similarly, Rutherford walked around with lumps of radioactive ore and vials of purified radium in his trouser pockets and stashed it in his desk. They didn't understand the consequences.

But Proteus knew his rationalization was a disguise for his guilt to make him feel better about robbing a brilliant scientist. Madame Curie had likely already received a cumulative radiation dose strong enough to ensure her death in scarcely ten years. And even if Proteus could steal all the radium in the world, it would not stop her from purifying more from the pitchblende ore.

The purity of the scientists' dogged pursuit of the secrets of the atom was both a blessing and a curse: two sides of the same coin. Curious moths to the atomic fire that would ultimately scorch the planet.

Proteus's eyes unfocused as his mind drifted.

His head smacked into the window as turbulence suddenly rocked the plane, startling him out of his trance. He looked down as his ears popped. The plane was descending through the clouds, and the ground appeared in swatches between the clouds zipping by. Beads of moisture formed and streaked horizontally across the window. The plane bumped again, and Proteus clutched the seat as he went weightless. Several people gasped in alarm.

"Just a bit of chop," yelled someone from the front, and Proteus looked up to see Mutton-chops grinning and flashing a thumbs-up from the cockpit. "We'll be on the ground soon."

Yes. That's certain, thought Proteus. *But in how many pieces?*

He closed his eyes and maintained his death grip on the wicker chair, which he imagined splintering into shreds when the aircraft plowed into the ground. There was a loud bang, and Proteus was forced down in his seat, and then in the next nauseating moment he was almost flung up to the ceiling. There was another bang, smaller this time, and a bounce — and then rumbling vibrated throughout the fuselage. He looked out the window and saw they were on a grass field, speeding along but gradually slowing. The engines roared, and Proteus was flung forward. And then the violence ended as the plane made the decision not to shred itself apart. They rolled along a taxiway toward a large building with white lettering reading *Aéroport de Paris– Le Bourget.*

Paris was more than ten kilometers from the airport, but all he needed to do now was clear customs and take a motor taxi downtown. Madame Curie had just returned from a speaking tour in Germany, and he was certain she would be buried deep in her laboratory at the Radium Institute.

$$\Psi$$

The motor taxi pulled up to the Louvre, and Proteus paid the fare. He shouldered his bags, stepped out of the taxi, and his eyes were caught by the glint of the afternoon sun off the windows of the old fortress-turned-museum. Proteus turned away and closed the passenger door. *"Merci,"* he said to the cloud of dust left behind as the vehicle sped off.

Although he longed to explore inside the museum, he didn't have the time. Madame Curie's institute was a bit of a walk from there, but he didn't want the taxi driver to remember an American who'd arrived by plane and been dropped off at the Radium Institute.

As Proteus went along the Quai du Louvre beside the River Seine, it struck him how different yet similar Paris was to London. There were the obvious differences he'd already noticed: the language, vehicles on the other side of the road, and the clothing. But the similarities were too large to ignore. Paris was a vibrant and historical city, split by a river, and full of people and culture. Proteus experienced the same wonderment in seeing so many people on these streets as he did in

London.

He thought back to his time period, the Colony huddled deep underground while the surface of the Earth burned.

How could humanity mess everything up so badly?

Proteus stopped to let the verve of the city wash through him. He absorbed the sights, smells, and noise — and tried to push away the thoughts of the Cataclysm.

After musing a few moments, he continued along the north bank of the Seine until he reached the Pont au Change and turned to cross over the bridge. The sun was dipping towards the horizon, and he cast a long shadow on the sidewalk. The lanterns rimming the streets of the City of Lights were of several designs: gas, arc light, and incandescent. Their different colors and intensities lent a curious, ever-shifting glow to the evening as Paris settled into nightfall.

Proteus stopped under a harshly bright carbon-arc lamp on top of an iron pole. The so-called Yablochkov Candle buzzed with the voltage arcing between the carbon rods behind the glass lens, spewing out visible and ultraviolet light. It was the discovery of the discrete atomic spectra emitted when different elements were torched with electricity, or flame, that had led to Bohr's model of the atom. The energy applied excited the atom's electrons, which quantum-jumped to a higher orbit, and when they fell back down they released photons of specific wavelengths.

Curiosity had driven scientists deeper and deeper into the atom, trying to unravel the mysteries. Why did different elements have different excitation spectra? What was going on inside the atom that it behaved thus?

Curiosity is an indelible facet of humankind, and we wouldn't be who we are without it. But it also killed the cat, and not just Schrödinger's. All of them. And us. Curiosity can never be suppressed, but it must be steered away from the precipice.

Pulling his eyes away from the painful light, he allowed them to adjust before continuing along the south bank of the Seine. The bells in the Notre-Dame rang a beautiful song and then chimed eight o'clock. As lovely as it was to hear, the music struck a sad note. The cathedral, too, would be turned to ash in the twenty-third century, along with everything else in Paris, if he failed.

The fear refocused Proteus's thoughts on his evening's work, and he moved into an alleyway to pull out the SDU from his satchel. He'd memorized the address for the Radium Institute, University of Paris, in the Latin Quarter, which was several blocks away — but he wanted to see what EM spectra he could pick up from here.

When the SDU had calibrated itself, Proteus gasped at the result: gamma radiation glowed and ionized the atmosphere above a cluster of buildings along the Seine with more intensity than he'd imagined.

He thought about the media articles yet to be written, a hundred years from now, about the heavy contamination in and around the Radium Institute — which some in the twenty-first century came to call the "Chernobyl on the Seine." Later in its history, the building had been renamed because Radium just wasn't so catchy anymore. Proteus marveled that the medical wing of the institute had already begun using radium to treat tumors. Ever since Becquerel had severely burned his skin from carrying a tube of radium in his vest pocket for two weeks, they'd known radiation could damage tissue. Unfortunately, knowledge of the full extent of the toxicity of radium, and the cancer-causing effects, lagged far behind its enthusiastic use.

Proteus put away the SDU and stepped out from the alleyway to continue toward his destination. He worried that he might find the building occupied by Madame Curie, or her assistants, working into the evening.

He passed by a sign for a bakery, *Le Petit Éclair*, and wondered if they might already have radioactive flour bits in the baguettes. *If I have the time, I can come back and warn them*, he thought, but then he realized that, although altruistic, it was a stupid idea. They would never be able to understand what he was trying to tell them.

His mouth became dry as he got closer; he rounded a corner and stopped to stare at a three-story French Colonial brick structure. The words *Université de Paris* were written above the front door. He exhaled a deep breath at seeing the lights were all off. The Radium Institute was deserted.

Proteus walked past the front then circled around toward the back of the building using dark alleyways to avoid the streetlights and found a doorway in the darkness.

$$\Psi$$

Proteus jiggled the back door and then probed with his tools, but the lock wouldn't yield. He gave up and smashed a glass pane, hoping the sound would blend in to the background noises of the city. Reaching through and releasing the latch, he was soon inside.

He located Curie's laboratories and found the purified radium, thorium, uranium, and polonium organized in compartments separated by lead bricks and malleable lead sheets. He put the latter into his backpack and molded them such that the lead shielding would be between his spine and the radioactive elements.

Once this was done, he turned his attention to wrecking the equipment. After a search, he located a fire-axe and a crowbar and then began hacking and prying apart cauldrons, steel pressure vessels, and retorts.

Next were the flasks and demijohns, which he shattered and punctured — spilling acids and alkalis onto the equipment, benches, and floors.

He circled through the various laboratory areas, reducing each to a broken, bubbling mess. Fumes stung his eyes, and he coughed. The reagents mixing on the floor began to smoke.

His heart hammered — he'd cut himself off from the route by which he'd entered, and the chemical reactions might soon spark a fire. He hefted the heavy pack onto his back, grabbed the crowbar, and ran toward the front of the building.

Out in the streets, he paused to breathe — and thought of where he might safely dispose of the radioactive stockpile on his back. His watch read 2:00 a.m.

He needed someplace deep and undisturbed.

$$\Psi$$

Descending into the cold catacombs beneath Notre Dame, Proteus shifted his heavy backpack to relieve the pressure on his shoulders. After an hour of hoisting it around, the weight had almost become an anchor, threatening to tip him over as he methodically worked his way down a spiral stone staircase into the depths.

The ancient stone walls squeezed toward him — he halted and began a breathing exercise to quell the claustrophobia. After a moment it ebbed, and he continued downward.

Arriving at the recessed threshold of an ancient sealed chamber deep beneath the cathedral, Proteus paused. He set the SDU to scan for infrared. It seemed unlikely that anyone would be down here at this hour, but he studied the display for several minutes before concluding it was safe to proceed.

He removed all of the tools from his pack and switched the SDU to an EM beam that would weaken the mortar. He rechecked the SDU and then focused a beam on a segment of brick, which he pulled away carefully from the rest of the wall with the crowbar.

Satisfied with the test, Proteus focused on a larger area, which he deconstructed like a jigsaw puzzle piece. Methodically, he worked it loose. He repacked his gear and squeezed through the hole.

Inside, he found a chamber with three sealed archways and a large stone coffin on a pedestal. The air was stale, and a thick layer of dust coated the floor. He approached the coffin. There were faint markings, but he couldn't understand them.

Proteus set his pack down and extracted the crowbar.

He leveraged up the edge of the tomb and pushed it to the side, clearing a triangular opening big enough for his arm.

He peered in and saw a shriveled skeletal foot. He wondered briefly who it might have been and then began transferring the radioactive stockpile into the coffin. When he finished this task, he added the lead sheets.

Then he resealed the tomb.

Proteus adjusted the settings on the SDU and carved a radiation warning into the tomb in several languages and with international pictographs. He had mixed thoughts about defacing the burial place, but his primary hope was that anthropologists, or others, wouldn't venture here any time soon. Unshielded, the concentrated contents in the coffin would crisp anyone who spent more than a few weeks in continual exposure.

Everyone should eventually understand the warnings he'd etched: *Lethal radiation.*

Proteus wormed back out of the chamber and then replaced the segments of the wall. He tried to reseal them as best he could using the SDU. The result wasn't ideal, but he had to keep moving.

His watch read 5:00 a.m. as he retraced his steps out of the cathedral.

38

May 4, 1926

Proteus looked about the office. There were only a handful of people in Providence this morning, when it should be bustling. He knew the reason as he joined the handful of people clustered around the radio, listening to BBC, in the communications room.

"A coal miners' strike started this morning, called for by the General Council on the Trades Union Congress, after weeks of negotiations failed. Hundreds of thousands of miners have stopped work, and the strike has quickly spread to other sectors of the economy, including transportation.

"Government officials estimate that there are now over a million and a half strikers across the UK.

"Everyday activities have ground to a standstill, and in some cases tempers have flared and violence has ensued. The government report that the military are on standby ..."

The front door opened. Nick, one of Proteus's researchers, entered, looking haggard.

"Trains and buses aren't running on time, and the Underground's stopped entirely," he said. "Folk can't get around."

Proteus nodded at Nick and then sequestered himself in his office with the reports that still needed to be reviewed. There wasn't much he could do about the strike.

Before starting his work, he picked up Carys's latest letter and reread it. He'd been in regular correspondence with her for the past year. Her letters were always filled with her love of discovering Nature's mysteries.

This letter was particularly special, though — his eyes flipped to the part where she said she'd be there in a fortnight to visit him.

Carys was due to graduate soon, and wished to pursue a doctorate with Professor Turley. She was quite excited and looking forward to telling Proteus about it in person.

Proteus grinned as he thought of the time they'd soon spend together. He'd show her Providence and some of the interesting places he'd discovered in London, but mostly he wanted to see her face and hear her voice.

He read the letter one more time. In just two weeks, they'd be able to speak in person, and he dreamed of where the conversations might go. He looked at the physics reports on his desk, back to Carys's letter, and thought about the irony of the scientific developments of the period.

The desire to understand the natural harmony of the Earth emerged at the same time as the desire to split the atom and unleash its destructive powers. If Proteus could gather up all the scientists on the planet and make them understand the need to pursue the former at the expense of the latter, before they uncorked the genie, before it was too late … but idle thoughts weren't a strategy. He turned to retrieve the first report.

Several hours later, he'd finished the report and had updated the objectives in the mission plot on the Data-Cube. He was achieving success, bit by bit. But he had a growing suspicion that there was far more going on than was apparent.

Ψ

The watchmaker closed the shop for the evening and went into the backroom. He sat at his bench and extracted a scrap of paper from the watch that'd been dropped off for repairs just moments ago.

The message was a long one, and whomever had crammed it in the gears had ruined the watch. He ground his teeth at the careless destruction of a timepiece.

His breath caught when he recognized that the message came from the Boss. It was the third day of the general strike, and hopes were high that the UK would be tipped over into revolution. After years of oppression and post-war depression, the workers were finally rising up against their capitalist overlords. It was glorious to be in the midst of change and on the right side of history.

The watchmaker's hands shook as he decoded the message. Something this length must contain a list of new strategic objectives to seize upon the tipping point the Soviets had worked so hard to achieve these past years.

But as he decoded each letter, his chest tightened. He backtracked to recheck: there'd been sparks of violence, but the dry tinder he'd counted upon hadn't caught. There was no Red May.

He reached for the bottle of nitroglycerine tablets and placed one under his tongue — and continued deciphering. *What went wrong? It seemed certain!*

In a flash, the watchmaker knew the answer. The counterspy, the American, had wrecked everything. MI5 had been in decline for years; they couldn't have exposed the Soviet network without the help of the American who'd killed or thwarted five of his assets.

The watchmaker decoded further: agents, rounded up; critical communications only; burn everything; vanish.

His pulse pounded his temples, and sweat dripped from his nose onto the paper, long before he had finished decoding the last part of the message.

We're all being hunted down, it said, and he imagined the Leopard of Rudraprayag bursting down doors and eating villagers.

"Not so amusing now, is it?" he said to himself.

"Time is running out. You will have to act fast and kill him. Svetlana has seen the car again."

He turned to look, but there was no one in the shop.

Now I'm muttering to myself — and answering. It's the stress of all of this ...

The watchmaker thought through the assets, short timeframe, and technical skills needed for a single clean hit. He wouldn't be getting his own hands dirty, of course, but reliving the days of his youth brought him pride.

The American, who's now an earl, must vanish in a tragic way. An accident.

39

The nerve center of Thames House bustled: telephone switchboards were flooded with incoming and ongoing calls, and operators feverishly plugged and unplugged patch cords to keep pace; every telegraphy unit was occupied with someone tapping an outbound message or transcribing an inbound.

The director of MI5 and tiers of assistant directors and their support staff hadn't slept in over twenty-four hours. The news had been grim but was thankfully improving by the hour.

The director leaned back in his chair and coughed, both to clear his mind and to attempt to clear some of the tobacco smoke from his face.

Nine days in, the British General Strike was waning to a resolution, but, more importantly, the veil had been lifted on the attempted revolution. There had been a few riots, targeted killings, looting, arson, and such, but there'd been no open rebellion. The military had stayed true to His Majesty, as the director's intelligence had predicted. The scales had tipped in England's favor; there would be no Red May in the United Kingdom.

He reread the front-page article in the *British Gazette*, especially the quotes from government ministers, and was certain that few knew how close the volatile situation had come to outright civil war.

As much as it enraged him to admit it, he had to admire the achievements of the Soviets. The British Communist Party and other Soviet mouthpiece organizations had gained footholds in the unions, universities, and newsprint. He had known this and had planned for it as best he could, despite the short-sighted winnowing away of his budget and cuts to his field assets. The same ministers that had pushed the reductions were the ones now posturing for "King and Country." That several of them now understood that England had almost been lost was of little consolation. He'd warned them months ago, and they'd done almost nothing.

The Soviets had made one colossal misstep, though. Their agents had completely misread the mood of the British military. The director's counterintelligence units had fed the Soviets a steady diet of exactly what they hoped to see in His Majesty's Armed Forces. All militaries had grumbling troops, but he'd been careful to spice this with exaggerated claims of near mutiny to lure Soviet agents deeper and expose them. And it had worked brilliantly. His small victory would earn him no promotion, medals, or recognition, but he now had the Soviets by the short-and-curlies and would see his operations through to the end.

Most of the spies, and a few of the assassins, that he'd tracked and cataloged for the past two years had been — or were in the process of being — rounded up. And he was certain the investigations into the British Communist Party and their cadre of compromised rich elites, academicians, moving-picture stars, and writers would bear even more fruit.

He thought of the quote from Winston Churchill, the editor of the *Gazette: It is very much more a difficult task to feed the country than it is to wreck it.*

He'd make a good prime minister, thought the director. *He has the fortitude to stand up and do the right thing. But no matter. The Soviets' actions in England have not tipped her over into revolution, despite the best efforts of the bastards. By the grace of God. I must see that they never get another chance.*

His thoughts turned to the upcoming conversation and the evidence he needed to present. He stood and put his hand on the shoulder of one of the telephone operators. "Please connect me with Prime Minister Baldwin, and patch it through to my office, please," he said and left the nerve center. Severing diplomatic relations and shutting down the Soviet embassy was not a trivial request, but he knew he had the data and the wherewithal to make it happen.

$$\Psi$$

Through his open office door, Proteus heard Freda greeting someone, and then Conrad's enthusiastic voice. He grabbed his satchel and joined them in the front office. Conrad was going to drive him to Woodchester, where they'd spend the night, and then tomorrow they would visit Oxford.

"Ah, good morning, sir," said Conrad. "Lovely day for a drive. She's fueled up and ready whenever you are."

"Great. Let's go," said Proteus, and they left the office together. He was running through the possibilities afforded by the publication of four papers on quantum mechanics by Schrödinger. There had been much chatter in the theoretical physics world about the implications of the wave equation that Schrödinger had assembled — and arguments were breaking out at lectures. Letters and telegrams had been exchanged, and the theoreticians divided themselves into camps following one interpretation or the other. And the fur was flying as they tussled.

Proteus strode past the lift, heading to the stairs at the end of the hallway, which was a much safer and less constricting way of getting down to the street. So far, the power in the building had stayed on, but he didn't want to be in the lift if it did go out. The strike had dragged on for a week now, but some normalcy had been restored and there were encouraging reports on the radio of hope for a resolution soon.

"I should have you in Woodchester by tea time," said Conrad as they left the building and walked toward the Vauxhall. Proteus's peripheral vision caught a brown blur, and he pivoted to see a dog slide to a halt in front of him and begin barking. The large dog had a collar and leash but no owner at the end. It did a playful bow and then ran off into an alleyway. A child ran toward Proteus and grabbed his hand. "Please help me get Alfy. Please, sir!"

Conrad moved to intervene, but Proteus waved him off. "It's okay, it'll just take a moment."

"I'll get the car," said Conrad.

Proteus allowed himself to be pulled into the alleyway. He couldn't see the dog, but then from around a group of trashcans it came charging towards him. Proteus was able to snag the leash as the dog ran past.

After reuniting dog and boy, he walked back out of the alley.

Conrad smiled, and waved at him from the driver's seat of the Vauxhall twenty yards away, and leaned forward to start the engine.

There was a bright flash, and Proteus was punched in the chest and thrown backwards onto the street. A loud ringing sounded in his head; dust and smoke shrouded his view. He rolled onto his side and saw a person staggering through the haze. Pain lanced into his chest and thighs; he looked down to see his clothes were shredded and he was bleeding from a dozen wounds.

Thick black smoke roiled upward. People were running, and some fell. The ringing in his head was replaced by screaming, whistles, and far-off sirens. Proteus tried to understand what had happened. Something was on fire where the Vauxhall had been moments before.

As the smoke cleared, Proteus saw that the wreckage engulfed in flames was the Vauxhall. "Conrad!" he screamed. He struggled to his feet and rushed towards the flames. "Conrad!"

Around the wreckage lay half a dozen bodies; and shop windows all along the street had been shattered. Two bobbies emerged from the smoke, pushing people away from the car, and one put his hand on Proteus's chest. "Get back, sir! Get back!"

"My friend Conrad!" shouted Proteus. "Conrad!"

Something hissed in the wreckage, and the flames flared brighter; heat blasted his face. The officer shoved, and Proteus stumbled backward, away from the conflagration. He was paralyzed as he watched the fire consume the vehicle.

The sirens grew louder. Proteus's vision began to grey, and dizziness forced him to sit down on the curb, shivering. A firetruck screeched to a halt, and firemen jumped off and uncoiled hoses to spray water onto the burning wreckage. Ambulances arrived, and medics began attending to the injured, covering the dead with sheets.

People on the street milled about in confusion. Reporters swarmed, and their flashbulbs strobed as they recorded the carnage.

Proteus waved away a medic who asked him if he needed help.

Suddenly, Freda appeared in front of him and helped him up and then inside the building. "Where's Conrad? What happened?" she asked.

Proteus shook his head slowly as his eyes brimmed with tears.

Ψ

After the funeral, the stack of papers on Proteus's desk grew. He couldn't bring himself to read the newspapers, nor could he muster the energy to read the scientific reports that Providence generated. He hadn't been out of his office in days except to shuffle to the hallway bathroom. Time blurred. Staff brought him food and water, and asked about his needs; Scotland Yard interviewed him; his glass and metal shrapnel wounds bled less.

Someone knocked at his office door, and he looked up. Sunlight streamed in through the windows, lighting the slowly swirling dust motes suspended in the air before striking a picture on the wall. It was one that Conrad had given him on his birthday several years ago: a photo of the two of them posed together in the Vauxhall, Conrad behind the wheel, both wearing straw boaters. Tears rolled down Proteus's cheeks and dripped onto his desk.

The knock was repeated, and then the door creaked open.

"Please, leave me alone," said Proteus.

"I know, sir — but it's a letter from Conrad's wife."

Proteus stood and then held on to the edge of the desk for support. He went over to accept the envelope being offered through the crack in the door and then returned to sit heavily in his chair, where he turned the envelope over and over.

His hands shook as he fumbled to open it. He thought about what the letter might say, and his throat tightened. *Why couldn't I predict the bombing? Why?*

Dear Mr. Proteus,

Earl of Nympsfield,

At this time of profound sadness in our lives, I wish to thank you for your generosity in the establishment of a trust for our family. Your barrister was kind enough to explain it all to me. Though my heart grieves now, my mind knows that time heals all wounds and that my daughter Rose and I have a future that will be bright. Through God's love we shall heal.

When we last met, you spoke of the power of education, and I wish you to know that Rose's insatiable curiosity will be challenged with the finest tutors and schools. It was Conrad's dream for her to go to university, and with the trust, she will. She's already learned her alphabet, and algebra is next, I reckon.

I also write to inform you that I don't blame you for my husband's death.

The world is full of blackguards and scoundrels, but I know your heart. You have a pure soul, Mr. Proteus. You gave Conrad the spark of enjoyment that he needed for growth. And you provided the means for us to save for our future.

Someone with only hate in their heart has taken Conrad from us in a heinous act of cruel murder.

I know in my heart that God's justice will prevail, and I believe in the good of humanity. My faith in the Lord has been strengthened by my Rose, my family, and my friends. I hope that you also have the comfort of those who love you.

In the Light of the Lord,

Allison

Proteus set the letter down on his desk and sobbed. The words struck him harder than any physical blow could have.

How can she be so strong?

He reread the letter, and his stinging eyes lingered on one word: *love.*

ACT 3

40

Proteus scanned the newspaper headlines and then stood from his desk to cross his office and open the windows. The damp morning breeze on his face sobered his mood, and he stood motionless, deep in thought.

His suffering was unlike anything he'd ever experienced. He was lost, empty, and angry all at once.

Scotland Yard had determined a bomb killed Conrad.

Proteus knew who'd done it, and he seethed at the thought: Russian spies. He'd become entangled with them in Rutherford's office and had later been stalked by Svetlana. They were the ones.

He also knew it was not coincidental. They were acting as agents of Time, which was trying to stop Proteus. Whether they were manipulated like puppets or understood on a conscious level mattered not.

Guilt gnawed at his soul — and there was no wound to bandage and no salve to soothe the hurt. Nothing he did relieved the pain.

His hands cramped, and he looked down to see them squeezing the sill, white-knuckled and trembling. Proteus relaxed his grip and pulled them from the window. He looked at the ever-growing pile of reports on his desk and then the letter from Conrad's wife.

Those who love you, Allison had written. In the past week, Carys had been all he could think about. Tomorrow, she was due to visit. She'd written as soon as she'd heard the news about Conrad, and her letter had expressed her desire to help ease his pain. *Can she truly help?*

Proteus went back to his desk, packed the SDU in his satchel and then grabbed his black overcoat on the way out the door. Freda looked up from her station with concern.

"I'm going home to my flat," said Proteus. "Call me if anything comes up."

"I will, sir. Please get some rest, and don't worry about Providence."

"Thank you, Freda."

Ψ

It was a dreary walk home, and Proteus didn't feel any better when he got there. He pulled the blinds closed and then noticed a yellow light blinking on the Retrieve-Unit. He went to the nightstand and picked it up.

The device was about the size of two decks of playing cards and had the same obsidian surface as the SDU. Proteus sat down on the couch to inspect it. The yellow light indicated the power supply had waned. A fully charged unit should last two decades, so this warning was unexpected, but he needn't be too concerned unless it changed to red, which meant only a few months of potential use remained. There were no signs of external damage, and he wondered what had gone wrong; its sealed container and shielding were impervious to the elements and EM spectra. It was his only way home and also beyond his ability to repair.

The Retrieve-Unit, when triggered, would relay a transmission home requesting a recall; when received, the Colony would utilize the space-time data sent to run the calculations for Proteus's return. They would then power up the wormhole and pull him through.

From Proteus's perspective, after he went through the unit's biometric security sequence and signaled the recall, it would take between a few minutes and several months, or perhaps even longer, until he was yanked back to his origin time. The probability variations needed in the calculations and the asynchronous flow of time accounted for the uncertainty.

Or I may never be pulled out. This thought led him down the well-trodden path he'd run many times before. If everyone in the twenty-fifth century was dead, or the technology failed, then there wouldn't be a recall. Proteus also had to consider the effects of his machinations in the early twentieth century. How exactly would this change the twenty-fifth century? The scientists had reassured him that, if he were successful, humanity would be living in harmony with Nature on the surface of the Earth.

But what if they're wrong? What if there's no utopia? What if technology no longer exists for a wormhole back? After all, necessity is the mother of invention. Existential fear led to the development of nuclear weapons, and existential desperation led to the pursuit of time travel at all costs. If the pressure for time travel is removed, then the wormhole technology may never have been developed. A paradoxical erasure caused by my actions.

Proteus's biggest fear, however, was that the closed time-loop theory was wrong, and there were actually many parallel instances of reality. He might trigger a recall, only to find himself back underground, beneath the surface of a dead planet, cooped up with the dwindling, dying remnants of humanity.

He had no answers, and this line of thought only deepened his funk. He could only follow his orders and hope for the best. The discovery of fission must be pushed into the future, until after the start of the Second World War. Once he was certain of that, he must activate the Retrieve-Unit. The people of his Colony did not, under any circumstances, want him to stay in the twentieth century. They reasoned that the power he possessed would be too tempting, and would eventually corrupt him.

The telephone rang, and he picked up the receiver. "Hello," he said. "Proteus speaking."

"Hello, Archie. This is Carys," said a woman's voice. Proteus was confused — and his heart skipped several beats. Woodchester didn't have a telephone yet.

"What ... how?" he stuttered. "Where are you?"

"I'm at Providence," said Carys. "I came to London a day early and went to your office. Freda said I should call you. I hope it's all right."

It's her. It's really her!

"Yes," said Proteus. "Yes, of course. I'll be right there." He dropped the telephone receiver and ran to the front door — then ran back and picked it up again. "Sorry ... don't go anywhere ... um ... bye-bye, see you soon." He hung up the receiver and then grabbed his satchel and overcoat and strode toward the door.

Mark Jenkins

41

Rutherford bellowed for his assistant and began sorting through the day's mail. A letter from Paris caught his eye, and he saw it was from the Radium Institute. He ripped it open and began reading:

My Dear Professor Rutherford,

Words fail me at present. Something dreadful has happened …

Rutherford stopped reading, put the letter down and thought back to the horrible accident in 1906 in which Pierre Curie's skull was crushed in the streets of Paris under the wheels of a horse-drawn carriage. *What could match that, I wonder?* He picked up the letter and continued reading.

All of the radium and thorium I was to send you is gone, stolen! I have no idea who would do such a thing. And …

At this point the lettering was smeared, making it difficult to read. Rutherford opened his desk drawer and retrieved a magnifying lens. He studied a mark on the letter surrounded by a halo of fading ink as if a drop of water had diffused it outward—

p

—and he thought of the vast empty sphere surrounding the atom's nucleus and how close they were to finding out what he *knew* in his bones was truly there. His guts squeezed as studied the next letters:

Processing equipment destroyed … All of it. I have no more for you or anyone! My laboratory has been ruined … all of it has been destroyed … everything that Pierre, God rest his soul, and I have worked on for decades. My students and assistant professors are beside themselves with anguish.

The letter fluttered out of Rutherford's hands to the dirty floor. He pushed back from his desk and slammed his large fists on the surface.

"Preposterous!" he said, and the windows rattled. He cleared his desk with a sweep of a large forearm. Glass crashed on the floor, and thick paper stacks flew, sending cascades of dust about the office. Rutherford stood and crunched across the office. Slamming the door closed behind him, he stormed into the hallway, bellowing for his assistant.

Pain stabbed his abdomen, and he gasped to lean against the corridor wall. He took in short breaths; his arms shook. It reached a crescendo — and then eased.

Rutherford's thoughts turned dark. *Everything is ruined. We're so close to teasing out the secrets within the atom. So close! First my laboratory notebook, and now Curie has been robbed. Who's doing this, and what are we to do?*

"Professor, are you all right?   asked Marco, startling Rutherford. "You look ashen."

"What the blazes are you doing, sneaking up on me like that?"

"You called for me, sir," said Marco.

"Yes, I did. How much radium do we have left?"

"I'll check, sir — but about two grams, I believe."

"Thorium?"

"None."

"Blast!" He leaned against the corridor wall and shook his head. *Why has this happened?*

42

Dear Albert,

I have just finished reading your letter and am stunned to learn of the theft of your notebooks and the erasure of your boards. I must admit to being entirely perplexed by the appearance of the mouse. And it's quite strange that the lads in Cavendish first began seeing mice in their experiments just recently, and now there's an appearance in your hall. Do you think any of those Rutherford chaps had anything to do with it? Were they trying to send you a message that your theories had best align with their experiments?

Regardless, I have faith that you can recreate much of your work and look forward to seeing the next evolutionary cycle of your unified field theory. I know this has been a challenging endeavor, and I have some thoughts to share next time we meet.

I have been puzzling much of late about the continued silliness coming out of Copenhagen. The idea that the very act of observing a particle forces it to make a decision into one state or another is absurd. I literally guffawed out loud when I read Heisenberg's latest paper. The quantum lads are really clinging to the bizarre notion that a superposition state exists until someone lays their eyes on it and — poof — it magically decides to spin null or spin one.

What poppycock!

Mind you, Denmark has always been a rather strange place, but their interpretation of the wave function collapse is silliness.

I hope you're doing well and enjoying time on your sailboat.

Until our next meeting, I wish you the best.

Yours in theory,

Erwin

43

Proteus's heart hammered as he sprinted up the stairs. Once he reached the hallway leading to Providence, he slowed his pace and tried to calm his breathing.

"Carys," he called out as he entered his offices. "Carys?"

"I'm here," she said. He turned to see her silhouette against the window in the communications room. Proteus went to her, and she put a hand on his shoulder, and her green eyes stared into his. "Oh, Archie, it's so dreadful. My father and I have been in shock since we heard. I know how much you cared about Conrad."

"It hurts so much, Carys," said Proteus.

Activity had stopped in the communications room, and Proteus looked around and coughed nervously. "Where are my manners ..."

"It's all right. Freda introduced me to everyone," said Carys.

"Ahh ... good," said Proteus. "Um ... let's go talk in my office."

She followed him in, and he closed the door, after thanking Freda.

"You said you'd been injured," said Carys.

"The wounds to my flesh have almost fully healed. But ..." He pointed to his chest. "Here ... I don't know what to do. I've never felt this way before. I can't sleep, and I can't think straight. Everything is —"

231

Carys stepped closer to him and said, "Have you never lost someone close to you before?"

Proteus shook his head.

Carys held out her hand, and Proteus accepted it. Her fingers squeezed, and she pulled him toward her. "Please, come and sit with me," she said. "I want to tell you about my mother and my father."

As he sat down with her on his office couch, Carys cleared her throat and paused.

"My father was an officer in the cavalry in the Great War, and eight years ago, my mother and I received a telegram that he'd been injured in a gas attack. He'd been maimed and was recuperating in a hospital in France. My mother and I were devastated. Months went by, and then we received a letter saying he was coming home," said Carys. "But she never saw him again. My mother became ill with the Spanish flu and died." She stopped, and a tear carved a track down her cheek. "It's still ... difficult to talk about it.

"When I did see my father, he had terrible weeping sores over his body, and he was ... changed, in other ways. He wouldn't leave the house or talk to anyone but me. And even then, only rarely. What he did say was too horrible to hear. As a young girl in her teens, I was frightened and alone. I needed love, but my father was a stranger.

"The war ended, and there were celebrations in the streets, but my father worsened. He was in constant pain from his wounds and began to say things about being abandoned by God and country. *If this is humanity*, he'd say, *I want no part of it.*

"I was confused and didn't know how to help him. I cried myself to sleep almost every night. One day I came home from school and he had a pistol in his mouth. I called out and rushed to him. I told him I loved him. I told him I needed him. I told him I didn't want to be alone.

"He put the gun down and sank on the floor, and then wailed. I hugged him and kept saying *I love you Papa*, over and over."

Proteus held his breath and looked into Carys's eyes, uncertain of what to say or do. Tears dripped from her chin and onto his hand.

"And then my father changed again. He walked me to school and then began walking me home as well. He turned his sharp mind toward helping me with my homework. Later, he said that my love had saved his soul."

Proteus sat in silence as he tried to understand the emotions coursing through him.

Carys turned to look into his eyes. "Some people say time heals all wounds. But that's only part of the truth. Time's passing is simply time's passing. But true healing requires love."

"I ..." stuttered Proteus. "I ... don't know what to say."

Carys pulled him close and hugged him. Her arms encircled his upper back, and he felt the warmth of her body. He'd never embraced another human in this way; his scalp tingled.

She released the hug, looked into his eyes, and said, "You're a caring soul. And perhaps that's why Lucy loves you. But I think there is more to you."

Proteus considered her words — and wanted to say so much, to tell her everything, but he sat mute.

"Perhaps one day you can tell me about your life growing up," she said.

"Yes. I should," said Proteus and thought about how he'd even begin to tell her his story. The silence stretched on, and he felt he should say something more. "One day I will tell you everything, I promise," he said. "My childhood. Everything." Then he wondered at his own words and the speed at which they'd tumbled out.

"I'd like that very much," said Carys.

Ψ

Proteus had arranged a hotel room for Carys, and after they'd finished the rest of the tour of Providence, they set off to walk there. The rain had yielded to a beautiful blue summer sky, and a weight had been lifted from his chest.

"Oh, I forgot — manners," said Carys and giggled. "Am I to use a title for the earl? Or some other such nonsense?"

Proteus laughed and said, "No. Archie is just fine."

He was buoyant as they walked. Even her suitcase felt light.

He'd selected the Charing Cross Hotel for several reasons: its proximity to his flat; the anonymity afforded by the swarms of people traversing the adjacent transportation hub; and the security and privacy of the suites on the top floor. It was also not known for ritzy parties. Proteus wanted no further risk to those he cared about. At this thought, his stomach churned. He couldn't let anything happen to Carys.

"Trafalgar Square," she said as they turned a corner and the plaza opened up before them. They crossed a street and entered the wide-open space lit with the warm late-afternoon sun. "I've always loved coming here."

They stopped near a fountain in a cool breeze. Proteus watched her eyes as she stood in the sunlight and looked around the square.

The hotel bordered Trafalgar Square, and after Carys had checked in, he swallowed his fear and rode the lift as he helped her with her luggage. She wished to "freshen up," so Proteus left to wait downstairs.

He avoided the lift and bounded down seven flights of stairs to the lobby, where he lurked in the corner, watching people, looking for anything that might be out of place or suspicious.

He wanted to keep Carys safely away from him yet close enough to protect her. The conflict in the logic puzzled him — and he couldn't explain it.

Musical notes sounded from the bar room, and Proteus cocked his ears to hear scales played on a saxophone. A bass drum thumped — and then a cymbal crashed. The band was warming up.

"Shall we go inside?" said Carys, suddenly appearing next to him. "I love music."

"Yes, of course," said Proteus. Carefree, he offered her his arm, which she accepted. Inside the room was a long bar — and behind it a mirror and more glass bottles than Proteus could count — and a low stage and a small dance floor. His enjoyment of Carys's company turned to fear at the thought she might want to dance and expose his lack of skills.

They sat down at the bar and Carys said, "Do you trust me?"

"Why, yes, of course," said Proteus, wondering what she was going to say next.

"Two salty dogs, please," Carys said to the bartender. She looked at Proteus and smiled. "It's my favorite."

After the drinks were served, she raised her glass, and he did the same.

"To good friendship," she said.

"To good friendship," he repeated and looked at the crystals on the rim as he tentatively took a sip. The taste of salt hit first, then the tang of citrus, and finally the burn of alcohol.

"Grapefruit juice, gin, salt on the rim, and rosemary," said Carys. "Do you like it?"

"Yes," said Proteus as his lips puckered. "It's delicious."

On the small stage, the drummer began a 4/4 beat on a snare drum, kicking the bass drum on the evens. He accelerated the tempo and crashed the high-hat cymbal to punctuate the building rhythm; people began to clap. And as if feeding off the energy in the audience, he began to add complexity to the drum solo.

A tall man wearing a blue beret and sunglasses shambled onto the stage holding a double bass; a cigarette hung loosely from his lips. He nodded at the applause and began thumping a rhythm that was varied yet completely wedded to the bass drum. The other musicians hung back at the curtain. People in the audience began to move their feet.

Then a tenor saxophone wailed, and people cheered as a trumpet and trombone joined in; and the band pounded out swing.

Goosebumps danced on Proteus's arms as the music flowed over him.

He turned to Carys and smiled. She was bobbing her head to the rhythm and grinning at him. Then she laughed. "So much fun," she said.

Proteus went giddy with delight.

44

"We are rather like children, who must take a watch to pieces to see how it works."
~ Ernest Rutherford

Rutherford sat in the corner of one of his laboratories and stared at the idle scattering equipment. His researchers had burned through the last of the radium and thorium, and it would be at least a year before Marie Curie could produce sufficient amounts to resupply him. He'd exchanged several letters with her, pledging his support and asking what he could do to help, and then the news had worsened.

The University of Paris was insistent that Curie begin charging for radioactive elements, when she could once again purify them in sufficient amounts, and the price tag was exorbitant. Repairing and replacing Curie's laboratories and equipment had been expensive and had happened during a time of overall financial difficulties for the university.

This left Rutherford in a terrible bind. His budget had been stretched thin even before his research had ground to a halt. And now, when the elements he needed were eventually available, he'd have to pay a small fortune. One he didn't have.

In these difficult economic times, requests for more funding would fall on deaf ears, just as they had the last several times Rutherford had tried. He couldn't stomach the thought of requesting more money from the provost and then listening to the man's smug reply. One of Rutherford's favorite quotes was, "We haven't got the money, so we have to think," and he knew the sniveling provost would delight in throwing it in his face.

Sharp pains stabbed into his abdomen, and he leaned forward to grip the edge of a workbench. He panted and his arms shook. Then, as quickly as they'd struck, the pains vanished.

It's not bloody fair. I know there's something dense and electrically neutral in the nucleus of the atom. I just can't yet prove it. We're so close, I can feel it in my bones.

Rutherford sighed as he looked around the lab. He was driving his teams to do as much as they could, but they were dejected. Some were so despondent, they'd taken to cleaning, and the place had never looked so good. It was a miserable state of affairs; he just had to find funding somehow. His very existence was centered around chasing the secrets of the atom, and it was wrong for him to be denied.

45

"The first gulp from the glass of natural sciences will turn you into an atheist, but at the bottom of the glass God is waiting for you." ~ Werner Heisenberg

The week that Carys spent with Proteus in London flew by too fast. He'd dropped her off at the train station that morning and still tingled from their embrace. She had a quick wit and a lovely laugh. Their conversations about science had shown her sharp analytical mind, and he longed to be with her again. Sitting in his office now, he was empty.

Proteus turned back to the reports stacked on his desk. Providence now had fully operational satellite offices in both Cambridge and Oxford, and his teams had become proficient in combing through, extracting, and compiling the information he needed. Conrad had trained them well; Proteus felt a pang of remorse at the thought.

He read the executive summary of the report on the top of the pile. Research into the atom had drifted slightly off course. Rutherford's group was at a standstill, as were all the other groups that depended upon Curie's purified radioactive elements. The Rutherford-Bohr model of the atom — which had electrons in orbit and protons in the nucleus — still dominated the landscape, and there were fewer and fewer references to something unknown in the nucleus. In the absence of new experimental data to tussle over, the theorists were cat-fighting with renewed furor. Einstein and Schrödinger insisted the universe must have physical laws that explained how it worked — and the quantum-jump team, Bohr and Heisenberg, insisted the mysterious atom had its own game of dice to play.

Proteus could barely contain his excitement. The direction of the combined search into the atom was just a tiny bit off, but it would be amplified by time. It was like a ship crossing the Atlantic on a heading that was erroneous by only a fraction of a degree; eventually it would arrive hundreds of miles distant from its intended destination.

Proteus thought of the timeframe he had left before he could consider his mission complete; his mind drifted through the events of the next decade, as recorded in the Data-Cube.

James Chadwick, working under Rutherford's guidance at Cavendish, discovered the neutron of the atom in 1932. The following year was called the *Annus Mirabilis* — the year of wonder — in theoretical and atomic physics. Discoveries avalanched as international teams raced each other by blasting neutrons into sundry atoms, eventually diving into the deep heavyweights like uranium.

These scientific advances occurred alongside the growing specter of totalitarianism in Nazi Germany and Soviet Russia. The crippling depressions and growing hopelessness stemming from the Great War proved fertile soil for Hitler and Stalin to rise.

Germany's National Socialists were consumed with twisted ideology and an obsession with Aryan purity. They viewed everything through a racial lens, and as they gained power, this fixation hardened into an addiction.

Their maniacal ideas of purity — their *idée fixe* — infested everything: government, industry, media, education, military, art, music, and scientific research. All were controlled by the Party, and ideological conformity was not a question: books were burned, businesses smashed, and scholars censored. All impure thoughts were persecuted.

Those who perceived the threat, and had access to a means of escape, did. A large swath of scientists fled Europe. In the 1930s, Rutherford and Einstein independently facilitated and financed the rescue of hundreds of them — a sort of Dunkirk for scientists, years before the military evacuation. Many of the displaced atomic physicists and theorists were drawn to England and America, like iron to magnets.

Eventually, a critical mass of minds were thrust toward one another — like the collapsing plutonium sphere in the Fat Man over Nagasaki — and a chain reaction of discoveries erupted.

Nuclear fission was achieved in 1938; the energy released was measured and quantified. The experiment was repeated in different laboratories in Europe and the US, all with the same conclusion: a small amount of uranium could power a city, and — if the theorists were correct — could also be fashioned into a bomb to destroy one.

The minds alone would not have been enough, but once World War Two broke out, the threat of annihilation drove everyone into a no-holds-barred battle for survival. Every country wanted its own super-weapons.

Weapons so powerful, they could end all wars.

This was neither the first nor the last turn of that phrase. The horrible gas weapons of the Great War (chlorine, mustard, phosgene, and others) had been morally defended as a way to shorten the war; to save lives.

The statement *Weapons so powerful they could end all wars* was a cyclical, linguistic reflection of an obsession — like a gramophone skipping on a scratch, replaying the last measures of a song over and over.

Repeating, until the Cataclysm presented humanity with its final moment of reckoning.

Proteus shuddered and turned his attention back to his plan. The last piece of the puzzle was his acceptance to the Royal Society, which he expected soon. The position would allow him to participate directly in decisions about research funding.

His first meeting with the chief steward had not gone well, but the last time Proteus had visited, the man had sung a different tune. Apparently, titles and money did talk.

46

May 1927

Borya Volkov paused his packing of the box on his desk in the embassy and read the communiqué again in disbelief. The bloody British had not only thwarted his plans, but had also tracked down and arrested many of his assets. Some were his spies and others were Englishmen in key positions who'd been recruited to the cause. How MI5 had moved so quickly was still a mystery to him, but that wasn't the only question he'd have to face back in Moscow.

He'd burrowed his entire network into the ground to avoid exposure and assured the Kremlin that they were hidden. However, MI5 had ferreted out several of his assets, like hyperactive terriers digging for rodents. And then it'd gone quiet.

Six months ago, he'd thought the embassy safely in the clear, confident that MI5 were not able to put any more pieces together — but then more agents were arrested. And then there'd been months of maddening silence and inactivity.

Up until now, almost exactly a year to the day from the failed revolution.

Last week, the British prime minister had presented a full dossier of captured and decoded documents to Parliament, fully implicating the Soviet Union in espionage. In the same week, the prime minister had moved swiftly to sever diplomatic relations. Borya had been recalled to an uncertain future. If he was lucky, he would be reassigned to a hellhole someplace, but if not it was the gulag and an early death.

Not wishing to be reminded of his failure any further, he tossed the communiqué in the fire. He stared at the box on his desk and became lost in thought. Since he'd received the news this morning, he'd had a growing suspicion that it was the American who had been the lynchpin of his downfall. The American whom he'd tried unsuccessfully, several times, to capture for information — and then kill — had turned the tables on him.

Borya was not yet without teeth. He pushed the box out of the way to compose a directive. He still had the power of his office, and he composed a message to mobilize assets. Ones that were heavily armed.

When he finished writing, he called for Pyotr.

The giant entered the room and stood at attention in front of his master.

"See that the man who makes clocks receives this message," said Borya and handed over the note. "Memorize, and tell him in person."

Pyotr studied the writing and grimaced, showing his brown teeth — then he stuffed the paper in his mouth and began to chew. Pyotr's eyes never left his master's as his facial muscles bulged. He swallowed — and then began to laugh. It was a rare breach of protocol, but Borya said nothing.

Pyotr's mirth trailed off, and he said, "It will be done." He cracked the knuckles of his massive hands. "Pyotr will see to it."

47

Proteus read the exciting news in Carys's latest letter. She had been approved for postgraduate studies in biology at Oxford, allowing her to pursue her dreams. She would start in the fall, glad to be able to stay at Oxford to be close to her father, and also glad that Proteus wouldn't be far away. She looked forward to seeing him.

He cleared away the reports he'd finished reading this morning and pulled out paper and pen to write her back. Proteus smiled as he thought of her warm embrace and began writing.

After a few paragraphs, he stopped and couldn't think of what to write. He set the pen down, unease nibbling away at the corners of his mind. It was a thought he'd been avoiding, but now that he had a relationship with Carys, it could no longer be denied. Proteus owed Carys and Gareth the truth of who he was.

Proteus wanted to be with Carys without the complications and entanglements of who he really was — and this paradox was becoming increasingly difficult to navigate. The thought kept him awake at night. His love for her kept growing, as did the guilt of keeping her in the dark.

He knew he'd have to tell her the truth, but he'd been forbidden to tell anyone; he also knew she'd never believe him.

He was an alien.

Ψ

Carys sat on the couch to read Proteus's letter and smiled. He was scheduled to visit Woodchester and had suggested they have a small celebration of her acceptance to postgraduate studies. Proteus also wrote of important information he wished to share. But would write nothing further and would tell her and Gareth in person after he'd arrived. The wording was curious, and she noted his penmanship had changed: the sentences sloped downward, across the page, when he wrote about this "important information." Whatever the news, it seemed weighty. Perhaps he was selling Woodchester and moving on. His decisions were difficult to fathom at times.

Carys became lost in thought — and hollowness grew in the pit of her stomach. She put down the letter and curled into a ball. *Why do I care so much about him?*

Our conversations have touched upon such breadth and depth in the sciences, and he makes me laugh with his odd wit and insatiable curiosity. He clearly cares about me, but who is he? When I ask about his schooling, he always says the same thing, about some university across the pond, but then won't describe much about the experience. Yet he hints about fields of research that seem fantastic and asks me about hypothetical ethical scenarios that —

"You all right, love?" said Gareth, startling her. "You're frowning."

She hadn't heard her father come into the den. "Yes, Papa, I'm fine," she said and smiled. "Just thinking."

Ψ

The drive west was a weighty mix of memories and anticipation, and Proteus's stomach churned. The trip to Woodchester would forever remind him of Conrad. He thought of him often, but times alone like this were especially hard. It'd taken him almost a year before he could contemplate buying another motorcar, and every time he sat in the seat of the Morris Motors MG, there was a sharp twinge of sorrow and guilt.

Thoughts of his destination were not much of a tonic to his mood.

His heart pounded as he thought of Carys and what he must tell her. As much as he longed to see her, he couldn't escape his growing fear of rejection.

Proteus pushed the car faster. The sooner he could get to Woodchester and see Carys, the better. He pressed the accelerator harder, and the tires squealed as he took a curve too fast. His mind ran through different scenarios of what he would say and how he might be received. Most of these pathways led to bleak outcomes, but in his heart there remained a glimmer of hope.

He drove the car hard into another turn; the rear end of the MG fishtailed, and Proteus nearly lost control of the vehicle.

Slow down! he thought. *You're no good to anyone as a corpse.* He reined in the speed and tried to push down his mounting anxiety and hold onto the dream of being accepted.

Ψ

It was early evening when Proteus arrived at Woodchester, and he ran up the trail to the cottage. He knocked on the door, out of breath, and was nearly bowled over by Lucy as Gareth opened it. After the dog had finished her greeting, Proteus shook hands with Gareth.

"Good evening," said Gareth. "You're just in time for supper."

Gareth excused himself to the kitchen, and Carys came into the den. Her sudden presence tied Proteus's stomach in knots, and his mouth went dry. He gave her a brief hug before holding her at arm's length and looking into her eyes. The pressure on Proteus's mind eased when he saw her smiling the same way she had the last time he saw her. She appeared as happy to see him as he was to see her.

Gareth called them to the table for dinner. All throughout the meal, which Proteus couldn't taste for some reason, he could manage little other than small talk. He stole looks at Carys and thought that it would maybe be better if he just kept silent. The status quo was the path of least resistance, avoiding throwing everything into chaos. Constructing different ways to tell Carys the truth had been so much easier at a distance, but with her here in front of him, the idea was mortifying. Even so, keeping her in the dark any longer would be wrong. She needed to know, and she needed to make her own decision about the dangers — as did her father.

Proteus looked down at his half-finished bowl of stew and said.

"This is delicious, but I'm afraid I don't have much of an appetite this evening. My apologies."

"Oh, that's quite all right," said Gareth. "We understand."

"Is everything well?" said Carys. She looked worried. "Your letter mentioned some news you wished to share."

Proteus took in a deep breath. *Here we go.* "After dinner, let's go into the parlor, and I'll tell you."

A short time later, Proteus found himself seated at the low coffee table while a nervous Carys sat watching him. Gareth finished up in the kitchen and sat down on the couch next to his daughter.

Proteus took a deep breath and rubbed his sweaty palms along his thighs. "So ... I need to tell you both the truth about why I'm here," he said. They both watched him in silence. "But it's so strange that you won't believe my words, and so I must show you."

He reached into his satchel and pulled out the SDU in its biblical wrappings.

"Is this a religious proposition?" said Gareth and frowned. "Because I've no time for that."

Proteus shook his head. He unbuckled the cover and placed the SDU on the table in front of them. The obsidian surface reflected the glare of the electric light.

"What the blazes is that?" said Gareth.

Proteus's eyes locked on Carys, who'd tilted her head sideways to look at it. "Data-Cube on," he said.

Carys flinched, and Gareth swore as the green cube hovered into view above the table. Carys's gaze jumped between the Cube and Proteus.

"What is this?" she said.

Cold sweat covered Proteus's palms as he measured his next words. He had to share the burden he carried and wanted to keep them safe; it was a violation of orders, but it was the right thing to do. He took another deep breath and said, "I'm from the future ... here to ... to stop the development of a terrible weapon." He tried to lick his dry lips but found no moisture. "What I'm going to show you is the next world war."

Proteus manipulated the controls, and a grainy black-and-white video began. Lettering flashed up: *Europe, 1939 — A BBC Production.* Gareth eyed him suspiciously, and Proteus paused the newsreel.

"How is this possible?" said Carys. "This technology can see the future?"

"No, it sees the past," said Proteus but then saw that he was only confusing them further. "I will explain when it's finished."

The newsreel showed long lines of German tanks streaming across lowlands. A narrator's voice took the viewer through the footage: "The Blitzkrieg began in 1940, and the combined armies of Britain and France were soon vanquished on the European mainland ..."

On and on it went: goose-stepping German soldiers on parade around the Arc de Triomphe, and then the Blitz. Gareth cursed at the fires raging in London.

On and on: Pearl Harbor, the frozen Eastern front. Soviet tanks. Japan's brutal conquest of China. Beheadings of prisoners. Germans in black uniforms rounding up people wearing the Star of David. Concentration camps. D-Day. Piles of bodies. The ruins of Berlin and the toppling of the German swastika from the top of the Reichstag.

Then the video switched to color, and a date flashed up: *Aug 6, 1945*. A lone four-engine bomber hovered into view; its silver fuselage glinted in the sunlight. The view flipped to a close-up of the markings on the plane: a large circle with an arrow on the tail; a five-pointed white star on a blue circle, with white and red ribbon in the background; the words *Enola Gay* and the number *82* were stenciled on the nose.

The scene flipped back to a view from much further away. The plane banked sharply as an object dropped from underneath.

The camera followed the speck down until it became lost in the grainy resolution of the footage. Proteus glanced at Carys and Gareth; both were fixated on the images.

Twenty seconds passed. A harbor could be seen far underneath.

Then the white balance of the camera was overloaded by a flash, and Carys gasped. As the camera's optics adjusted, a sphere of white filled the screen and rose, dwarfing the harbor below. An enormous mushroom cloud blossomed into the sky.

The footage switched to the ruins of a city. People crawled in the debris, and children lay dead in the dust. One image showed a flashed outline of a human silhouette etched into a stone wall. Another showed a trembling woman with horrible burns lying in a hospital bed.

The narrator continued: "From this single bomb, 80,000 Japanese men, women, and children in the city of Hiroshima were killed instantly, and 35,000 were wounded. Radiation burns and sickness claimed another 60,000 lives over the next four months."

"Gods above," said Gareth.

Carys sobbed and buried her head in her hands. "This can't ... be real," she said.

"This was the first nuclear-fission device to be used as a weapon," said Proteus. "Three days after the bombing of Hiroshima a second nuclear weapon was dropped on the city of Nagasaki. World War Two ended only days later, but Pandora's Box had been opened.

"The blast you saw was the equivalent of 15,000 tons of artillery explosives. Can you conceive of two million British eighteen-pounders all going off at once in a space smaller than this room? Beyond the damage from the blast, the soil was laced with radioactive toxins that poisoned for generations."

Gareth shook his head and stared at the floor.

"Eighty percent of the buildings in that city of a quarter of a million residents were destroyed with one bomb, dropped from one plane. But we didn't stop there. This one bomb was but a grain of sand compared to the destructive power we developed. And then, one day, we dropped so many, we cracked the Earth and set the surface on fire."

"Wait ... this doesn't make sense," said Carys. "You're speaking in the past tense, as if—"

"—it has happened," said Proteus. "Or will. I don't know."

"What do you mean, you don't know?" said Gareth and stood. "You either know the future or you don't. Don't play games with us!"

"I've been sent here to halt the beginnings of what I've just shown you. In humankind's future, there is nothing. Nothing! I'm from that future. We're all dying underground because we blew ourselves up with fission and fusion weapons."

Proteus realized he'd risen from his seat and was now pacing. He stopped and studied Carys's face; he realized he needed to clarify. "My mission is to interfere with the scientists working on splitting the atom, which is the technology used to develop that bomb. The longer I can delay it, the greater the chance that the Cataclysm will never happen. And when I'm certain my mission is complete, I'm to send a signal to my time period, and they'll reverse the process that sent me here to return me home. Hopefully to a world that's not an ash heap."

Gareth sat down. Carys frowned and looked away.

After a few moments, she said, "How will you know if you've done enough? Won't the scientists just keep working?"

"The critical period is 1933, the so-called *Annus Mirabilis* — the miracle year in atomic physics. If artificial fission is not achieved by the start of World War Two in Europe in 1939, governments will not be able to pour vast amounts of money into a bomb project. If the technology just isn't ready, there won't be a race to develop a weapon. Eventually, the scientists will succeed, but hopefully far enough in the future that humanity will have evolved beyond the desire to create doomsday weapons."

"I need a drink," said Gareth. He stood, went to the kitchen, and returned with a bottle and three glasses. "Jameson's whiskey," he said and held up the bottle. He uncorked it and poured each of them a generous splash. Proteus took a sip and shuddered as it burned his throat.

They sat in silence for several minutes.

Gareth frowned and said, "Does this have any relation to the bombing that killed Conrad?"

A familiar pang struck Proteus. He set his glass down and stared at the table. "Yes," he said after a moment. "I believe so. I think it was intended for me."

"Who did it?" said Gareth. "I'd assumed with the violence that'd erupted around the general strike that it was a random act—"

"Who would want to hurt you?" asked Carys.

"It's not who, but more of a question of what," said Proteus. He saw their puzzled expressions and considered how to describe Time-resistance.

"Time — this period we're in — doesn't want to be changed," said Proteus and explained the paradox of a closed time-loop. "So the work I do can only be in very small increments. If I'm too successful, too far beyond what might happen naturally, there is opposition. And that opposition can be dramatic, which is why I've been nibbling away at this for years. It could be a seemingly accidental event, perhaps a gang of street thugs, but Time wants to stay on its course."

Proteus described the horse carriage accident and the encounters he'd had with Russians in Cavendish, and Svetlana.

"Russians? Were they spies?" said Gareth. "Did they plant that bomb?"

"I suspect so. I became of interest to them — I'm certain it was intended for me, but it cost Conrad his life."

Proteus paused and recalled the minutes directly before the explosion. The happenstance encounter with the boy and his dog that had delayed him from being in the car. A jolt ran through him as he considered that it might not have been as haphazard as he initially thought. It had nibbled at the edges of his consciousness for some time, but he hadn't conceptualized it until now. *Was it Nature? Is Nature herself rebelling against Time, to prevent Earth's extinction?*

"Are you all right?" asked Carys.

"Umm ... yes," said Proteus. "Why?"

"You stopped talking, and you've had a far-off stare in your eyes for several minutes," she said.

"Oh ... sorry," said Proteus. "I had a strange thought just now."

"You seem to have a lot of them," said Gareth and chuckled; but moments later, he scowled. "Is Carys in danger?"

The question smacked like a blow, and his throat tightened. "I worry about that," he said and turned to Carys. "I couldn't live with myself if anything happened to you."

"How will you prevent it then?" said Gareth.

"Nothing's going to happen to me," said Carys. "Or you, Papa."

"You don't know that," said Gareth. "Let him answer the question."

"The *opposition* seems to ebb and flow based on my actions and their consequences," said Proteus. "I'm at a point now where I don't need to do much more other than monitor the atomic research. Following my earlier actions, the scientific community is confused and drifting away from the discovery of the neutron and fission." He paused to look at Carys and continued, "I believe that if I keep a low profile, then the risk to you is lower, but I cannot promise anything."

"So you think the Russians, or whoever, will leave you alone now," said Carys.

Proteus nodded.

"I've never trusted Russians, and I detest the Bolsheviks," said Gareth. "I'm glad the prime minister's expelled the bastards. That was the right thing to do. Hopefully, you're in the clear now."

"Hopefully," agreed Proteus. "But I need to keep my footprint small."

Gareth looked at him for a moment before returning his attention to the fire.

The conversation dwindled, and Proteus gazed into the fire. Gareth stood to adjust a log with long iron tongs; the fire sparked and popped. Proteus turned to look at Carys, who was staring into the fire as well. *I wonder what she's thinking? Am I an alien to her forever?*

Gareth stood. "I'm off to bed. I don't know what to think anymore." He bent to receive a kiss from Carys.

"'Night, Papa," said Carys.

Ψ

In the tortuous moments that Proteus waited for Carys to say something, his eyes flicked between her sitting next to him on the couch, and the fire, and Lucy snoring on the floor.

"Do you have any family in your future?" said Carys. "Parents?"

He exhaled slowly and said, "No."

"Someone that cares about you, perhaps?"

"No. I have nothing."

"I see," said Carys. She smoothed her dress with her hands and stared into the fire. "Will you really leave here and journey to your time when you are finished?"

"That's what I've been ordered to do," said Proteus.

"What if you get there, to your future, and it's the same?" she said.

"I don't know," said Proteus. "That thought tortures me. I never want to go underground again. After what I've seen and experienced here, I think it would kill me." He reached over to take her hand as he looked into her eyes. "I want stay with you."

She squeezed his hand and smiled. "Stay, then," she said. "I can't bear the thought of your dying alone in some bunker."

"Carys, I love you," said Proteus. "And I will do everything in my power to be with you."

"I love you, too."

Proteus leaned forward, and they kissed. After a moment, they embraced, and then sank back slowly onto the couch in each other's arms.

48

Autumn 1927

As twilight neared, the watchmaker sat alone at a table near the hearth in the Anchor and Hourglass and sipped his India pale ale. He'd chosen this table because the warmth of the fire helped ward off the chill settling into his bones and the window gave a view of the waterfront street and the harbor beyond. The masts of moored ships swayed from side to side in the winds of the approaching storm. But his aching joints had warned him of the impending change hours ago.

The door to the public house opened, admitting a chilly gust and two sailors. He looked at them briefly before deciding these were not the ones; then he glanced at one of his pocket watches. The ship was overdue — and this was not *correct*.

He looked around the pub. A few of the tables were occupied by bearded men in wool caps, smoking pipes and nodding at each other; at the bar was a lovesick couple and a trio of drunken sailors. The latter group slobbered over meat pies. Two men played darts in the corner; the bored publican read the paper.

Is that couple at the end of the bar looking at me?

He clenched the pint glass, relaxed his fingers, and squeezed again. As he repeated the motion, he timed it against his own heartbeat. The rhythm helped him think. Familiar patterns, precisely repeated, were necessary for ordered thought, and recently his had been fragmented. Sometimes words and images intruded into the back of his mind, and he couldn't shake the suspicion that he was being watched.

He reassured himself that it was only natural. MI5 was most certainly looking for his network of operatives, and even though the one-time ciphers were unbreakable, the disruption of leaving his shop for a last minute "holiday" would foul anyone's thinking. And, he reasoned, his highly ordered mind and precise hands needed the challenge of repairing timepieces. The withdrawal of his routine had dulled his normally precise calculations. An elite swordsman needed ceaseless development of his skills and meticulous care of his blade.

The watchmaker's thoughts would be back to normal when he'd taken care of this task and things had settled down enough for him to return to his shop. He pictured Father Time's display of clocks, each set to the exact same time; their second hands sweeping together. He could hear the delicate ticking of their controller wheels rocking back and forth. The ticking grew louder and he looked up from his beer.

The noise stopped. The watchmaker looked around the room with suspicion. There was an old ship's brass clock mounted above the bar, and he noted with disdain that it was several minutes slow. He ground his teeth. It couldn't have duplicated the noises of the clocks in his shop, which had been so clear a moment ago.

Perhaps MI5 is broadcasting the sound to play tricks on me, to flush me out.

He checked a different pocket watch and looked through the window again. Twilight had descended, making the sky indigo, and fat flakes of snow drifted down like ash against the faint light of the silvery, moonlit harbor and yellow dock lanterns. He'd been waiting in the pub too long.

They're watching you.

The door opened and closed. The watchmaker adjusted his focus to use the window pane as a mirror: he watched a large block of granite approach the bar; behind this man was a small, thinner man. He knew the larger one, Pyotr, from the embassy (former embassy, he corrected himself). His hands stopped their rhythmic clenching on the glass, and he drank the remaining beer. The watchmaker studied the new arrivals, wary for any signs that something might be amiss. Pyotr had a rucksack slung over his left shoulder and gripped a red log book in his right hand, which he set on the bar as he spoke with the publican. The small man hung back beside the front door and put his overcoat on one of the pegs as he glanced around the room.

The watchmaker stood and left his table, carrying the empty pint glass. He approached the bar and set his glass down, paused, then extracted his pocket watch and studied it. This was the signal that all was well; without making eye contact, he walked past Pyotr, retrieved his coat, and left the pub.

Despite the cold weather, the meeting would take place at the docks in exactly thirty minutes. He checked a different watch and walked toward the docks.

"People see you — they know!" The voice was so loud that it startled him, and he stumbled and fell to the ground. He looked around, but there was no one; the alleyway was deserted.

"I hold the truth! I can help you," the voice thundered in his head.

He turned again—

—and the voice said, "Time is Purity."

The watchmaker panted. The slick-cobbles dug into his back as the snow drifted down. The words were undeniable. *Time is Purity. Purity is Time.* And the voice was as clear as a bell. But could only the watchmaker hear it?

"Proteus must die."

The watchmaker then realized that this must be why Pyotr was here. He carried with him the order from Borya, and in twenty minutes he would learn the details of the plans. But there could be no negation of the power of the voice. After years of being a steward of time, he'd been chosen. The universe suddenly made sense, and the flash of insight was intoxicating.

Nothing must deviate from the pre-ordained. It has been willed. Order must prevail over chaos.

The watchmaker rose to his feet and, for the first time in memory, he didn't fear Pyotr.

I've been chosen.

49

"Look deep into nature, and then you will understand everything better."
~ Albert Einstein

In the morning, Proteus opened his eyes and listened to the wind in the trees outside the cottage. He heard a noise from the kitchen and rose from the couch to find Carys pouring hot water into a pot. She turned to look at him, standing silently. After a moment, she walked over to embrace him.

Proteus returned the hug. Her soft warmth was intoxicating. "I never want to let you go," he said.

"It seems so fantastic," she said.

"I want to be with you, always."

"Will the people from your time come after you?"

"I don't think so," said Proteus. "If I never return, they'll think me lost in time like the others. And if by some miracle the Earth is vibrant and healthy in the future, I'll likely be forgotten anyway."

Carys reached out and gently stroked Proteus's cheek. The touch made him tremble, and he leaned forward to kiss her.

"I want to help you stop the next war," said Gareth's voice from the doorway, and Proteus jumped.

"Father!"

"I've thought it through, based on what we heard last night, and I think I understand it pretty well," said Gareth. "I have a number of ideas on how we can undermine the Germans as they go down this National Socialist pathway — and disrupt the Soviets as well."

"I can't do anything about that. It's not why I'm here," said Proteus.

"You'll at least hear me out," said Gareth. His eyes fixed on Proteus, who understood he'd have to listen. Proteus hadn't expected this turn of events and saw no escape.

"I'll pour some tea and warm some scones," said Carys.

"Best grab the Jameson's as well," said Proteus.

Ψ

"I understand the Gordian Knot," said Gareth. Carys rose from her seat, stretched, and went into the kitchen. Their discussion had consumed the morning and half the bottle of whiskey, interrupted only by breakfast and short breaks, and now they were moving on to lunch.

"You push too hard, and Time's minions come after you," said Gareth. "Thus, you have to take baby steps. And that's why you can't just take a sniper rifle and kill this Hitler person, or Stalin, to stop the next war. But if you do nothing to stay safe from harm, then nothing about the disastrous future will change. Millions of people will die in a terrible war."

"It's true," said Proteus. Carys returned with a large plate of sandwiches and set it down in the middle of the table.

"You've agreed my ideas are good," said Gareth. "And that there is a way forward."

"In theory," said Proteus.

Carys sat down, picked up a sandwich, and observed their exchange.

"Then let me start," said Gareth. "Help me, with the information you have. Let's do this together."

"I can't," said Proteus. "It's best if we stay away from this topic until I'm finished with fission. I have too much innocent blood on my hands as it is. I care deeply about you, but I can't risk your lives with direct involvement in a new direction."

"Seems to me that's my choice," said Gareth. "And Carys's." He stood, and paced, and stopped at the mantle. Gareth reached out and picked up a red ribbon. He held it up and a metal cross swung from its end.

Proteus glanced at Carys, but her attention was fixed on her father.

"The Victoria Cross. *For most conspicuous bravery, a daring act of valor or self-sacrifice, or extreme devotion to duty in the presence of the enemy,*" said Gareth. "Hundreds of my lads died bravely in that war, and for what? You speak of innocent blood on your hands — I remember each and every one of their faces and will carry those memories to my grave. That I saved more from the same fate and turned the tide of battle won't bring back the dead.

"We believed what we were doing was just. But the things that kept most of us going were the mate by your side and thoughts of surviving to see loved ones back home, and the hope that our misery and sacrifice meant something.

"*The war to end all wars* — I knew it for the politicians' horse manure it was. Mankind is too barbaric, and there was no *happy back home* for us. I lost my wife, and I nearly lost my daughter and myself."

Gareth spun to point at Proteus. "And you bear this ... knowledge about what's about to come ... the madness of an even bigger world war, genocide, and these ... *nuclear weapons*, and tell *me* I can't help because it's too dangerous? To hell with that."

Proteus shrank back from the onslaught, and his mouth went dry. Gareth towered over him; his green eyes pinned Proteus to his seat.

"I ... um," he said. "I understand your logic, and I agree with you." Gareth remained motionless — staring and waiting. Proteus swallowed and continued, "I promise you we will plan together when I'm done with my mission."

"Aye, but aren't you leaving, then, when your work's done?" said Gareth.

"No," said Proteus and looked at Carys — and she met his eyes. "Not anymore. This is where I belong."

$$\Psi$$

In the afternoon, Proteus and Carys went for a stroll in the woods and along the trail to the pond they'd visited before. Gareth had gone down to the barn to attend to the horses and had taken Lucy with him.

The sun filtered through the trees and onto the trail, and Proteus smiled as the wind rustled the leaves. He adjusted his satchel and said, "I have such fond memories of this trail."

"Me too," said Carys, and laughed. "You asked about every plant and animal you saw, like an inquisitive child, and now I know why."

"And what do you think about it all now? About the future, and time travel, and me?"

Her expression changed, and she walked in silence for a while. Then she said, "Your time period is horribly tragic, and I can't believe you grew up in such a terrible place. I wouldn't be able to live like that." She swept her arm in an expansive gesture and continued, "This nature, all around us, flows in my soul — and I understand why it's so magical for you. It makes me profoundly sad that mankind will stumble and destroy it all. I'm glad you're here to prevent that."

They continued along the trail and arrived at the pond. Carys picked up a flat rock and skipped it across the water. Proteus laughed, and she skipped another.

"How delightful," he said.

"Ducks and drakes," said Carys, laughing. "Try it."

Proteus set his satchel down, puzzled over the ballistics of the projectile and the hydrodynamic properties of the surface of the water, and picked up a rock. He began explaining the physics to Carys, then turned, and threw. It plunked.

"No. Like this," said Carys and laughed again. "You've got to spin the stone. Flat ones work best." She showed her hand position on the stone and then flicked it. Her rock skipped four times before it sank.

After two more tries, Proteus's stone kissed the surface and hopped once. He jumped on the spot and cried, "I did it!"

The next thirty minutes were spent playing ducks and drakes.

When they'd finished, Proteus said, "Here, wait a second." He trotted to fetch his satchel. "I've one more for the pond," he said as he returned.

He held out the Retrieve-Unit with its flashing red light.

"What is that?"

"The device to summon me back," said Proteus. "Its power is fading."

Then Proteus flung it; it arced in the air above the pond — then splashed and sank. He watched the ripples widen and fade. The sunlight reflected off the water, blinding him; he blinked as he turned to Carys. He found her standing next to him, and they embraced.

50

"Welcome home, my husband," said Anne.

"Thank you, dear," said Erwin.

"How was your visit to Cambridge?"

"The English are a bit stuck-up, but I had some enlightening discussions. I believe that there are indeed some brilliant minds here at Oxford and Cambridge with whom one would expect to have lively conversations. But do you know, I had the most remarkable interaction with someone from a completely unexpected quarter. One of Rutherford's bench monkeys, the loud chaps that strut about while doing experiments with high-voltage equipment and radiation, muttered something that at first seemed utterly incomprehensible and completely unrelated to my wave equations and this quantum nonsense in Copenhagen. However, as I listened, he made me think of something positively brilliant. Not his intent, of course. He's probably still blathering about vacuum tubes and cloud chambers, but I had a stroke of genius."

"That's lovely," she said and stepped closer for a kiss.

"I have constructed the most remarkable idea for an experiment," said Schrödinger, and pecked her on the cheek. "Have you seen Fritz?"

"He was chasing rodents earlier, I think. Perhaps he's out back in the garden with Marie."

"Ah," said Schrödinger. "Thank you — I shall seek them out." He mounted the few steps to the cottage and went in by the front door. He strode through the entryway, past the kitchen, and through the back door to the garden.

"Hello, dear. How was your visit to Cambridge?" asked Marie, his mistress. She sauntered over and planted a big, wet kiss on his mouth, then curled an arm behind his back.

"Splendid," said Schrödinger as he looked around the back garden. "Have you seen Fritz?" He turned to peer under the rose bushes.

"He went over the fence just a moment ago. Hunting little mice, no doubt," said Marie, and then pouted her lower lip. "Why would you want that silly cat, anyway?"

"I need Fritzy because I've a brilliant idea for an experiment. Just a thought experiment, of course, but quite ingenious. I want to rub his belly, give him a treat, and tell him he's a good cat for inspiring me."

She reached up and gently stroked his earlobe in a way that made his spine tingle.

"Oh, yes. Quite right, my dear," said Schrödinger and coughed. He suddenly straightened. "I forgot my manners. Perhaps there's something we should attend to inside?"

She giggled, accepted his arm, and they strolled towards the back door. Erwin shot a look back over his shoulder one last time as he looked for Fritz, and then followed Marie inside the cottage.

Ψ

Dear Albert,

I have come up with the most incredible idea for a thought experiment.

First I put a vial of poison gas in a box, and then add an extremely sensitive Geiger counter. A hammer is poised above the vial, with a trip switch connected to the Geiger counter. The hammer will fall, smash the vial, and release the poison gas when it senses the gamma decay from the radioactive atom.

I then add a cat and seal it all up.

Whichever radioisotope you choose (and considering its corresponding half-life) at some point a gamma ray will fire off and the hammer will fall, releasing the gas and killing the imaginary cat.

According to the Copenhagen imbeciles, the radioactive atom exists, simultaneously, in two states — it hasn't yet decayed, and it has — until someone measures it. This means that the cat is both dead and alive at the same time, until I open the box and take a peek. How absurd. I wish I could see their faces as they try to philosophize their way around this one. I am quite certain they couldn't reason themselves out of a wet paper bag with a butcher's knife!

Isn't it positively brilliant? It's as absurd as buying your wife or mistress a present, wrapped up in a small box with a colorful ribbon, and declaring it could be anything from a lovely necklace to a lump of lead and that the present is still deciding until she opens it.

On another note, if I do accept the position at Oxford, I think that perhaps my cat Fritz could help with the mouse problem that you and Rutherford seem to be having. It's a kind offer to be a Fellow of Magdalen College at the University of Oxford, but my Irish-Austrian roots are waving a flag of caution because the English are strange people.

How were your travels to the California Institute of Technology? And New York? How are the Americans compared with the British? Your missive indicated that they are much more open to honest, critical thought, and less stuffy, but it's difficult to know from Vienna. I remain uncertain. For example, I recently learned that some cartoonist in America named Dusty or Dizzy has apparently been keenly following the experimental developments in Cavendish. Did you know that he has produced a short animated cartoon featuring a whistling mouse on a steamboat? Indeed, these are strange times. When a cartoonist feels bold enough to mock men of science, I wonder about the future of humanity. Every time I see the mouse posters, I think of your chalkboards.

This leads to my final topic. I grow increasingly concerned about the changes occurring in Germany. The National Socialists gaining political power have an unhealthy obsession with racial identity, and I fear the mob may come for you and I before too long.

Take care of yourself, my friend.

Erwin

51

"What the devil!" said Rutherford after reading the letter. His booming voice rattled the glassware in the lab; people studiously kept their heads down.

"The bloody Soviets can't bloody do this," he said, speaking to no one in particular. "Kapitsa has been ordered to stay in Moscow. One of my protégés is practically under house arrest. I won't allow it!" He stood and shook the letter above his head, as if he could force the letters into a better arrangement.

Everyone within earshot, which encompassed most of the people in the building, wanted to be someplace else.

Kapitsa is one of the brightest students I've ever had, thought Rutherford. *They think that by keeping him there they can gain the secrets of the atom for their own twisted purposes. Well, no good will come of it.* He reached into his pocket to grasp the pitchblende sample he carried everywhere. *Science can only advance through an open exchange of ideas. It can empower humanity to higher levels, but only if we work together to allow it to bloody happen. This nationalistic paranoia of the Soviets and the Germans will lead to more wars.*

"I need to write to Lord Kelvin," he said and reached into his jacket pocket. "Blast, I've lost me bloody pen again."

Mark Jenkins

52

Proteus, Carys, and Gareth sat at the dining room table in the great hall of Woodchester, eating Christmas Eve dinner, while an early winter storm began dropping its first snowflakes. The fire in the hearth crackled; Lucy sat in front of it, watching them for signs of a dropped morsel. The goose that Gareth had prepared was succulent and spiced with black pepper and herbs that he'd grown in his garden and was served with potatoes and carrots. Carys had promised a surprise for dessert.

The great hall was one of the few rooms not still cluttered with sawhorses, carpenters' tools, and stacks of timber. The new table was piled with plates full of food, or at least it had been half an hour ago. Now the plates were mostly empty. His full belly and the wine relaxed Proteus as he smiled and looked at Carys. The conversation had turned in many directions, but Proteus was most interested in hearing more about Carys's studies, and kept steering the discussion that way.

Suddenly, Lucy growled and stood, her hackles bristling.

"What is it, Lucy?" asked Gareth and rose from his seat to peer outside through the window. Lucy continued to growl and then paced back and forth at the front door.

"It's all right, Lucy," said Gareth. "I don't see anything."

Lucy's growl deepened, and she began to snarl.

A sound of breaking glass came from the adjacent library. Carys stood, and Proteus jumped, knocking his seat over. Gareth used hand signals to communicate that they should keep still and quiet. He began to move silently toward the library. Lucy followed her master.

An explosion shook the mansion.

Proteus's ears were ringing; his pulse hammered in his head.

Gareth staggered back toward them through a dust cloud. "Get under the table!"

Another explosion shook the building, smaller this time.

Proteus dove under the table as the glass of the windows burst inward. Pops of gunfire echoed. He looked to find Carys, then crawled toward her. Panting, he reached out a hand, and she gripped it. She stared at him, wide-eyed.

Bullets impacted the wall of the dining room.

Proteus shielded Carys with his arm and craned his head to locate Gareth. He saw Lucy first; both were sheltered in a deep corner of the room.

Gareth made eye contact and then yelled, "On my signal, keep low and follow me." He peered through the shattered window and paused, tilting his head.

"Now," he said and hunched as he ran toward the hallway. Lucy went next, and then Carys and Proteus followed. Another boom sounded, but from farther away.

In the hallway, Gareth halted them and said, "Carys, go upstairs to the telegraph, keep sending S-O-S — you've got ten minutes until the power is cut. Lucy, go with Carys!"

"Papa, I—"

"Hush!" said Gareth. "No time for talking — they'll breach the front door next. Go, quickly and quietly." He turned to face Proteus, and said, "Follow me, and then you're headed to the basement to the electricity board. Check your watch. In ten minutes, I want the power off." Proteus's heart hammered.

Carys went upstairs after Lucy, who was already at the first landing. Proteus wanted to rush after her to protect her. Loud thuds sounded against the door.

"Come," hissed Gareth. Proteus turned from watching Carys and then crept after Gareth down the hallway. At the stairs leading to the basement, Gareth motioned him over. "Time?"

Proteus hands shook as he checked his watch. "One minute," he said.

"Good — now go. And after the power's off, wait for me. I'll come for you." Then he turned and left. After he'd gone a few steps, Proteus could no longer hear Gareth.

He waited several heartbeats and then descended into the basement. The dim light bulbs were spaced far enough apart that darkness covered the steps between them. The walls pressed toward him.

Proteus put his hand on the cold stone and stood motionless, listening. His ears picked up footsteps in the distance, and he willed himself to descend. The infrared of the SDU would have been invaluable, but it was upstairs in his second-floor suite.

As he resumed moving downward, the walls in the stairwell narrowed. His throat tightened, and each step became harder than the last. Halfway down, he stopped. His heartbeat hammered in his ears, and he began to sweat. He reached for his pocket watch and almost dropped it. Seven minutes to go.

Come on — keep moving.

Ψ

Under a gentle snow, the watchmaker followed the arc of the grenade as it crashed through one of the massive windows and into Woodchester Mansion. Although he was at a safe distance, he pressed his fingertips into his ear canals as he waited for the explosion.

The entire window frame bowed outward; then it burst like a bubble, spraying glass shards.

The *crump* of the shock wave pulsed into his chest.

It saddened him that those assigned to him were of limited intellect and knew only one tool: the hammer. Their crude, imprecise tactics, while direct, were messy and invited complications. Although they were in a remote area in the Cotswolds on Christmas Eve, someone might hear and summon help.

Also, the explosions could make it harder to determine whether Earl Proteus was dead. It seemed unlikely that the fools would collapse the stone mansion entirely with their bombs and fire, but mangled bodies were sometimes difficult to identify — and he required certainty.

And that was the only thing that mattered. It had been commanded: Proteus must die.

The divine voice spoke to him again, and he marveled at the clarity and wisdom of the words. He knew in the marrow of his bones that it was God. An electric shiver passed through him at the thought.

He watched another grenade arc into the mansion and sighed. The fact that these were the only louts Moscow could arrange for him set his teeth on edge. In his earlier years, he could have entered the mansion and slit all the occupants' throats without a sound; but he was long past those years now.

Any moron can toss a Molotov, but ordered thought and precision are the foundations of a disciplined mind.

And Time is exacting.

And beautiful.

And God has chosen me.

One side of the barn briefly flared yellow as a petrol bomb exploded. The watchmaker saw muzzle flashes and heard the pops of rifle fire. He limped forward on his cane toward the mansion, thankful the grenades had stopped. The mansion was an ugly, Gothic-revival architectural design, but it deserved a better fate. Perhaps one single large implosion rather than these superficial bullets and bombs.

He limped closer and saw his troops battering at the front door with sledgehammers. To the left, a fire had begun to grow on the wall of the barn, and more rifle shots sounded. The people inside the mansion were penned in, yet the wolves of chaos snapped at him.

Order must prevail. Find him and kill him.

He'd seen no response from within the mansion — and that worried him. Proteus was either alive or dead, but he needed certainty. Then he thought about finding him half-dead and torturing information from him; he smiled. He limped toward Woodchester's entrance, where his louts were still hammering away. He wondered if the front door was thicker than their heads.

Ψ

Rifles and grenades, thought Gareth as he stalked toward the back entrance. *These bastards are attacking Woodchester with rifles and grenades. No one threatens my family.*

His mind dove into the tactics he should use. The size of the force was unknown, but they possessed military weapons, and his firearms were up at the stone cottage. His current advantage was that he knew the terrain and the interior of the mansion like the scars on the backs of his hands.

He checked his watch. Six minutes until the power would go off; hopefully enough time for Carys. *The darkness and construction clutter will hinder them, but I need time, weapons, and luck.*

Gods above. I'll hunt these bastards down.

Gareth turned off from the hallway and into the kitchens. He strode to the mantelpiece and retrieved his cavalry sword from its mounting above the hearth. Sliding the oiled 1912 pattern from its scabbard, he glanced at the thin, straight blade; red embers from the hearth reflected in the steel.

Not my family.

Gareth stepped back out into the hallway. Footsteps and hushed whispers echoed from the front of the building, where he'd been eating dinner only minutes earlier.

He stalked toward the rear exit and then saw a sickly yellow light cast upon one side of the stone corridor. As he got closer, he saw it was coming through the windows of the back door to the kitchens. Then his heart caught in his throat.

The barn was on fire. *My horses!*

He kicked open the door.

Instinct warned him that he was one step from a killing field — and he spun back to dive deeper in the hallway as rifles cracked and bullets impacted the entryway.

Gareth rolled onto his feet and bolted from the hallway into the antechamber of the chapel. More rifle fire sounded and rounds hit the walls behind him.

He held his sword up, squeezed past a pile of stacked timbers to enter the chapel, and hurried toward the pulpit and stained-glass window at the far end, stepping around ladders and scaffolding and over piles of stone, mortar, and tools.

The pillars and peaked archways flew past as he thought of his horses.

At the front of the chapel, Gareth entered a small corridor leading outside. As he opened the door, a man holding a rifle appeared, scarcely six feet away. Gareth lunged and impaled him in the throat. The rifle fired twice, but Gareth had already pushed the barrel aside. He hugged the man close with his left arm as his right hand twisted the sword.

He pulled his sword free and let the body collapse; then he turned to look at the barn. Flames were licking upward along one wall, and he could hear his horses squealing in terror. He also heard the shouts of men in Russian.

Gareth held the blade in front of him, tip first, then took a deep breath. *Speed is of the essence.* He breathed again and then sprinted in the shadows of the burning barn. He saw a silhouette against the blaze, firing a rifle into the mansion, and veered toward it.

A moment later, Gareth's sword burst through the man's chest. He spun to free the blade and continued his charge.

He flung one of the barn doors wide open and stalked inside. One wall glowed with heat, and smoke was beginning to fill the air, but nothing inside was yet on fire. Gareth went to each stall and began to free his horses: the first two galloped out of the barn, toward the hill, but the third, the roan, reared in fear and wouldn't calm. The way was clear but the roan was spooked.

A chill went along Gareth's spine, warning him, and he pivoted 180 degrees. Illuminated by the glow was a giant of a man headed toward him from the other end of the barn. Gareth yelled at the roan to go —

— and lost sight of the giant.

The roan bucked and stomped and then ran from the barn.

Gareth held his sword poised to thrust and paced in a slow circle, trying to locate the man. His ears warned him too late as the giant tackled him, pinning his sword arm against his side, and slammed him to the floor.

The man circled around to try to grasp Gareth's neck from behind. Gareth released the sword, rotated toward his opponent, and countered the impending chokehold. They were now face to face. The giant's right arm wrapped around the back of Gareth's neck, and the crook of the elbow gripped like a vice. The other arm circled around Gareth's back.

Gareth's left arm was trapped, but his right forearm pressed into the man's neck, under the jaw. For the moment they were locked in a stalemate. Cold grey eyes bored into Gareth's — and the giant grunted a word: "Death."

The smoke in the barn burned Gareth's eyes, and flames flickered on the barn wall. The man was huge and much more powerful than Gareth. The giant snarled, revealing brown teeth, and squeezed harder. Suddenly the weight shifted as the man maneuvered to wrap his massive legs around Gareth's waist — and began crushing him.

Gareth planted his right foot on the floor and thrust his hips up, creating a small gap between their torsos. During this brief separation, he freed his left arm and drove it up to cross over his right. Both forearms were now pressed against his opponent's throat like a pair of scissors.

The giant pulled Gareth close and resumed squeezing with all four limbs. Gareth struggled to breathe; his vision blurred red.

He grunted as he forced his forearm-scissors deeper into the giant's larynx. The man's face contorted into a grimace and turned purple. Gareth pushed with all his might, his arms shaking with fatigue.

Suddenly, the giant released his grip and rolled away.

A flaming timber crashed to the floor as the conflagration intensified; smoke filled the barn. Gareth leapt to his feet, and the giant faced him from ten paces away. Gareth's eyes darted to his sword on the floor behind the man, but the giant must have seen his eyes shift, because he glanced down — and then turned back to Gareth. The bald head reflected the yellow of the fire, and he gave his brown-toothed rictus smile as he stepped backward and slowly squatted to retrieve the blade.

Gareth backed into one of the stalls.

The man's dark frame approached the stall entrance, backlit by the blaze. He held the sword over his head like a club. *He doesn't understand the weapon*, thought Gareth still backing away. His hands closed on the shaft of a pitchfork.

The giant took one step forward, then another. He was still grinning.

As he raised his arm higher to strike, Gareth lunged forward and drove the tines of the pitchfork into the giant's face and neck — then leapt to one side to avoid the descending sword.

The blow missed, and the giant turned towards him, spraying blood.

The giant stumbled to one knee and pointed the sword at Gareth. *Death*, he mouthed — then he swayed, dropped the sword, and fell to the ground.

"You bloody bastard!" said Gareth.

More timbers crashed around him.

He bent to retrieve his sword and leapt over the man. Dodging the flames, he coughed and choked his way toward the open door. A crash sounded above, and the roof collapsed as Gareth dove forward.

$$\Psi$$

Carys sat down in front of the telegraphy terminal and switched it on. She checked her wristwatch. It had been four minutes since they'd separated. She adjusted several switches and then began tapping on the Morse key: dot dot dot; dash dash dash; dot dot dot; then the code for Woodchester, and the words *under assault*. Then she repeated the entire SOS. Her key finger flew with certainty, but fear clutched her chest, and she could take only short, panting breaths.

Lucy stood guard just inside in the communications room facing toward the second-floor hallway, her ears perked forward and her tail stiff.

Carys tapped the message for the tenth time, and glanced at her wristwatch. Only a minute to go until Proteus cut the power. Her finger cramped in pain as she tapped faster.

The lights went out and the telegraphy unit went dead.

She sat in darkness and tried to slow her breathing. She heard Lucy's paws on the stone as she approached Carys, who reached out for the dog to lick her hand. Carys put her hand on Lucy's neck and bent close. "Stay with me, please," she whispered.

Carys couldn't risk a candle or electric torch, so she listened carefully. She shivered, and wondered about her father. The rifle shots had stopped, and she feared what that meant. Her eyes adjusted to the darkness, and in the feeble light coming through the window she could make out the dark rectangle of the doorway.

Distant voices and regular footsteps echoed from the threshold.

They're coming up the stairs.

Lucy could see much better than any human in this light, so Carys pulled her close and slipped her fingers under the collar. "Upstairs," she whispered and stood to allow Lucy to lead her into the hallway.

Her fears were confirmed as she saw lights playing off the walls of the stairwell to the first floor. There was a loud crash, and Lucy tensed. The footstep stopped, but then voices rose in argument.

Carys whispered to Lucy, and they headed for the stairs to the third floor. Carys explored each step carefully with the tip of her boot as she and Lucy ascended. At the top, she had to remind herself that there was no banister. The renovations on the third floor were still in progress, and the area was replete with hazards in full daylight; in darkness it was a minefield. Lucy led her on, and they moved along the hallway at a timid pace, careful to avoid the scaffolding and the piles of stone without making any sound.

Carys thought of the men pursuing her; she could hear them now on the second floor. Her heart pounded, and she strained to pick out the sounds in the dark. She knew Lucy must hear them too, and marveled at the dog's discipline to keep silent.

A light beam snapped on, and a man's voice said, "Stop! Don't move!"

Carys flinched and spun to see a man with an electric torch in one hand and a pistol in the other.

"Hands up!"

She raised her arms slowly and looked down for Lucy but found her gone.

"Where is the earl?" said the man.

"I ... don't know," said Carys. She began to tremble.

"You will come with me downstairs, and we will find him together, yes?" he said and then waved the gun. "Move!"

Carys walked in the direction he pointed, back toward the stairs, and he pivoted to keep her in the torchlight. She heard his steps behind her and a faint growl from the darkness.

The pistol fired — and a scream pierced the air. Carys spun, and her eyes followed the electric torch as it hit the floor. Crimson mist sprayed into the beam, and she saw the man enter the light as he was jerked about like a rag doll.

Lucy's jaws were latched onto his wrist.

He screamed again and dropped the gun as Lucy wrenched his right arm from side to side. The man pushed at Lucy's head with his left hand. Lucy released her jaws — and then quickly grabbed his left wrist and resumed yanking.

Carys picked up a piece of metal scaffolding and swung it at the man's head.

The shaft bucked and vibrated in her hands like the impact of a solid polo mallet strike. The man collapsed.

Lucy released her grip. Carys ran to the torch and called Lucy over. She played the beam on the man, who was motionless and bleeding severely from his mangled forearms.

Carys pulled Lucy close and checked her for injuries but couldn't find any. "You're a very brave girl," she said, hugging the dog around her neck.

The man moaned, and Carys directed the beam at him again. Then she saw the pistol on the floor and went to retrieve it. It was unlikely he'd be able to use it, but she wanted to leave nothing to chance.

"Lucy, let's go," she said and moved toward the stairway. When she got there, she flicked the torch off and listened for sounds from below.

After a few moments of silence, she crept down the stairs. She moved carefully along the hallway of the second floor and then jumped when she heard pops of gunfire from deeper within the mansion, and then another shot. She held on to Lucy's collar and moved toward the set of stairs leading to the first floor.

Ψ

Proteus stood in complete darkness next to the fuse box. It had been a minute since he'd turned off the power, and Gareth had told him to wait for his return, but the sounds of rifle shots outside and the footsteps echoing in the halls above, were too much to bear. Carys was up there.

Even in pitch blackness, Proteus found his eyes had adjusted enough that he could see the rough shapes of doorways. He began to retrace his steps slowly, moving faster as his anxiety rose. Arriving at the bottom of the staircase, he heard gunshots and a man's scream from upstairs. He started up the steps. The scream echoed again, and then there was silence.

At the top of the stairs, Proteus paused and listened. A shuffling sound attracted his attention, and he saw a dark figure move around a corner. He followed and entered the chapel. There was an eerie yellow glow coming through windows along one side, and Proteus realized that the barn was on fire. Mindful of the scaffolding and masonry materials that lined the pointed arches and vaulted columns inside the central chamber, he moved slowly forward and scanned for the man who'd limped in here moments ago.

The stained-glass window behind the altar began to glow with moonlight as the cloud cover thinned. Then a man wearing all black stepped from the shadows behind the altar.

Proteus hesitated.

A shiver passed through him, and he spun back toward the entrance to see a man raise a rifle to his shoulder and aim.

Proteus dove into a side chamber as the rifle barked twice — rounds cracked into the limestone column where'd he been standing. He crouched, keeping a stone column between him and the rifleman.

"Stop!"

The voice reverberated around the stone chamber. Proteus turned to look at the man in black in front of the stained-glass widow.

"Order and Time must prevail," said the man. "It has been willed by God."

The stained-glass window brightened further; the man limped forward into the moonlight streaming through. He wore a black homburg, and his midnight cape hung almost to the floor. In the light from the circle of the rose window, the man cast an indigo, halo-clad shadow on the floor of the chapel.

"You are a changeling — a hell-spawn of chaos," said the man.

Proteus heard the sound of the rifleman's feet stepping softly and moved backward into the shadows. He removed his boots silently as he struggled to understand what the man was saying. After a moment, he said, "Who are you?"

"You don't know me?" exclaimed the man. "Interesting. Yet I know so much about you. And that brings up an interesting question. Is the leopard blind to its hunters? Can the leopard only see prey?"

"I don't understand," said Proteus. His heart hammered as he thought of Carys.

"Let me help, then," said the man. "I have four words. Svetlana. Vauxhall. Conrad. Boom." He chuckled. "I am the Watchmaker, Guardian of Time, and you have been judged a heretic of Time!" The man in black stepped forward and raised a long-barreled pistol. "There is no escape."

Proteus snarled.

His ears caught the light footsteps of the rifleman creeping closer, and he padded towards him, keeping a column interposed between them. Proteus's eyes darted to the heavy scaffolding structure extending to the ceiling and the stones on its platforms.

"I wonder if Conrad felt anything," said the Watchmaker. "Or did he just go poof? Funny how we never know when it's our time."

Proteus judged the distance to the structure, and when he saw the rifle barrel emerge from behind the column, he leapt.

As he landed, he yanked the lowest portion of the scaffolding toward him. The segment broke free, and Proteus rolled behind the column as the Watchmaker's pistol fired.

He turned to see the upper fifteen feet of the scaffolding collapse, burying the rifleman. Something burned in his thigh, and he reached down to feel wetness. He put his fingers to his mouth — and tasted his own blood.

"And then a clumsy lout died, leaving just us two," said the Watchmaker. "The fledgling chaos of Nature. And the enduring order of Time."

Proteus heard a sound of stumbling and calculated the Watchmaker's location. He pressed a palm against the wound that had creased his thigh like a knife slash.

"Whom do you imagine will win?" asked the Watchmaker.

Proteus crept in the deep shadows, behind the columns, drawing closer to the voice.

"You see, in the end it's futile, because everything becomes extinct. You, me, this planet. We all die. And there's nothing you can do to change that. You don't belong in this time. The past is immutable."

Proteus sprinted, then leapt — and grabbed the Watchmaker's long cloak as he slid behind him on the floor. The Watchmaker turned to aim the pistol; Proteus yanked hard as he landed in a crouch.

The Watchmaker spun off balance and fell backward. A crack sounded as the back of his skull hit the edge of the marble altar. His pistol fired into a column, and he collapsed in convulsions.

Proteus rose; he stepped on the Watchmaker's wrist and removed the pistol from the twitching hand. He knelt to look at the Watchmaker's face and saw he was struggling to breathe. The convulsions had stopped and the Watchmaker lay still, eyes locked on Proteus.

He wasn't breathing. Proteus could see the realization mounting in the man's eyes as he slowly asphyxiated.

"Your neck is broken," said Proteus. "Soon, the shock will fade and you will be at peace." He leaned in close. "I do belong here in this time. Nature is with me — just as Time is now against you."

Proteus turned and ran out of the chapel, looking for Carys.

Ψ

Gareth opened his eyes. A stone building was tilted sideways, and smoke drifted across his field of vision, stinging his eyes. He tried to remember what had happened and reached for his gas mask. Panic gripped him. *My mask is gone!* Something heavy was on his back, and he lifted his head to see several large, broken timbers. *A German artillery bombardment ... the bunker's collapsed ...*

I ... must ... see to my troops.

He pushed the wood beams, pulled himself along a few inches, and then repeated this action until he was clear. Metal glinted in the dirt, reflecting the light of the fire behind him. Gareth crawled on all fours toward his sword, and grabbed it — and then stood slowly. He staggered as he looked in a slow circle, surveying the battle area and looking for his men. It was strangely quiet.

Two figures emerged from the darkness ahead and converged on him. He held up the tip of his sword.

"Papa? Papa!"

He lowered the weapon. "Carys?" *Why is she on the battlefield?*

His vision swam — and the stone building shifted and blurred to become Woodchester Mansion. Carys appeared and hugged Gareth. He trembled and his ears buzzed. The fog lifted from his senses, and he squeezed her tight. The memory of Christmas dinner and the attack flooded back—

"Are you hurt, lass?" His voice sounded loud in his head.

"No, Papa," she said. "You're injured!" Then he heard her gasp. "The horses—"

Gareth spun to look at the barn. "I got them out," he said.

"Gareth, let me help," said Proteus, and he felt the shorter man's strong grip and shoulder to help prop him up. "Let's get you inside."

"Yes," said Gareth and looked again at the smoking ruins of the barn. "Bloody bastards!"

53

Captain Hopkins, the head of Gloucestershire County Constabulary, couldn't believe the reports coming in. There had been some sort of attack on an estate near Nympsfield, and on Christmas morning to boot. He'd been disturbed in the wee hours of the morning by a call from Scotland Yard in London, which had received an SOS and had sent constables out to investigate.

The report back from his constables had been stunning: there were seven dead bodies at the scene. Thankfully, none of corpses were residents of the estate, who had somehow fought off a paramilitary group armed with Molotov cocktails, rifles, and grenades. Who these people were, and why they were attacking the estate, was a complete mystery.

His lieutenant interrupted his thoughts, handing him another dispatch. Circling buzzards had alerted the constables, and with help of the townsfolk they had discovered the remains of three more of the paramilitary group in the hills around the estate, apparently ripped apart by wolves.

The entire thing was too ghastly to comprehend.

"Get my car ready, we're going down there to take a look," the captain said to his lieutenant.

Ψ

In the cottage, Gareth dozed on the couch by the fire. Carys and Proteus were talking quietly at the table over a pot of tea. Earlier, in the mansion, they'd checked Gareth for more serious injuries, and after bandaging the nicks and cuts, they had helped him up the trail to the cottage. Gareth tried unsuccessfully to shoo them away, insisting he'd been through much worse — which was true — but Proteus could see he'd been through hell. Large areas on his back were swollen and already turning purple, and Proteus was amazed his spine wasn't shattered by the roof collapse.

Proteus consulted the first-aid instructions on the SDU, which had, amongst other things, recommended a large increase in fluids for Gareth to help flush the proteins released by the damaged muscles out of his system. He and Carys had taken turns filling his cup until Gareth had fussed at them and then fallen asleep. When he started snoring, Lucy had curled up on the floor to guard her master.

Then it was Proteus's turn, and he too tried to minimize his injury. The superficial bullet crease on his thigh had stopped bleeding hours ago, but Carys was insistent until he gave in and let her dress the wound.

One of the farmers from down the road had helped round up Gareth's horses and was taking care of them. The police were combing through the estate, gathering evidence and removing the corpses. There wasn't much else for Carys and Proteus to do at present, so the conversation turned to the future.

"So what happens now?" said Carys. "Is that the last of them?"

"I hope so, but I don't know," said Proteus. "I thought we were done before, but this entire Time-resistance thing is convoluted."

"You're a master of understatement," said Carys.

"I think I'm at least a full professor of understatement," said Proteus. "And speaking of which, I think I should keep a very low profile, and you should bury yourself in your doctorate studies. I have a lot of work with Gareth, when he recovers, to repair the mansion and build a new barn. And once we get a full array of telecommunications gear set up, I'll be able to monitor the work in Providence remotely."

Carys stood and walked around the table to stand in front of him.

He looked up into her eyes. "You said bury," she said. "I think we should bury ourselves in each other's arms for a bit."

54

Dear Albert,

I am grateful to be out from the midst of the deranged National Socialists and am quite appreciative of the Fellowship at Oxford. And, of course, learning that I was to be awarded the Nobel Prize along with Paul Dirac was incredible.

However, since then, all has not been well. I've been disinvited from Oxford. Booted, I believe, is the term. Not because of academic strife or conflict about our theories, mind you.

Indeed, my colleagues and I are having the most inspiring conversations, although they can be as snooty as you warned me. The Oxford elite are quite distrustful of anyone who didn't cut their academic teeth on the Oxford bread. And I've discovered that the same holds true in Cambridge.

How do you tolerate their xenophobia? Aren't we all scientists trying to discover the truth?

No. I've been asked to leave because of my domestic situation — and this is none of their damn concern. I live with my wife and my mistress. That is fact. And this is the heartfelt wish of Anne and Marie as well.

What is wrong with the British? I'm a prominent international theorist, not some crazed Viennese pimp.

If I may explain in a different vein. My work with you, by correspondence, *on the unified field theory centers around understanding and uniting three things: gravity, electromagnetism, and atomic forces (weak and strong).*

I see my life in exactly these terms. The three forces must live together harmoniously. If we're to hope to understand the complex relationships within the universe and model them into equations, then all three parts must be considered thoroughly. A balanced, unified three-part structure, as are Anne, Marie, and I.

It makes sense, does it not?

In any event, I am departing Oxford in a fortnight.

I cannot return to Austria. The National Socialists are initiating a clampdown, and censoring or expelling those of our ethnicity. All our livelihoods are in jeopardy, I fear.

Hitler's ideas of purity are as sickening as the ever more deadly chemical weapons that Fritz Haber and Otto Hahn cooked up during the war.

And did you know that Hahn is now probing into the atom? It gives me chills, Alfred. Nothing good will come of it.

You were right to leave Germany when you did. I was saddened to learn that they'd raided your property and stolen your sailboat, Porpoise. The times we spent on the water were very relaxing. For me there has always been something soothing about waves.

Perhaps this Princeton that you talk about so much would be a good fit for me. I'll contact them as you've suggested.

I wish you good health.

Your eternal friend,

Erwin

55

In his London office, Proteus unfolded the July 5, 1934 edition of the *Times* to the international section and scanned the headlines:

America Celebrates Independence Day;

Jordanians Revolt in Amsterdam;

Madame Curie Dies: Famed Nobel Prize winner succumbs to illness in Paris;

Hungarian Physicist Szilard Missing.

Proteus turned to the article on Marie Curie, and after reading it, he folded the paper on his desk. *If only they'd known the health and societal dangers beforehand.*

Proteus reached into the top drawer of his desk, retrieved the letter he'd composed, and rang for Freda.

"You called for me, sir," she said from the doorway.

"Yes. Please send this to the French minister of health," said Proteus and handed her the letter.

If he ignores me, I have another one for the press.

Ψ

"*Mon Dieu!*" said the minister and set the telegram down. His office in the French ministry of health had a lovely view of the Seine, and he rose to look out the windows as he contemplated the message. It was from the same Royal Society member in England who'd been hounding him with letters and phone calls for weeks — he was obsessed with the Radium Institute. But something niggled at the minister. *Could it be true?*

A knock came at the door.

"*Oui!*"

His chief adjutant entered. "Sorry to disturb you, but there is a reporter from Paris-soir here to speak with you."

"I've no time at present, Leopold. Ask him to schedule an appointment with the undersecretary," said the minister.

"He said this might convince you to meet with him," said Leopold and held out a scrap of paper that appeared to be torn from a notebook. The minister accepted it, and the adjutant stood motionless, eyebrows raised, as the minister adjusted his glasses to read the note:

Tomorrow's Headline: Poisonings in Paris. Children near Radium Institute sickened.

You may speak with me now or after the paper goes out tomorrow morning.

The minister felt sick. He looked at the telegram in his left hand and back to the reporter's note in his right. *How?*

"Show him in, please," said the minister and buried his face in his hands as the adjutant left.

Moments later, Leopold returned with the reporter.

"Thank you for seeing me on such short notice, Minister. I shall not trouble you for long, but I wish for a statement from the ministry of health about the clusters of sick children around Madame Curie's laboratory. I first began investigating a series of reports of unusual illness in children in the Latin Quarter months ago, when my niece became ill. And I've spoken with several parents whose children also became mysteriously ill. Tragically, some of the children have died.

"At the parents' insistence, I've spoken with the physicians caring for the children. The doctors report a ..." He stopped to consult his notebook. "... a malady of the blood and bone marrow, which they say is rare but not unheard of." He closed his notebook and looked at the minister. "What is unheard of, however, is the occurrence of so many cases so close together in time and place. And, of course, this made me think that there may be something more than random chance." He paused, waiting.

The minister stared at him.

The reporter cleared his throat, pulled out a map, and began to unfold it. "I've plotted out where the children live and play, and behold!" He handed over the map.

The minister recognized the streets of the Latin Quarter, and his eyes were drawn to a series of concentric circles centered on the Radium Institute. Yellow and red dots were clustered within the circles. The minister looked at the reporter and said, "And?"

"The red dots are deceased children, and the yellow dots represent the sick ones. You'll notice that—"

"Yes, I can read a map."

"—I've also put a time and date on this copy, in case some of the sickened children die or new illnesses develop."

"All the same illness!" said the minister. "How?" He sat in his chair and ran his fingers through his receding hairline, trying to clear his thoughts. After several moments he looked up at his adjutant. He opened his mouth and took in a breath—

"There's a theory," interrupted the reporter; both men turned to look at him. "I've been in communication with a colleague in England and learned of a Royal Society member who's been looking into clusters of illnesses in, or near, places where radioactive materials are used."

At the mention of the Royal Society, the minister became ill. *The communications — everything he said is true.*

"I've exchanged several letters with Earl Proteus and have learned the most remarkable things. For example, there have been scores of women workers made sick — and over a dozen deaths — at a factory in the US that paints watch dials with radio-luminescent paint. And guess what's in the paint?"

"Radium," said Leopold.

"*Exactly!*" said the reporter. "I learned there have also been unusual illnesses in and around a physics laboratory in Cambridge, England — and did you know that the Radium Institute has been sending them radioactive elements for decades?" He paused; his gaze flicked between the minister and the adjutant, as if trying to stare them both down at the same time.

The adjutant sat down. The minister's nausea worsened, and he became faint.

The reporter said, "Earl Proteus has suggested the widespread use of a new, advanced Geiger counter as a way to investigate our outbreak. And has offered help. What is the minister's response? What should we add to our story?"

"I've been there many ..." The minister paused. *This is what I feared when I first heard of the wonders of radioactivity.* "You may quote me as saying that this office will investigate fully. I will have more information for you tomorrow, and my adjutant will help you schedule an appointment. Now you must excuse me, for I must get to the bottom of this."

After the reporter left the office, the minister looked at the polished wooden box of the table-phone on his desk. He sat unmoving for several minutes, then picked up the handset and spun the crank on the side. "Connect me to the president's office," he said into the mouthpiece.

$$\Psi$$

Antonin Bertrand, director of the Radium Institute, Université de Paris, looked up from his work distracted by the voices arguing outside his office. He rose from his desk and took a step toward the door when it suddenly banged open and a short man strode in, waving a document.

"I am Leopold de Qúervin, chief adjutant to the minister of health. You are hereby ordered to cease all operations within this institute," announced the man. He tossed the paper he'd been waving onto the desk and glared at Director Bertrand.

Bertrand's secretary arrived on de Qúervin's heels, and she pointed a finger at him. "I tried to get him to make an appointment," she said. "But he would *not* listen."

"What's all this about?" asked Director Bertrand. His eyes caught the seal of the office of the president on the document as he picked it up and began reading.

"It's all there, Monsieur Director," said de Qúervin before Bertrand had finished reading. "You are to cease operations at once."

"I report to the ministry of education, not the ministry of health. Perhaps you are in the wrong building, no?"

"You'll note the president's seal and signature at the bottom."

Director Bertrand reread the document and studied the official seal. "It appears authentic, but there must be some mistake," he said. "I must check with the university." He was going to say more but was interrupted by a burbling sound from outside the building.

He went to the window and looked down onto the street to see a score of people on the street below. Some held signs, and more were joining from the ends of the street and the alleyway. He spun to look at de Qúervin and then his secretary. "What is happening?"

Both joined him at the window and looked at the gathering crowd.

The secretary gasped and put a hand to cover her mouth. "That sign: *Murderers!*"

"What do they want?" asked Director Bertrand.

Below, a woman began chanting; she repeated her phrase, and then others joined in.

The office was silent as they all listened.

"Justice for the children," said the secretary.

"They were outside the president's office earlier," said de Qúervin. "They're angry at the deaths of their children, and they blame radiation from this institute."

"Impossible! Radiation is safe," said Director Bertrand. "I'll go down there and tell them in person. Superstitious peasants."

Something banged the window next to his head, and he jumped in alarm. "They're throwing stones—"

"That's also another excellent reason to follow the president's order. Stop all operations now," said de Qúervin. "For the health of France." He leaned close and whispered, "I was at the meeting. The president is concerned about riots and doesn't need further tinder ignited. My God, children have died! You will comply, and I will tell this crowd that you have stopped work."

Director Bertrand knew he had no choice. He nodded.

$$\Psi$$

"I'm sorry but I think this is the best option," said the provost.

"But I've no interest in going on sabbatical," said Rutherford. "You told me — in writing, I might add — that if I could raise sufficient funds to purchase purified radioactive elements from the Radium Institute, I could restart my work, and I've done it."

"Yes, but there's a problem."

"Don't you dare try to back away from your word," said Rutherford. "I've got your letter right here." He began rifling through the mess on his desk. He dove deeper and began organizing piles of paper into strata based upon age, as though it were a geological filing system.

The provost cleared his throat.

"I've almost found it," said Rutherford.

"The letter isn't the issue," said the provost and sighed. "Look, Ernest, your previous work and Nobel Prize are remarkable achievements. Then, when the Great War broke out, you answered your country's call and put aside the atom to work tooth and nail on the antisubmarine detection system that saved so many lives. Without your sacrifice, the Jerry U-boats would've sunk our island."

"Blast! I can't find it," said Rutherford.

"Ernest!" said the Provost. "Listen to me."

"Well, there's no need to shout," said Rutherford. "I hear you fine — but you're talking about the past, and I'm thinking of the future. We're on the cusp of understanding the inner workings of the atom. The energy is there, within that atom. *Power*, as Einstein has theorized — and I've demonstrated — is there. We can split a proton off the atom, but there's more there, so much more. I'm certain there's a dense neutral particle in the nucleus. And the heavier atoms hold the key." He reached into his pocket, pulled out his pitchblende talisman, and began tossing it in the air. "Right here in these atoms."

"What is that?"

Rutherford scowled at the reminder that the head faculty administrator in front of him was a mathematician; someone who didn't get his hands dirty with experiments. "This is pitchblende, the raw material for radium, thorium, and uranium," he said. "This is where the future lies."

A strange expression appeared on the provost's face, and he backed slowly to the door. "I wouldn't play with that so much if I were you," he said.

Rutherford laughed. "Why? Are you afraid?"

"That's the other reason I'm here."

Knives stabbed into Rutherford's belly; he gasped and dropped the pitchblende. He panted short breaths, and the pain faded, as it had every time before.

He coughed and bent to retrieve his talisman. "And what would that be, then? Beyond the shortsightedness you've already demonstrated. I've raised the funds to buy the radioactive elements."

"There won't be any more *elements* for a while."

"Marie Curie's death, God rest her soul, won't stop the wheels of science, and she wouldn't have wanted it to," said Rutherford. "The Institute continues, and her daughter, Irène, follows in her footsteps."

"If you would just stop and listen," said the provost. "The news I have from the University of Paris is dreadful. Children have become ill and died from exposure to radium, and it's also what killed Madame Curie."

Rutherford went to his desk and sat down heavily as the provost began telling him about illnesses in Paris and the sickened and dead workers in America.

"My God, is this true? It's horrible," said Rutherford after the provost had finished his story. He coughed, and then another round of pain gripped his guts. After it had passed, he said, "What should I do?"

"Take the sabbatical at the University of Birmingham. They're doing remarkable work with radio waves — trying to use them to calculate the precise velocity and position of aeroplanes in the sky and ships at sea. They'll pay a generous salary. It's just your cup of tea. And while you're there, we'll look into this radiation issue. I've met with a sharp lad in the Royal Society named Proteus who seems to know a great deal about illness from radiation and has offered to help."

"Proteus, hmm?" Said Rutherford. "Haven't met him."

"American," said the Provost. "But he seems trustworthy and doesn't talk all the time like some of them."

56

August 1934

Big Ben chimed six, and Proteus looked out over the Thames from his favorite spot by the window in the Providence communications room. The last of the employees had gone home for the day. Carys was seated at one of the desks, reading a report, and music played on the radio. The summer sun glinted off the river, clouds gathered on the horizon, and the open window allowed in a cool breeze, along with the sounds of the street below.

Proteus thought of his childhood dreams and where they'd ultimately led. He shook his head and then smiled as he remembered the first time he'd met Conrad, and the Mark Twain quote he'd recited: *"The two most important days in your life are the day you are born and the day you find out why."*

"This is great news," said Carys, interrupting his musings. "Rutherford's gone on sabbatical."

At the magic of her voice, Proteus smiled. *We're two years beyond the previous timeline for the discovery of the neutron.*

"Yes, it is," he said and after a moment added, "They'll resume, but hopefully the gap between their comprehension of the atom's dangers and lure of its mysteries will have narrowed — and they won't go rushing headlong after its powers."

"So what's next?"

"Well, Carys," said Proteus. "Or should I call you *Doctor* Carys?"

"Only if you want me to start calling you *Lord* Proteus," said Carys and laughed.

Proteus winked at her and walked over to the desk. Outside, the clouds built and the sky darkened with an approaching storm. "Well, I have to continue helping with the radiation cleanup in Paris and Cambridge, we have a wedding to plan, and I've a promise to keep to your father about trying to head off the next war."

"Wait ... did you say wedding?"

"Yes. How does *Lady* Proteus sound?"

Carys rolled her eyes and then laughed again. She popped up from her chair and gave him a long kiss. "I think it sounds marvelous," she said as their lips parted.

Lightning flashed outside, and the electric lights flickered. A deep, rolling boom washed over the building, and the first fat spots of rain tapped on the glass.

The song on the radio reached its end, and a BBC announcer came on with the news. Proteus listened for several minutes to information about the world's continued economic depression, and then his ears perked up when he heard the news about Germany.

"... Germany's President Hindenburg has died. Chancellor Hitler has combined the office of chancellor and president and has named himself Führer. Scarcely a month after the Night of the Long Knives, in which he consolidated power through the murders and imprisonment of those who might stand in his way, Hitler has made Germany into a de facto dictatorship.

"Prime Minister MacDonald has condemned the seizure of power, as have many Members of Parliament. However, in Germany there are celebrations in the streets, and several of her allies have expressed support at the change toward stability, both politically and economically ..."

Proteus crossed over to the radio and turned it off. "And so it accelerates," he said. "The march toward war."

"Will it ever stop?"

"One day, I hope," said Proteus. "One day."

Thank you for reading *Saving Schrödinger's Cat.*

Now that you have finished, I would love if you could take a moment to leave a review on the site where you purchased the book, and/or on Goodreads.

*

Want to keep up with what's fun and happening in my writing world? Please visit **MarkJenkinsbooks.com** and consider signing up for my periodic newsletter. Also on the website you'll find interesting backstory from both this novel and previous works.

*

As a final thought, some secrets are best shared, so please feel free to spread the word about *Saving Schrödinger's Cat* to family and friends, and on social media. The Cat will love it and so will I.

Author's Note.

Saving Schrödinger's Cat was both fun to write and a struggle. The early 20th century was an incredibly rich time of discovery, chockfull of scientific giants trying to determine the true nature of the atom and the universe: Curie, Einstein, Rutherford, Schrödinger, Bohr, Heisenberg, de Broglie, Lord Kelvin, Geiger, Marsden.

And that's just the tip of one iceberg.

There were also brilliant minds who applied themselves to understanding nature and biology. In 1912, Casimir Funk proposed the term *vitamine* to describe a class of newly discovered essential biochemical micronutrients, and in 1935 Arthur Tansley, at Oxford, first coined the term *ecosystems*.

In telling this tale of science, nature, and time, science-aficionados and historians might (and probably will) chastise me for my choices — as well as my inaccuracies — but this is the fictional story my Muse told me to write. And for that I have no apology.

I have the uppermost respect for the historical scientific giants appearing in this novel. My love of science began in high school and was firmly rooted in learning about these inquisitive minds and their experiments/theories.

In writing this book, I researched biographies of these great humans, and learned of their experiments, writings, and personalities. But, of course, *Saving Schrödinger's Cat* is fiction and I hope readers will understand my flights of fancy and historical transgressions. The scientists' letters, characterizations, and actions are completely fabricated and one shouldn't judge the actual historical figures through the lens of this novel.

Blame the Muse.

If you've been stimulated to learn more about these people and their scientific inquiries then I've achieved one small thing in telling this tale. There are many wonderful biographies and factual accounts of their tremendous work, and I encourage you to explore.

Primarily, I hope you — the reader — enjoyed the whole of the story, because it's in a vein of love and respect that I have written *Saving Schrödinger's Cat.*

ABOUT THE AUTHOR
MARK JENKINS

Mark Jenkins is a British-American author of speculative fiction — primarily sci-fi, thrillers, and historical fiction. He is a physician and life-long seeker of knowledge, who thrives on deep dives. Mark is as excited by the challenge of exploring a new subject in a book, as he is by learning to solo-climb glaciated stratovolcanoes — and centers these moments of discovery in his fictional works. He is the author of *Klickitat - and other stories* (speculative mountaineering fiction tales), and the novel, *Saving Schrödinger's Cat* (Sci-fi/time travel/historical fiction - Fall 2021).

Mark is an avid cyclist, open water swimmer, and admirer of seals. He currently lives in the Pacific Northwest where he and his wife, Joanna, enjoy hiking, climbing, stand-up paddle boarding (when Mark can stay upright), photography, and quiet walks in nature.

Lightning Source UK Ltd.
Milton Keynes UK
UKHW011857271121
394709UK00001B/178